MAIL-ORDER VISCOUNTESS

LORDS OF THE ROCKIES

BOOK THREE

MISTY BELLER

Mail-Order Viscountess

MistyMBeller.com

Cover design by Evelyne Labelle at Carpe Librum Book Design: www.carpelibrumbookdesign.com

ISBN-13 Trade Paperback: 978-1-965918-46-3

He tends his flock like a shepherd:
He gathers the lambs in his arms
and carries them close to his heart;
he gently leads those that have young.

Isaiah 40:11 (NIV)

CHAPTER 1

February, 1870
Butte, Montana Territory

The crate hit the wagon bed with a satisfying thud, and Thomas Balfour scraped a sleeve across his forehead as he turned for another. The morning sun had climbed higher over Butte's ice-hardened streets, melting some areas into slush. Though his breath still formed small clouds as he moved, loading supplies for the ranch had burned through the cold in his limbs.

The physical exertion felt good. Better than standing still. Better than thinking.

"That's it for the baking goods." His older brother James hefted another wooden box alongside where Thomas placed his. "Mrs. Wang will be happy they finally have these spices back in stock."

Thomas grunted and pushed a crate of nails and tools in next to the others.

James had been acting strange all morning—cheerful in that forced way that meant he was hiding something. And James's wife, Rose, had been glancing at Thomas with an expression he couldn't quite read. Pity, maybe. Or concern.

Were they hiding something from him?

The mercantile's back door stood propped open despite the cold, and Rose's voice sounded from inside, discussing fabric with the shopkeeper.

It didn't seem like all three of them had needed to come on this supply run, especially since Butte lay a full day's wagon ride from their ranch.

Thomas could have handled it alone, or James and Rose could have made a holiday of it—newlyweds that they were.

But his oldest brother, Enoch, had insisted. Something about having help if the weather turned bad and the road became impassable. At least coming to town had given Thomas the chance to order the last of the supplies he'd need for the trip west.

A familiar wagon rolled past the alley, and Thomas glanced up to take in the pair on the bench. Two Stones and his wife, Heidi.

These two traveled the area sometimes, trading for specialty items, though their home was farther west. Good people, these. They'd brought Enoch's wife to the ranch last year when she'd been injured and in need. No telling how many others they'd helped in their travels.

Two Stones reined in his team beside their wagon, his expression as unreadable as ever, though his dark eyes held a friendly glint. Heidi raised a gloved hand in greeting, her smile as warm as her husband's was hard to read.

"Good to see you both." James stepped forward, brushing his hands on his trousers. "How's the trading?"

"Fair enough." Two Stones's voice carried that quiet steadiness Thomas had always appreciated about the man. "Heading south to the Bitterroot before the passes close."

"You two should stop by the ranch next time you're

anywhere close." Thomas moved in beside his brother. "Mrs. Wang would think it's Christmas if she had the chance to feed you for a night or two."

Heidi chuckled and leaned against her husband's arm. "We might just take you up on that."

Two Stones gave one of his rare almost-smiles—little more than a softening around his eyes—and dipped his chin. "We'll find you."

The pair rolled on, their wagon disappearing around the corner toward the livery, and Thomas turned back to the supplies. He gripped the edge of another crate and hauled it toward him. The wood bit into his palms even through his work gloves.

"Thomas." James's voice came from too close behind him. "Leave that one. We need to talk."

The hair on the back of his neck prickled. What now?

"Plenty of time for talking on the ride home." He grabbed the box and swung it up. "Still got half a wagon to fill."

"The supplies can wait."

Something in James's tone made Thomas drop the crate into the bed harder than necessary. He turned and pulled off his gloves. "What about?"

James shifted his weight, glanced back toward the mercantile door, then met Thomas's eyes. "There's a reason we wanted you to come with us to Butte."

"Obviously." Thomas crossed his arms. Now they'd finally get down to it.

James scrubbed a hand through his hair—the movement was a sure sign bad news was coming.

"Just say it." Thomas leaned against the wagon, crossing one boot over the other in a show of casualness to hide the clenching in his gut.

"We've, um… We thought… That is, Enoch, Robert, and I discussed it, and we felt…"

"Spit it out, James."

His brother's shoulders straightened, taking on that older-brother-knows-best posture Thomas despised. "You've been different since the knighting ceremony. Restless. Taking more risks than usual." James held up a hand before Thomas could protest. "Don't deny it. That business with that three-year-old stallion last month? You could have been killed."

"But I wasn't." He kept his voice level, though it took everything inside him. "I broke the horse, and now he's bringing a good price from that rancher in Helena."

"That's not the point."

"Then what is the point, James?" He spat the words. "You brought me all the way to Butte to lecture me about my horse training methods?"

Rose stepped from the mercantile, a wrapped parcel in her arms. Her face blanched when she saw them, and the look she and James exchanged stoked the fire burning in his chest.

This had nothing to do with horse training.

James turned back to him, and his voice dropped to a no-nonsense tone. "We've arranged something. Something we think will be good for you."

Arranged something.

Thomas could count on one hand the number of times his brothers had arranged anything for him that turned out well. Usually their planning involved more responsibility at the ranch, more reasons to stay put, more ways to keep him from the life he actually wanted. A life in California.

"What kind of something?" He clenched his jaw to keep his anger in check.

"A bride."

The world tilted sideways for a moment. He had to have heard wrong. "A what?"

"A mail-order bride. She's arriving on the afternoon stage."

The words burned in the cold air between them.

Thomas stared at his brother. He had to have misheard.

The sounds of Butte filtered through—a wagon rattling past on the street, someone shouting about fresh deer meat, a hammer striking metal at the smithy.

Normal sounds. Ordinary sounds.

But James had said something impossible.

Thomas finally forced out words. "A bride?"

"A mail-order bride. For you."

A mail-order bride. What in the Bitterroot Mountains were they thinking?

His brothers had summoned a woman all the way out here, presumably from back East, and hadn't bothered to ask him first?

Heat flooded through him, flaring hot and fast. The nerve of them. The absolute gall.

"No." The word came out flat. Final.

James stepped closer, hands raised in that placating gesture that made Thomas want to hit something. "Just listen. We're worried about you. Ever since you came back from Fort Benton with that new title, you've been—"

"Been what? Myself?" Thomas pushed off from the wagon. "Sorry if that's inconvenient for you all."

"Marriage settles a man." James glanced at his wife. "Gives him something to live for. Something to—"

"So you bought me a wife?" The absurdity of it choked him. "You think shackling me to some stranger is going to make me want to stay? I don't need settling." Thomas clenched his hands into fists. "I need to be left alone to live my life."

"You don't know what you need." Rose spoke for the first time. She set down her parcel in the wagon bed. "Thomas, I understand how you feel. Truly, I do. But sometimes the very thing we think will trap us is actually the thing that sets us free."

He barked out a laugh. "That's easy to say when you chose your husband. When you had a say in your own future."

The hit landed—he saw it in the way Rose's face tightened—and a sliver of remorse slid through him. Given her past, that was an especially low blow.

Yet his chest felt like it might crack open. His brothers had betrayed him. All of them. Enoch, Robert, *and* James. Even their wives, and probably Mrs. Wang too.

They'd sat around discussing his life, his *future,* as if he were a problem to be solved rather than a man with his own mind. Sure, he was the youngest in the family, but how incapable did they think him?

"When does this stage arrive?" He bit out the words.

James glanced at the sun's position. "Three hours. Maybe four."

Three hours until some unsuspecting woman showed up looking for her new husband. A husband who hadn't asked for her, didn't want her, and sure as Montana winters were cold wouldn't marry her.

"You'll send her back." He grabbed his gloves from where he'd dropped them and started toward the main street.

"We can't do that." James moved to block his path. "She's traveled all this way. Given up everything—"

"Not my problem." Thomas shouldered past him. "I didn't invite her. I didn't write to her. I didn't make her any promises. You did."

The rage felt good—clean and hot and righteous. Better than the hollow feeling that had been eating at him for months. Ever since that ill-fated event in Fort Benton with the queen's cousin that ended with him being knighted for failing to protect a man.

He stomped down the alley between buildings, splashing through half-frozen puddles. The main street of Butte stretched before him, crowded with freight wagons and miners and the usual chaos of a town flush with silver money.

Somewhere in this mess of humanity, there had to be a saloon. Not that he'd drink more than coffee. He'd never been able to stand that rot-gut whiskey. But he needed to lose himself somewhere.

James called after him, but Thomas didn't turn back.

James, of all people, should have understood. James had been the one who listened when Thomas talked about California, about starting fresh somewhere nobody knew the Balfour name or cared about English titles that meant nothing out here. James had nodded and said he understood the restlessness.

Apparently understanding and respecting were two different things.

Thomas shouldered past a group of miners arguing about claim boundaries. The smell of unwashed bodies and stale tobacco smoke hung thick in the winter air.

A painted sign swung from chains ahead—The Silver Strike. Good enough.

The interior was dim after the bright winter sunlight, and Thomas paused inside the door to let his eyes adjust. The place reeked of whiskey and sawdust, with an undertone of something sharper. Cigar smoke, maybe, or the particular desperation that clung to men who spent their days underground working for barely enough to survive on.

A handful of men clustered around tables, nursing drinks despite the early hour. A few glanced up at his entrance, their gazes watching—the way men in rough towns always sized up strangers.

He ignored them and headed for the bar.

The barkeep, a grizzled man with more scars than teeth, wiped at a glass with a rag that looked dirtier than the glass itself. "What'll it be?"

"Coffee. If you have it." He'd need his wits to get out of James's trap. Especially without saying or doing something he'd regret.

One eyebrow climbed toward the man's receding hairline. "Coffee."

"That a problem?"

"No problem at all." The man set down the glass and turned to a pot sitting on a small stove behind the counter. "Just don't get many asking for it."

Thomas leaned against the bar and tried to let the anger drain out of him.

Not an easy feat.

Every time he thought about James's face—that earnest, we-know-what's-best-for-you expression—the fury climbed higher in his throat.

A mail-order bride. As if he were some pathetic recluse too inept to find his own wife. As if he even wanted a wife.

The bartender slid a chipped mug across the scarred wood. The coffee inside looked thick enough to stand a spoon in and smelled like it had been sitting on the stove since yesterday. Perfect.

He wrapped his hands around the mug's warmth and stared into the dark liquid. Somewhere a few miles from here, a woman traveled toward a future that didn't exist. Some poor soul who'd believed the letters his brothers wrote—probably full of descriptions of the ranch, the mountains, the life she could have here.

All lies.

Well, not lies exactly. The ranch existed. The mountains were real enough.

But the husband? That was pure fiction.

He took a sip of the coffee. The brew tasted as bad as it looked—bitter and burnt—but at least it gave him something to do with his hands besides put them through a wall.

"Trouble with a woman?"

Thomas glanced sideways. The bartender had returned to his glass-wiping, though his attention remained fixed on Thomas with the knowing look of a man who'd seen every kind of misery parade through his establishment.

"Something like that."

"Always is." The man chuckled, a sound like gravel in a tin can. "They're either the cause of your problems or the solution. Sometimes both."

Thomas didn't respond. The last thing he needed was philosophy from a saloon keeper.

What kind of woman agreed to marry a stranger sight unseen anyway? Someone desperate, probably. Or running from something.

That thought pricked his conscience. She came all this way, expecting...what? A home? Security? Love, even?

He shoved the thought aside. Not his problem. He hadn't made her any promises.

He had his own plans.

California. Only a few more weeks before he'd have his supplies gathered and be ready to head out. Stake a claim on his own land. Start his own ranch.

His own future.

Not one mapped out by his brothers or dictated by family duty or trapped by some English title he'd never asked for.

A burst of laughter erupted from a corner table, harsh and mean-edged.

He glanced over. Four men sat hunched around a table in the corner, cards spread between them. The kind of men who looked like they'd been in Butte too long—faces hard with disappointment, clothes worn past decent.

One of them held a woman on his lap. She couldn't have been more than eighteen, dressed in a faded calico dress that had seen better days. Her eyes darted around the room like a trapped animal looking for escape, and her smile was fixed in place with the brittle quality of something about to shatter.

The man holding her had one meaty hand clamped around her wrist, his other arm wrapped tight across her waist. He said something Thomas couldn't make out, and his companions roared with laughter.

The girl's smile never wavered, but her fingers clutched the edge of the table until her knuckles went white.

He should look away. Not his business. Butte was full of hard men and women trying to survive however they could. He couldn't solve everyone else's problems when he couldn't even settle his own.

The girl's face had gone pale beneath the rouge on her cheeks.

Thomas set down his coffee mug.

"Those aren't men you want to cross." The bartender's voice held an unmistakable warning.

"I'm just going to have a friendly word." He was already moving away from the bar. The anger burning in his chest since James's revelation found a new target, and he welcomed the shift.

He could actually do something about this situation.

The four men didn't look up as he approached their table. Too focused on their cards and their captive audience.

Up close, the girl looked even younger—maybe sixteen. A smudge of dirt marked her jaw beneath the powder, and the dress hung loose on her thin frame. Her eyes flicked to Thomas for a half second, and something in that look—hope mixed with terror—made his jaw tighten.

"Gentlemen." He kept his voice easy, his posture relaxed. He'd learned years ago that the appearance of calm could diffuse most any situation. "Wondering if I might borrow the lady for a minute."

The man holding the girl finally looked up. His face wore hard angles and old scars, with eyes that had gone flat from too much whiskey or too much disappointment. Probably both. "We're in the middle of a game."

"I can see that." Thomas smiled—the charming, harmless

smile that made people underestimate him. "Won't take but a minute. The lady's employer is looking for her."

"Her employer?" The man tugged the girl a little, and she winced. "That would be Nelson, and he's right here."

Thomas slid his gaze to the man he'd called Nelson—a wiry fellow with thinning hair and a mouth like a knife slash. The one who'd laughed loudest at whatever crude joke had been made.

Nelson eyed him. The gleam in his eyes that said he might be willing to hand her off to Thomas if that increased the profit in his pocket for the girl's time. Would buying an hour—or an afternoon—really do much to help her though? She needed a new home. A new life. And he couldn't give her either. Probably.

Or could he? If he bought her freedom, would she have a place to go? Friends or family back East?

What was he thinking? He couldn't rescue every girl in every mining town saloon in the Montana Territory.

But the way her fingers trembled against the table edge...

"How much?" He pulled two coins from his pocket—money he'd brought to buy supplies for California, for a fresh start that apparently his brothers were determined to prevent.

Nelson's eyes lit up. "Depends on what you're wanting."

"Just her time. For the afternoon." The words tasted sour, but he kept his expression neutral. "I'll pay double your usual rate if you let her go now."

The man holding the girl—the one with the scarred face—tightened his grip. "We ain't done with her yet."

"Jake." Nelson leaned forward, his gaze fixed on the silver in Thomas's hand. "Let the man have what he's paying for."

"I said we ain't done."

The temperature in the room shifted—that moment when a situation teetered between resolution and violence. The other two men at the table had gone still. Waiting to see which direction this would tip.

He'd talked his way out of worse situations than this. He could do it again.

"I'm not looking for trouble." He kept his hands visible, the money in his open palm. "Only want to spend some time with the lady. You'll get your cut, I'll get her, and everyone walks away happy."

Jake's chair scraped against the floorboards as he stood, still gripping the girl. He was a big man—taller than Thomas by a few inches and built like someone who'd spent years swinging a pickaxe. The kind of size that usually ended arguments before they started.

Thomas didn't move. Just kept an easy smile in place.

The bar lay behind him—maybe eight strides away. The door to his left, blocked by another table. The other two men were still seated, but they'd be on their feet in seconds if this went bad.

"You think you can walk in here and take what you want?" Jake's breath hit his face, reeking of whiskey and decay.

"I think I offered fair payment for the lady's time." He shifted his weight so he could move if needed. The girl had gone rigid in Jake's grip, her eyes wide. "I imagine Nelson will give your money back."

Jake's mouth twisted into something that might have been a smile on a friendlier face. "Maybe I don't want the money."

The other two men stood now. Chairs scraped across floorboards. The sound seemed far too loud in the sudden quiet. All other patrons had gone still. Waiting.

His own pulse surged through his body, but he kept his breathing steady.

He'd been in worse spots than this. That time in Fort Benton when he'd accidentally insulted a trapper's wife. The cattle thieves two years ago. The stallion that had nearly crushed his ribs.

Though looking at Jake's fists—each roughly the size of a loaf of bread—maybe this ranked higher on the list of stupid decisions than he'd initially thought.

"Then what do you want?" He kept his tone conversational. Just discussing the weather.

Jake released the girl with a shove that sent her stumbling against the table.

She caught herself but didn't run. Just stood there frozen, like a deer that had spotted the wolf but couldn't remember how to move.

"I want you to mind your own business." Jake stepped closer, crowding into Thomas's space. "And get out of my saloon."

Was it this man's saloon? Or did he simply spew big talk?

Still, retreating now would be like showing your back to a mean dog—it only made them bite harder.

Some distant part of his mind whispered that this may be exactly the kind of recklessness James had been talking about—walking into a situation that could get him killed over a girl he didn't know.

But he'd already opened his mouth. Already charged the bear. No backing down now.

"Actually..." He let his smile sharpen just enough to show teeth. "I think this is exactly my business now. Seeing as I've already paid for the lady's time."

The first punch came faster than Thomas expected—a wild haymaker aimed at his jaw. He ducked sideways as the wind of it passed over his head. His shoulder crashed into the table edge, scattering cards and coins across the floor.

The girl screamed.

Thomas straightened in time to catch Jake's second swing on his forearm, the impact jarring all the way to his shoulder. Pain bloomed hot and immediate, but he shoved it aside and drove his fist into Jake's gut.

Like punching a barrel. The man barely grunted.

Then Jake's companions were moving. One grabbed Thomas's left arm, yanking it behind his back. The other came at him from the front with a fist raised.

Thomas drove his boot down on the instep of the man holding him. Bones crunched, and the grip loosened enough for him to wrench free. He spun, using the momentum to throw an elbow that connected with someone's face. Cartilage gave way with a wet crunch.

Someone howled.

The room tilted as something slammed into the side of his head—Jake's fist, probably, though everything had gone a bit fuzzy around the edges.

Then the distant crack of a rifle echoed through the air.

CHAPTER 2

The stagecoach wheel dropped into another rut, and Kate's shoulder slammed against the side panel hard enough to add another bruise to her collection.

Three months of steamships and ice floes and bone-rattling wagon rides across the frozen prairie, and now this final torture device disguised as a stage. The leather seat had long since stopped providing any cushioning—or perhaps her body had simply run out of places that didn't already ache.

She shifted, trying to find a position that didn't press on the worst of the bruises. Nothing helped though. At least the end was in sight.

Butte sprawled ahead through the grimy window, buildings rising from the mountainside like tombstones in a particularly crowded cemetery.

It wasn't South Carolina. It wasn't even close.

But it was here, and that meant the end of this nightmare journey.

"Oh, Kate, look!" Clara leaned across her, pointing at something through the window. Strands of her honey-blonde hair had come loose from their pins hours ago, and dust streaked her traveling dress—the blue one Kate had spent two weeks sewing, with the tiny pearl buttons Clara had fawned over. "Is that a theater?"

Kate followed her sister's finger to a false-fronted building with peeling paint and a crooked sign. "I think that's a saloon."

"Oh." Clara settled back against the seat, though the disappointment lasted only a moment before her smile returned.

Kate glanced at the bench across from them, where Mrs. Hartwell—Audrey, as she'd insisted they call her—slept on her husband's shoulder. Somehow, the woman had managed to remain immaculate despite the journey. Her traveling suit showed barely a wrinkle, and her dark hair stayed perfectly arranged beneath her hat. Almost like she had a lady's maid hidden in her reticule.

Mr. Harwell shifted, and his wife stirred but didn't wake. He'd proven himself a decent traveling companion despite his obvious wealth—quiet, unassuming, and patient with his wife's enthusiasm for every landmark they passed. He caught Kate's eye now and offered a small, friendly nod.

Kate returned the gesture and looked back out the window. The buildings grew denser as the stage rolled deeper into Butte. More substantial too—brick and stone replacing the rough lumber of the outskirts. Signs advertised everything from mining equipment to French millinery, though she doubted the millinery was actually French.

Still. The variety meant opportunity. The wealth pouring out of these mountains had to go somewhere.

Her hand moved to the pocket where she'd tucked Audrey Hartwell's calling card, just to confirm its presence. The cardstock was thick and expensive beneath her fingertips. Real. Not a dream conjured by exhaustion and desperation.

She had a commission. A real one, from a woman who could afford to pay well and whose recommendation could open doors throughout Butte's social circles. The kind of opportunity she'd hardly dared imagine when they'd left South Carolina. The kind of opportunity her stepmother had made clear was never meant for women like her.

Lord willing, Clara would be well settled with her new husband—a God-fearing rancher, if he turned out to be as he advertised. And Kate could live in Walnut Springs and build her own business as a seamstress. She'd only need to travel to Butte once a month or so for fittings and deliveries and such. She could manage that.

The stage lurched again, and her stomach protested. When had she last eaten? That morning's dried beef and biscuits, probably. Her mouth tasted like dust and something foul.

"I hope we'll have time to stop at the hotel first." Clara's voice sounded bright despite the exhaustion that showed in the shadows beneath her eyes. "We could freshen up. And maybe take a bath?"

Washing sounded like heaven. Kate's skin itched beneath layers of travel grime, and her hair stiffened with dust. How many days since she'd been properly clean? She'd lost count somewhere between when they'd been forced off the wrecked steamboat on the barren prairie and here.

But would Mr. Balfour be waiting for the stage? The last wire she'd been able to send had been from Fort Benton, eleven long days ago. She'd communicated the schedule the stage line posted, which had her and Clara arriving yesterday. Had he come to meet the stage then? Was he disappointed when the rickety contraption never rolled into town?

When she sent him their arrival date, she'd not realized how challenging this last stretch of the journey would be—and how much better she and her sister would feel after a few minutes' respite before meeting the man Clara would marry.

The stage slowed, and buildings pressed closer on either side. Men crowded the wooden sidewalks—miners mostly, from the look of them. Rough clothing and thickly bearded faces. A few glanced at the stage as it passed, but most ignored it.

Just another stage. Just another day in Butte.

Except it wasn't just another day for her and Clara. This was a new beginning for them both.

The stage rolled to a stop, and the driver's voice carried from above. "Butte! End of the line!"

Mrs. Hartwell stirred, blinking awake with the grace of someone who'd merely been resting her eyes rather than sleeping through the last hour of travel. "Oh, are we here already?"

Her husband smiled and patted her hand. "Indeed we are, my dear."

The driver appeared at the door, yanking it open with a force that sent cold air rushing into the cramped interior. Kate's lungs seized at the shock of it—sharp and clean after hours of breathing stale air thick with the stench of unwashed bodies and leather.

"Watch your step, ladies." The driver offered his hand, his lined face creasing into something that might have been meant as a smile. "Ground's a bit icy."

Clara went first, gathering her skirts with the natural grace she'd somehow maintained despite these three months of torture. Kate followed, accepting the driver's callused hand and stepping down onto—

Her boot hit the frozen ground, and her foot nearly went out from under her. She caught herself on the stage's doorframe, her fingers screaming protest at the sudden grip. Every joint in her body felt rusted shut.

"Steady there." The driver's hand gripped her elbow. She would have shaken him off but didn't trust her legs yet.

The street stretched before her, wider than she'd expected. Buildings rose on either side, most two stories tall with painted signs advertising wares she couldn't quite make out through the film of exhaustion coating her vision. Men moved along the wooden sidewalks, their voices a low rumble beneath the sharper sounds of hammering somewhere in the distance and the creak of wagon wheels.

So many people. After weeks of empty prairie, the sheer mass of it all made her head spin.

"Kate?" Clara touched her arm, concern flicking across her face. "Are you all right?"

"Fine." The word came out too sharp. She worked for a smile. "Just finding my legs."

The Hartwells had already descended, Mr. Hartwell directing a porter about their luggage, clearly a man accustomed to being obeyed.

Mrs. Hartwell turned back to them, her face bright despite the journey. "Katherine. Now, you have my card, yes? You must come call on me once you're settled. We'll discuss the designs for the winter gowns, and I can introduce you to some friends who are simply dying for a skilled dressmaker."

"Of course." Kate forced another smile through her stiff face. "Thank you again, Mrs. Hartwell. For everything."

"Audrey, please." The woman squeezed Kate's hand, and the gesture felt genuine. "I have a feeling we're going to be great friends."

Friends. The word sat strange in Kate's chest. She didn't have friends—just Clara, the one grace that came from her father's remarriage.

Friends required trust, and Kate had learned the steep cost of that particular commodity. Still, Audrey Hartwell's recommendation could mean the difference between scraping by and actual success. She had to nurture the connection, even if friendship felt like too generous a word.

"I look forward to it." This time, the smile felt more real.

Mr. Hartwell tipped his hat. "Ladies. Best of luck to you both." He offered his arm to his wife, and they swept away toward a waiting carriage, its roof already loaded with an impressive stack of luggage.

As she turned to scan the street, the cold bit through her traveling dress—layers of wool that had seemed adequate in the heated confines of the stage but now proved laughably insufficient. Her teeth wanted to chatter. She clenched her jaw against it.

Somewhere in this chaos of people and commerce, a rancher would be coming to meet Clara.

Thomas Balfour. The name signed on the letters Clara had shown her. Letters that promised stability, faith, and a home in the mountains.

She could only pray he would be the man he seemed. Reality had a way of disappointing.

"Do you think he's here?" Clara's fingers twisted in her skirt, betraying the nerves her bright smile tried to hide. "Mr. Balfour?"

Kate studied the crowd of men moving along the sidewalk. Most paid them no attention, intent on their own business. A few glanced their way—the kind of looks that made her want to wrap her cloak tighter.

Then a woman appeared through the bodies, striding with intention toward them. A tall lady in a deep green dress—a simple cut, but the color brought out the rich auburn in her hair. Beside her walked a man—broad-shouldered and dark-haired, his hand resting at the woman's back.

Kate's stomach tightened. Something about the way they moved, the deliberateness of their approach, spoke of purpose.

That couldn't be Mr. Balfour though, right? Not with the possessive way he touched the lady.

The woman's eyes found Kate's, and she smiled—warm and genuine in a way that didn't quite belie the tension visible in the set of her shoulders.

"Miss McKinney?" The woman's voice carried clearly despite the noise of the street. "Miss Clara McKinney?"

Clara stepped forward, her chin lifting in that way she did when nerves threatened to overwhelm her. "Yes, I'm Clara McKinney. And this is my sister, Kate."

The woman's face broke into a smile that looked genuine enough, though Kate had learned long ago that smiles meant nothing. She stepped forward beside Clara and waited.

"I'm Rose Balfour." She gestured to her companion. "And this is my husband, James. We're Thomas's brother and sister-in-law."

Brother and sister-in-law.

Not Thomas himself.

The knot in her middle pulled tighter. A man who sent his relatives to meet his mail-order bride—what did that say about him? Nothing good. Nothing that made her want to hand Clara over to his keeping.

"It's wonderful to finally meet you both." Rose's words tumbled out. "We've been so looking forward to your arrival. Thomas is—he's waiting at the hotel. We thought it might be easier this way, given the crowds and all the luggage."

Kate's jaw tightened. Easier for whom? Not for Clara, who'd traveled three months to meet this man. Not for Kate, who needed to assess this Thomas Balfour with her own eyes before she'd let her sister anywhere near him.

"How thoughtful." The words came out a bit too flat. She couldn't usually manage warmth when her instincts screamed warning.

Rose's smile faltered at the edges. "I know this must seem—well, unconventional. But Thomas is just—he's been—" She glanced at her husband, maybe for help.

James Balfour offered a smile their direction, and he motioned back the direction the couple had come. "My brother's looking forward to meeting you. The hotel's just down the street. We have rooms reserved for you also."

As she and Clara followed the pair toward the boardwalk, she kept her hand firm on Clara's elbow. Whoever this Thomas Balfour turned out to be, and however excited Clara was about this new life gleaming before her, Kate wouldn't turn her sister over to him without proof he deserved her.

If he turned out to be another disappointment—another man who promised one thing and delivered another—then she and Clara could make their own way right here in Butte. Kate's sewing could support them both.

The commission from Audrey Hartwell was just the beginning. She'd build a clientele, establish a reputation, and Clara would never have to marry anyone out of desperation.

The thought settled deep in her chest. A backup plan. An escape route if Thomas Balfour proved unworthy.

CHAPTER 3

His coffee had gone cold an hour ago, but Thomas kept his hands wrapped around the cup anyway.

His left cheek throbbed in time with his pulse, and the gash over his cheekbone stung every time he moved his face. Rose had wanted him to stop at the doctor's clinic to have it stitched, but Thomas declined. The cut would heal fine with salve.

James's gunshot had stopped the fight before Jake and his friends could do real damage. Thomas had gotten off with just the swollen cheek and the cut—and a set of bruised ribs that protested every deep breath. Could've been worse.

Would've been worse if his brother hadn't shown up when he did.

The girl had disappeared in the chaos. He'd looked for her afterward, but she'd vanished into whatever shadows had spawned her. Probably for the best. What would he have done with her anyway? Brought her back to the ranch like some kind of stray?

Though that would've been less insane than what his brothers had actually done—ordering him a wife like she was a cookstove from a catalog.

The café door opened, and Thomas straightened, despite the protest from his ribs. But it was just a miner, shoulders hunched against the cold, making his way to the counter.

Not James. Not Rose. Not the poor woman they'd summoned across half the continent to marry a man who'd never written her a single word.

His stomach twisted, and he pushed the cold coffee away.

What was he supposed to say to her? *Sorry my brothers are meddling fools who can't mind their own business? Sorry they used my name to make promises I won't be keeping?*

The door opened again.

This time it was them—James and Rose, and behind them…

Two women.

His mind stuttered. Two?

He pushed to his feet, manners drilled too deep to ignore even when his world was falling apart. The movement sent a spike of pain through his side, but he kept it off his face.

Both women followed James and Rose into the cafe, approaching his table. The shorter one possessed honey-blonde hair escaping its pins, delicate features, and eyes that went wide at the sight of his injured face.

The taller woman beside her had hair the color of pale wheat and a spine like an iron rod. Her hazel eyes swept over him with the kind of assessment usually reserved for livestock, and her mouth thinned to a hard line when her gaze landed on his cheek.

They stopped in front of him, but all he could do was take them in. He should say something. Welcome them. Apologize for his appearance. Explain about the fight.

Instead he stood there like an idiot while his face throbbed and his tongue forgot how to form words.

Rose stepped forward, filling the awkward gap. "Thomas, may I present Miss Clara McKinney and her sister, Miss Kate

McKinney?" She motioned to the shorter woman first, then the taller.

Sister.

The word clicked into place, and the situation clarified itself. Clara was the bride. Kate was the chaperone—the protective older sister who'd come along to make sure her younger sibling wasn't being delivered into the hands of a frontier monster.

Based on the look Kate McKinney was giving him right now, she'd already decided which category he fell into.

"Ladies." He managed a nod to each of them, though the movement made his cheek sting. "Please, sit."

Clara moved first, her step hesitant as she settled into the chair James pulled out for her. Her gaze kept darting to Thomas's face, then away, then back again. Like she couldn't quite believe what she was seeing but couldn't stop looking either.

Kate remained standing a moment longer, that assessing stare never wavering. Then she took the seat beside her sister with the rigid posture of someone preparing for battle.

James and Rose claimed the remaining chairs, and Thomas lowered himself back into his own. His ribs protested, and he had to focus to keep the wince off his face.

The silence stretched long enough to become uncomfortable. Rose opened her mouth—probably to launch into some prepared speech—but Thomas raised a hand to stop her.

If he was going to do this, he'd do it honestly. No more games. No more half-truths or careful omissions.

"I apologize for my appearance." He kept his voice level despite the way his jaw ached with each word. "There was an altercation earlier. Nothing to do with—" He gestured vaguely at the table, at the situation, at the disaster his brothers had created. "Nothing you need to worry about."

Kate McKinney's eyebrow climbed. "An altercation."

The way she said it—flat and disbelieving—made it sound like he'd claimed the sun rose in the west.

"A disagreement that got out of hand." He met her gaze and held it, though something about those hazel eyes made him want to look away. "I was helping someone. It escalated."

"Helping someone." She repeated his words again, stripping them of meaning through her clear skepticism.

"Yes." He spoke a little too forcefully. Something about her tone—the way she made everything sound like an accusation—set his teeth on edge. "A girl was being mistreated. I intervened."

"How noble." Still that flat delivery, though her fingers had moved to rest on her sister's arm. Protective. Possessive, even.

So similar to Jake's movements in the saloon and yet entirely different. Gentle where Jake's had been brutal, reassuring where his had been controlling.

Still. The comparison lodged in his mind and wouldn't shake loose.

Rose cleared her throat. "Perhaps we should order some food? I'm sure you ladies are hungry after your journey."

"We're fine, thank you." Kate's words cut across Rose's suggestion. She leaned forward, and he had the distinct impression of being pinned by a hawk. "Mr. Balfour, I think we need to discuss the nature of this arrangement."

His stomach dropped. She knew. Somehow she already knew this whole thing was a sham.

He glanced at James, but his brother's face had gone blank. No help there.

"The nature of the arrangement." He repeated the words to buy himself time to think. His cheek throbbed, and the pain made it hard to focus. "Yes. We should discuss that."

Clara's hand moved to clutch her sister's arm now, fingers white-knuckled against the dark fabric. Her face had gone pale beneath the travel dust, and something about that look—hopeful and terrified in equal measure—made his chest tighten.

She'd come all this way believing in something that didn't exist. Believing in him, or at least the version of him his brothers had invented in their letters.

"Miss McKinney—both of you—there's something you need to know." The words tasted foul. He'd never been good at disappointing people. That was supposed to be his gift—the charm that smoothed over rough situations, the easy smile that made people like him even when they shouldn't.

But there was no charming his way out of this mess.

Kate's eyes narrowed. "Go on."

"I didn't know about this arrangement." The confession came out blunt and graceless. "My brothers made it without consulting me. I never wrote those letters. I never asked for—" He stopped himself before he could say something truly rude. "A bride."

The words landed like stones in still water. Clara's face crumpled—just for a moment before she caught herself.

But he saw it. The hope draining away, replaced by something that looked like humiliation.

His throat tightened. This was worse than getting punched. At least with Jake's fists, the pain had been clean and straightforward.

"You didn't know." Kate's voice hadn't changed—still that same flat skepticism—but her fingers tightened on Clara's arm. "Your brothers arranged a marriage without telling you."

"That's correct." The admission burned worse than the cut on his cheek.

James shifted in his seat, and Thomas could feel his brother preparing to launch into some explanation. Some attempt to smooth this over and make it all sound reasonable.

He couldn't let that happen.

"My brothers—all three of them—decided I needed settling." The words came easier now that he'd started. Like lancing a wound. "They wrote the letters. Made the promises. Set up this whole arrangement without telling me."

Clara made a small sound—not quite a gasp, not quite a sob—and pressed her hand to her mouth. Her eyes had gone bright and glassy.

Thomas forced himself to hold Kate's gaze rather than look at her sister's devastation. Cowardly, maybe, but he couldn't bear to see what his honesty did to her.

"I see." Kate sat back in her chair, and something about the movement reminded him of a general reassessing the battlefield. "And what exactly do you intend to do about the situation now, Mr. Balfour?"

What did he intend? His ribs ached with each breath, his cheek throbbed, and his brothers had just blown apart any remaining trust he'd had in them. California looked better than ever—his escape route, his fresh start, his chance to finally live life on his own terms.

But seeing Clara McKinney's devastated face—even as he tried not to—made California feel less like freedom and more like running away.

"I won't hold you to any arrangement I didn't make." He forced the words out steadily. "We'll escort you both to our ranch so you can rest and recover from your journey. You can decide what you want to do from there. If you choose to return East, I'll pay for your passage."

Kate's expression didn't soften. "How generous."

The sarcasm stung worse than the gash on his cheek.

"Kate." Clara's voice came out small and tight. She dropped her hand from her mouth and gripped the edge of the table. "Perhaps we should—"

"We should get the full picture before making any decisions." Kate's attention never left Thomas's face. "Mr. Balfour, tell me about this ranch. How many people live there?"

The shift in topic caught him off-balance. "My three brothers, two with wives, and our oldest has a newborn babe." He shot a look at James. "Plus our housekeeper, Mrs. Wang. And me, obviously." Though not for long, if he could manage it.

"How many bedrooms?"

"Eight." Where was she going with this?

"And the nearest town?"

"Walnut Springs. About an hour and a half ride."

Kate's mouth pressed into an even thinner line. "So if we go to this ranch, we'll be trapped there. An hour and a half from civilization, surrounded by your family, with nowhere to go if we need to leave."

Trapped? She thought he'd bring them to the ranch and—what? Hold them prisoner? Force Clara into a marriage she didn't want?

The injustice of it burned hotter than the cut on his face. He'd just told them the truth, offered them a way out, promised to pay their way back East. And still she looked at him like he was some kind of predator circling wounded prey.

"You'd be guests in our home." He kept his voice level despite the anger climbing his throat. "Free to leave whenever you choose. We'll provide safe transportation any time you ask. I give you my word."

"Your word." Kate's laugh held no humor. "Forgive me if I find that less than reassuring, given that your family's word brought us here under false pretenses."

The accusation hung between them, and Thomas couldn't argue with it. She was right. His brothers had lied, and now their dishonesty stained him too.

Clara's fingers had gone white where they clutched the edge of the table. A single tear tracked through the dust on her cheek, and she brushed it away quickly—like she hoped no one had noticed.

And the sight of it made something twist in his chest.

"You're right. My family's word brought you here under false pretenses. I can't undo that. But I can give you my word—*my* personal word, not theirs—that you'll be treated with respect at the ranch. That you'll be safe. That you'll have choices."

Kate's expression didn't change, but something flickered in those hazel eyes. Not trust—he hadn't earned that—but maybe a tiny bit less hostility.

"I'd like to see this ranch before we make any decisions." Her tone remained businesslike, stripped of warmth. "If what you say is true, then we'll need to understand what we're dealing with."

Rose leaned forward, her voice gentle. "Of course. We thought we'd stay here in Butte tonight—let you both rest after your journey—then head to the ranch in the morning. It's a full day's ride."

Clara's face went another shade paler. These women had likely already traveled two or three months to get here, and now they had to face another day of hard riding into the mountains.

All for nothing. All because his brothers couldn't leave well enough alone.

"That's acceptable." Kate's fingers finally loosened on her sister's arm. "We'll need rooms, of course. And time to refresh ourselves before dinner."

"Already arranged." James spoke for the first time since the introductions, his voice carrying that careful warmth he used when trying not to make things worse. "A room on the second floor. The hotel has baths available as well."

Kate's face showed no reaction to the words. Just that same assessing stare, like she was calculating angles and measuring distances in case she needed to make a quick escape.

He couldn't blame her. If he'd been in her position—dragged across the continent on false promises, only to discover the whole thing was a lie—he'd be suspicious too.

Still, the constant scrutiny made his jaw tighten. Every time her gaze swept over his battered face, judgment seemed to drip from her eyes. Like the fight proved something about his character. Like helping that girl made him reckless or dangerous instead of decent.

"Thank you." Clara's voice came out barely above a whisper. She'd been so quiet he'd almost forgotten she was there—which was ridiculous given she was the whole reason for this disaster. "That's very kind."

Rose stood, smoothing her skirts with the kind of grace that came naturally to her. "Why don't I show you to your rooms? You can rest, and we'll meet for dinner later. Say, six o'clock?"

Kate rose as well, one hand reaching to help Clara up from her chair. The movement was protective—the way she positioned herself between Clara and the rest of them.

Thomas stood as well. The movement made his vision blur, and he gripped the edge of the table until the room steadied.

When his eyes focused again, Kate was watching him with that same calculating expression. Like she was cataloging every wince, every sign of weakness, storing it all away to use against him later.

Let her look. He had nothing to hide. Well, except for the fact that he'd be heading to California as soon as he could manage it—but that was his business, not hers.

And the day he'd leave couldn't come soon enough.

CHAPTER 4

The stairs creaked under Rose Balfour's weight—a sound that matched the exhaustion pulling at Kate's bones.

"Your rooms are just down this hall." Rose glanced back over her shoulder, her auburn hair catching the light from the oil lamps mounted along the papered walls. "They're not fancy, but they're clean. Mrs. Kendell keeps a respectable establishment."

Kate's fingers tightened on the handle of her carpetbag. Respectable. The word meant different things depending on who spoke it. In Columbia, *respectable* had included her stepmother's drawing room—all silk and mahogany and cruelty dressed up as polite conversation.

The hallway stretched ahead, dimly lit and narrow. The wallpaper bore faded roses that might have been cheerful once, before years of frontier dust had dulled them to brown. Better than some places they'd stayed on the journey. Worse than others. At least it didn't reek of unwashed bodies and stale tobacco.

Rose stopped at a door near the end of the hall and produced a key from her pocket. "Here you are. We can request another room if you'd each rather have your own." She pushed the door open and stepped aside.

The room was small. A double bed dominated the space, covered in a faded quilt. A dresser stood against one wall, complete with a chipped porcelain basin and pitcher and a small mirror above. A single window overlooked the street below, its curtains drawn against the afternoon light.

Kate stepped inside, Clara close behind her. "This will be fine." The bed would be adequate—they'd shared smaller in worse places. At least this room had a door that locked. She'd check the mechanism before they slept tonight.

"The bathing room is downstairs." Rose remained in the doorway, her hands clasped in front of her. "I can let Mrs. Kendall know you'd like baths drawn?"

"Please." Her voice scratched, so she cleared her throat. "That would be appreciated."

Rose's smile flickered—uncertain, like she wasn't sure whether to stay or flee. She'd been kind enough on the walk from the stage depot, filling the silence with commentary about Butte's growth and the weather in the mountains. But kindness didn't erase the fact that her family had lied to Clara. Had brought them here under false pretenses.

Had summoned a mail-order bride for a man who'd never asked for one.

Kate set her carpetbag on the floor beside the dresser, her muscles protesting the sudden lack of motion after hours confined in the stagecoach. Three months of travel had taught her body to expect constant jarring movement. Standing still felt wrong somehow, like the floor might drop away at any moment.

"I'll have Mrs. Kendall send up tea as well." Rose shifted her weight, still hovering in the doorway. "Unless you'd prefer coffee?"

"Tea would be lovely, thank you." Clara's voice carried that bright politeness she always used when trying to pretend everything was fine.

Rose's smile warmed a fraction. "I'll see to it then. We'll eat dinner at six in the dining room, but if you'd rather have trays sent up—"

"We'll come down." Kate kept her voice level. Hiding in their room would solve nothing. She needed to observe Thomas Balfour more, assess whether his pretty speech about choices and respect held any truth. Men said all kinds of things when their backs were against a wall. Following through was another matter entirely.

"Of course." Rose's fingers worried at her skirt—a nervous gesture that seemed at odds with her otherwise composed demeanor. "I know this situation is...unconventional. Thomas truly didn't know about the arrangement. My husband and his brothers meant well, but they should have consulted him first."

Meant well. As if good intentions excused lies.

The words sat bitter on Kate's tongue, but she swallowed them. Antagonizing Mrs. Balfour would accomplish nothing. The woman seemed genuine enough—nervous, certainly, but that could mean anything. Guilt over her family's deception. Concern for how this disaster might unfold. Simple discomfort with strangers.

Kate had learned not to trust her first impressions. People showed only what they wanted you to see.

"I'm sure they did." She kept her tone neutral, offering nothing that could be used against them later. "We'll see you at dinner."

After that clear dismissal, Rose's smile tightened at the edges, but she nodded and withdrew, pulling the door closed behind her with a soft click.

The silence that followed pressed against Kate's ears after weeks of constant noise—wind and wagon wheels and the endless chatter of fellow travelers. She moved to the door and tested the lock. It slid into place smoothly enough. Not much of a barrier if someone truly wanted in, but better than nothing.

When she turned back, Clara had sunk onto the edge of the bed, her shoulders curving inward. The afternoon light filtering through the curtains caught the tear tracks on her cheeks—fresh ones, joining the paths the earlier drops had carved through the travel dust.

Kate's chest tightened. She crossed the room and sat beside her sister, close enough their shoulders touched. "We don't have to stay."

"I know." Clara's voice came out thin, like she'd worn it down to nothing. "But where would we go?"

The question hung between them. Back to Columbia? Back to the man more than two times Clara's age, whom her mother had chosen—the perfect next step on her insatiable climb to the top of Columbia society. Never mind that he'd buried two wives already and looked at Clara like she was a brood mare he was purchasing.

No. They couldn't go back there.

Fort Benton sat behind them—a rough river town where they'd waited three days for this stage. They could return there, find lodging, and wait out the winter. Except their funds wouldn't stretch that far, not with the prices these frontier towns charged for everything.

"We could stay in Butte." She forced the words out steadily, though her mind raced through calculations. The money left in her reticule—enough for maybe two weeks of lodging if they were careful. A month if they found somewhere cheaper than this hotel. "I have the commission from Mrs. Hartwell. That's a start."

Clara's head lifted, and something flickered in her eyes. Hope, maybe, or just the desperate need to believe Kate could fix this like she fixed everything else. "One commission?"

The doubt in her sister's voice stung, though Kate couldn't

argue with it. One commission wouldn't support them through a Montana winter. Not in a mining town where prices climbed as high as the mountains surrounding it.

"It's more than one commission." Kate kept her voice firm. "It's an introduction. Mrs. Hartwell moves in society here—she said so herself. If I do good work for her, she'll recommend me to others. I can build a clientele."

"How long will that take?" Clara worried at a loose thread on her cuff. "A month? Two? What do we do in the meantime?"

She had no answer—not one that would satisfy either of them. The truth sat heavy in her stomach. She reached for Clara's hand, stilling the anxious picking at the thread. "We'll manage. We always do."

Clara's fingers curled around hers, small and cold without her traveling gloves. "What about the ranch?"

The ranch. Where Thomas Balfour's family waited—the brothers who'd orchestrated this disaster, their wives, and a housekeeper. All of them complicit in dragging Clara across half a continent for nothing.

But Rose had seemed kind. Nervous, yes, though there'd been genuine warmth in her smile when she'd greeted them at the stage depot. And she'd called Thomas's brothers out for their deception without hesitation. That counted for something, didn't it?

Or maybe Kate was just desperate enough to see kindness where none existed.

"The ranch is an option." She forced the words past the resistance in her throat. "Thomas Balfour said we'd be free to leave whenever we wanted. That he'd pay for our passage back East if we chose to go."

"Do you believe him?"

Did she? He'd sat there with his face battered and swollen, his ribs clearly paining him with every breath, and admitted the truth. He could have lied—let them believe he'd written those letters, gone through with the wedding, and dealt with the fallout later. Or simply refused to marry Clara, pretending he'd changed his mind.

Instead he'd confessed. Offered them choices. Promised to pay their way home.

The cynic in her—the part that had learned to trust no one except Clara—whispered that words meant nothing. That men said whatever suited them in the moment and changed them once they had what they wanted.

But the part of her that had watched him flinch when Clara's face crumpled—that part whispered something different.

"I don't know." The admission tasted like failure. "But staying in Butte means spending money we don't have while I try to build a business from nothing. Going to the ranch at least buys us time to figure out what comes next."

Clara's thumb traced circles against Kate's palm—a habit that revealed she was thinking. "What if they won't let us leave?"

The worry in her sister's voice pulled something tight in Kate's chest. She'd spent years shielding Clara from the worst of her mother's manipulations, their father's weakness, the reality of how little protection women had in this world.

And now they sat in a hotel room in the Montana Territory, discussing whether to trust strangers who'd already proven themselves capable of deception.

"Then we'll find a way out anyway." She closed her fingers around Clara's hand. "I won't let anyone trap you. Not them. Not anyone."

Clara's fingers tightened around hers, holding on like Kate was the only solid thing in a world gone liquid and uncertain. "Promise?"

"I promise." Kate's throat constricted around the words. Clara needed steady right now, even if Kate's insides churned with uncertainty.

She pulled her sister closer until Clara's head rested against her shoulder.

She'd kept Clara safe this far. Through Clara's mother's schemes and the suffocating drawing rooms of Columbia society. Through steamships and frozen rivers and endless prairie. Through everything that had tried to break them.

She hadn't failed yet, and she wouldn't do so now.

CHAPTER 5

The leather reins had frozen stiff between Thomas's fingers, cold enough to bite through his gloves.

He guided the team out of the livery's wide doors, the wagon bed creaking under the weight of supplies they'd loaded last night. The horses' breath formed white clouds in the barely dawn air, and their hooves rang sharp against the frozen ground.

Butte still slept around him—most of it, anyway. A few workers stumbled along the street, heading toward the mine shafts. Smoke curled from chimneys against a sky the color of old pewter.

The cold settled into his bruised ribs with every breath, a dull ache that matched the throb in his cheek. He'd barely slept, what little he managed punctuated by dreams of Clara McKinney's devastated face and Kate McKinney's razor-sharp eyes.

Two women. His brothers had ordered him one mail-order bride and gotten two women instead—one who'd come expecting marriage, and one who looked at him like he was something she'd scrape off her boot.

He pulled the team to a stop in front of the hotel and set the brake. Through the dining room windows, lamplight spilled onto the boardwalk. James would be in there already, probably working on his second cup of coffee while Rose picked at whatever breakfast Mrs. Kendall had set out.

And the McKinney sisters would be there too. Preparing for a full day's ride to a ranch they'd once thought would be their home. At least...Miss Clara's home. Where had Kate McKinney planned to live? He should have asked that. Maybe it didn't matter now. They would be leaving together eventually.

Unless... The idea that had dawned sometime around midnight crowded in once more.

Robert.

He should be the one to marry next anyway, as the older brother. Why in cotton they thought Thomas needed a bride more than Robert was still a mystery. They must think him a truly desperate case.

But this could all turn out for good. He could match Robert with one of them—Miss Clara, probably, since she was the one who'd come expecting a husband.

Robert was steady, responsible. The kind of man who'd make a decent husband once he got his head out of whatever book of law cases currently occupied it. And if Robert married Clara McKinney, Thomas could leave for California with a clear conscience.

The plan had seemed brilliant in the dark hours before dawn. Now, sitting in the cold with his ribs aching and his face throbbing, it felt less likely.

He climbed down from the wagon seat, his boots hitting the frozen ground with a jolt that shot pain through his side.

The dining room's warmth hit like a wall when he pushed through the door. Heat from the cast iron stove in the corner had already chased away the worst of the morning chill, and the smell of coffee and frying bacon made his stomach clench with hunger he'd been ignoring.

James sat at a corner table with all three women, and they all looked up at Thomas's approach.

Clara wore a traveling dress the color of dark green pine needles, her honey-blonde hair arranged in some complicated style that had probably taken her an hour. She looked bright and cheery, despite the early hour and the months the pair had been traveling.

Kate sat beside her in a dress of deep blue wool, simpler than her sister's but well-made. Her blonde hair was pulled back into that same severe style she'd worn yesterday, not a strand out of place.

Rose smiled at him from across the table, though the expression carried a note of caution. Like she wasn't sure whether he'd bolt or cause a scene.

Fair enough. He'd considered both options last night.

"Good morning." He aimed for the empty chair at the table's end. Sitting pulled at his ribs again, and he had to concentrate on keeping his breathing steady as he settled.

Kate's gaze tracked every wince, every careful shift of position. Tallying his weaknesses again. "Morning." James pushed a cup of coffee across the table toward him. "Wagon loaded?"

"Most of it." Thomas wrapped his hands around the cup, letting the warmth seep through his gloves. "Still need to add the trunks and tie down the canvas in case the weather turns."

"It will." James glanced toward the window, where gray light filtered through the frost patterns on the glass. "Could start snowing any time."

Perfect. A full day's ride in potentially worsening weather. At least it would keep conversation to a minimum. Hard to make small talk when your face was numb, and the wind cut through every layer.

"We should eat quickly then." Rose gestured to the serving dishes arranged in the center of the table—bacon, eggs, biscuits that steamed when Clara broke one open. "Get on the road before it gets worse."

Thomas reached for a biscuit, though his appetite had vanished somewhere between walking through that door and sitting here under all these stares. The bread, still warm from the oven, felt dense in his hand.

He forced himself to take a bite. Chew. Swallow. His body needed fuel for the long day ahead, whether his stomach wanted it or not.

"How long to the ranch?" Kate's question cut through the silence, directed at James but sharp enough that Thomas felt the blade.

"Eight to ten hours, depending on conditions." James set down his coffee. "We'll have plenty of blankets in the wagon, and we'll stop halfway to rest the horses and eat a meal. There's a spot with some shelter if the weather turns."

"And if conditions become worse before we reach this spot?"

The challenge in her tone made Thomas's jaw tighten. Everything she said carried an edge, like she was constantly preparing for the worst possible outcome. He'd never liked a pessimistic outlook. Why hunt down trouble before you'd even crossed its path?

"We'll manage." James's tone carried that careful patience he used when trying to keep peace. "I've made this trip in worse conditions."

Kate's mouth pressed into a thin line, but she didn't push further. Just reached for her own cup and took a deliberate sip, her gaze never leaving Thomas's face.

He looked away first—coward that he was—and focused on the biscuit in his hand. The bread had gone dry in his mouth. He forced himself to swallow and reached for his coffee.

Clara cleared her throat. "Will there be other travelers on the road?"

"Unlikely this time of year." Rose offered a warm smile.

"Most people stay close to town once the weather turns. But that makes it safer in its own way—no other traffic to worry about."

Safer. Thomas nearly laughed. They were about to spend a full day trapped in a wagon together, heading toward a ranch full of his meddling family. Safe wasn't the word he'd use.

He drained his coffee in three swallows, the heat scalding all the way down. The burn felt good—something real to focus on besides the weight of Kate McKinney's stare and the careful way Clara picked at her breakfast.

"I'll start loading the trunks." He pushed back from the table. The scrape of his chair against the floorboards covered whatever Rose started to say.

After another half hour or so of time-wasting, they finally rolled out of Butte. James opted to drive the team, and Thomas sat on the bench with him while the ladies tucked into the empty nook he'd reserved for them in the bed of the wagon—as protected from the wind as he'd been able to make it.

In a few hours, Rose might want to come up to the bench with her husband. Thomas could stretch his legs at that point and warm up by walking behind the rig.

The wagon lurched over a frozen rut, and he grabbed the side rail to keep from sliding into his brother. His ribs shot a spike through his left side that made his breath catch.

"Sorry." James didn't look over, his attention fixed on the road ahead. "Ground's worse than I thought it'd be."

Thomas grunted and settled back against the bench to find a position that didn't make everything hurt. The cold had worked its way through his coat and shirt, settling into his bones with the kind of deep ache that promised a long day ahead.

Behind them, the murmur of women's voices drifted forward—too quiet for him to make out words, but the tone carried clearly enough. Rose's warm reassurance. Clara's tentative responses. Kate's determined tone.

She might be a wrinkle in his plan to match Clara with Robert. Maybe. What had she planned to do when her sister married Thomas? Surely those intentions wouldn't shift just because the name of the groom changed.

Perhaps he should mention his idea to her though. She was likely already plotting their next step, where they would go from the ranch. He needed to plant this idea before she all but bought tickets to travel elsewhere.

Mayhap he could pull her aside when they rested the horses at midday.

CHAPTER 6

At first glance, the river had looked nearly covered over by the snow piled up along both banks. But now that Kate stood at the edge, the expanse of ice they'd have to cross stretched as wide as the Missouri.

Snow fell in thick curtains now, swirling over the frozen mass and blurring the far bank into gray nothingness. How long had it been snowing? Half an hour? Longer? The flakes had started as occasional visitors, but now they came in earnest, whipping around her shoulders and catching in her eyelashes.

"We crossed this two days ago on the way to Butte." James's voice carried from where he stood by the horses' heads. "Ice was solid then. Should be even thicker now with the cold we've had."

Should be. The words did nothing to ease the knot twisting in her middle.

The white coating over the river's surface should be reassuring. But all she could see was the dark water that must flow beneath—cold enough to kill in minutes if the ice gave way. Cold enough to swallow Clara whole before Kate could reach her.

"I'd like to walk for a bit." The words came out steadier than she felt. "Take a bit of exercise."

James glanced back toward the wagon, then at her. "You'll want to keep close. Snow's coming down harder."

"I know." She turned to the wagon bed where Clara sat bundled under blankets, her face barely visible beneath the hood of her cloak. "Clara, come walk with me."

Her sister's nose wrinkled. "I'm finally warm. Can't I stay here?"

The refusal shouldn't have stung—Clara had every right to prefer the relative comfort of the wagon. But the thought of crossing this river with her sister trapped in that heavy rig made Kate's chest tighten until breathing hurt.

"The fresh air would do you good."

"I'm better here." Clara pulled the blankets higher. "Really, Kate. I'm comfortable."

Kate opened her mouth to argue, then caught the shadows under Clara's eyes. Three months of travel had worn them both down, but Clara looked more exhausted than Kate had seen her since Fort Benton. Forcing her to walk in the snow and cold just to ease Kate's own fears seemed cruel.

"All right." She stepped back from the wagon. "Stay warm."

Thomas appeared beside her as James guided the team toward the ice. When had he climbed down from the bench? She hadn't heard his approach over the wind.

"Mind if I walk with you?" He didn't wait for an answer, just fell into step as she moved to follow a few steps behind the wagon.

The last thing she needed was company—especially his. But sending him away would require conversation, and she had no energy for it.

The wagon's wheels hit the ice with a hollow sound that carried too well across the frozen expanse. The knot in her middle pulled tighter.

"There's a frozen waterfall about five minutes upriver." Thomas's voice cut through her spiraling thoughts. "Beautiful this time of year. The spray freezes as it falls, creates these formations like icicles but wider. Fan-shaped."

She glanced at him. His breath formed white clouds in the cold air, and snow had already gathered on his hat and shoulders. The bruise on his cheek stood out darker against his wind-reddened skin.

Was he trying to distract her? Did he actually see how nervous this situation made her and was trying to ease the worry? The realization settled over her like the snow—cold and unwelcome but undeniable.

"That's nice." She kept her eyes on the wagon ahead, watching the way it swayed across the ice. Did it always creak so much? Or was that just her nerves making every sound ominous?

"The formations catch the light when the sun hits them." Thomas kept talking, his voice carrying that easy quality men used when they thought words could smooth over reality. "Like diamonds. Though I suppose you can't see much in this weather."

She couldn't. The snow had thickened until the far bank disappeared entirely into swirling white. Even the wagon ahead had started to blur at the edges, though it couldn't have been more than ten steps away.

The groaning sound came again—not the wood maybe, but something deeper. Something beneath the wheels. Her breath caught, and panic rose in her middle.

"It's just settling," Thomas said beside her, though she hadn't asked. "Ice does that. Makes all kinds of noise when there's weight on it, but that doesn't mean—"

The crack split the air like a gunshot.

Her heart stopped. The wagon lurched, its back end dropping with a sickening crunch as the ice gave way beneath it. The rip of splintering wood mixed with Clara's scream, and Kate was running before her mind caught up to her body.

"Clara!" The name tore from her throat as her boots hit the ice. She slid, caught herself, and kept moving.

Snow whipped her face, burning her eyes, but she could see the wagon—tilted at an angle now, its rear wheels disappearing into black water that churned around the broken ice.

Clara. Clara was in that wagon.

Her feet went out from under her. Her hip slammed against the ice, and a burst of pain shot up her side. Scrambling forward on hands and knees, she clawed at the slick surface. Her gloves did nothing—just slid uselessly across the frozen river.

"Kate, stop!" Strong hands grabbed her shoulder and arm. Holding her back.

She twisted against his grip, but his fingers dug into her coat sleeve. "Let go!"

"The ice won't hold you." His voice cut through the wind and her panic. "You'll go through too."

She didn't care. Clara's scream still echoed in her head—that terrified sound that cut through every rational thought. Her sister was in that wagon, and the wagon was sinking into water black as death.

"I have to—" She wrenched away, gained a single step before Thomas hauled her back again. Her boots scrabbled against the ice, slipping. "Clara!"

James had reached the horses' heads, fighting to keep them focused as they screamed and threw their weight against the traces. The front of the wagon stayed on solid ice, but the back end tilted lower with each passing second.

At the front of the bed, Clara's head rose above the tarp. Kate couldn't breathe as her sister climbed up on the bench, Rose following close behind. As James fought with the horses to pull the rig out of the churning water, the two women slipped from the death trap and crept onto the ice.

Past the horses. All the way to the safety of the far bank.

Kate's lungs burned, her breath coming in sharp gasps that tore at her throat. Clara stood on snowy ground now—alive, whole, not drowning in black water. The relief hit so hard her knees buckled. Only Thomas's grip around her kept her upright.

Then the ice beneath her feet shifted.

Not a crack—not yet—but a slight movement that sent her stomach plummeting. Every instinct in her screamed.

"Ease backward." Thomas's voice came urgent near her ear. "Slow. Don't run."

Her body craved to run. To bolt toward the bank, toward safety, toward anything solid. But her boots stayed planted, frozen by fear as much as sense.

"Kate!" Clara's voice carried across the ice, high and terrified. "Get off the ice!"

She took one step backward. Then another. Each movement felt like walking on glass about to shatter. The snow swirled thicker, coating her eyelashes and blurring everything beyond a few feet. She could barely see Clara anymore—just a dark shape on the shore.

And the wagon. Had the horses pulled it out of the water?

She couldn't tell through the snow. The shapes had dissolved into a gray and white blur—horses screaming, James shouting, the dark bulk of the wagon...but she couldn't tell if it was tilted at that horrible angle.

Another step back. Thomas moved with her, his hand locked around her waist now. His breath came hard beside her. A glance up showed his face had gone pale beneath the bruising. But his grip never loosened.

Another step. Her heel caught on something—a ridge in the ice, maybe, or just her own clumsiness born of terror. She stumbled, and Thomas's arm tightened around her middle, keeping her upright.

"Steady." His breath hit her cheek, warm against the biting cold. Then, under his breath, "God, help us." It sounded almost like a prayer.

Kate swallowed. She'd stopped looking to God a long time ago. Stopped expecting Him to answer.

And yet Thomas spoke like help was as real as the frozen earth under her boots.

They kept edging backward. The shore felt impossibly far away, though it could be only a few more steps. Every hands-breadth of ice between here and solid ground might as well have been a mile.

The wind shifted, and for a moment the snow cleared enough that she could see the distant shapes more clearly. James had gotten the horses under control. And somehow...miracle of miracles...they'd pulled the wagon up onto solid ice. The rig eased forward, one slow step at a time, to cover the final distance to shore.

Rose stood with Clara on the far bank, both of them dark silhouettes against the swirling white.

Safe. Clara was safe. The others were safe. Even their belongings.

The knowledge should have brought relief, but all she could feel was the wrongness of the ice beneath her feet and the way Thomas's breathing had gone ragged beside her ear.

Her boot hit something solid—not ice but frozen earth covered in snow. The shift registered somewhere in the panic clouding her mind, and her knees gave out completely.

She hit the ground hard, the impact jarring through her already-sore hip. Snow cushioned the fall some, but not enough to keep her teeth from clacking together.

Thomas went down beside her—or maybe she'd pulled him down. His arm still gripped her waist, his weight heavy against her side.

"Are you hurt?" His voice came out tight.

Was she? Everything ached, and yet she could feel nothing, her body caught in that strange numbness that came after terror.

Her hands shook where they pressed against the frozen ground, trembling so badly she couldn't make them stop. "I'm fine." The lie scraped her throat raw.

CHAPTER 7

Thomas pushed himself to his feet, though his ribs screamed at the movement.

The ice wouldn't hold—not here, not with the break already spreading cracks through the surface like spider webs.

Kate still crouched in the snow beside him, her shoulders heaving with ragged breaths that sent white clouds into the swirling air.

"Can you stand?" He kept his voice level despite the way his side felt like someone had driven a knife between his ribs and twisted.

She nodded, though the movement looked more automatic than certain.

He gripped her elbow and helped her up, his fingers finding purchase through the thick wool of her coat. She swayed when she found her feet, and he steadied her with his other hand at her back. "We need to go upriver."

She lifted her head, those hazel eyes finding his through the snow. For once, the suspicion had drained from her face, leaving only exhaustion and the remnants of terror. "Upriver?"

"Above the waterfall." He released her arm but kept his hand hovering near her elbow in case she swayed again. "The ice should be solid there."

Understanding flicked across her features. She glanced at the river—at the jagged break that had nearly swallowed the wagon—then nodded.

He glanced to the far side. The wagon had made it safely to the far bank, thank the Lord. The horses stood with their heads down, sides heaving, while Rose and Clara clustered near the wheels.

All safe. Everyone accounted for.

Except him and Kate, stranded on the wrong side of a river that had just proven itself deadly.

He cupped his hands around his mouth and shouted across the ice. "James! We're going upriver to cross."

His brother's response came faint through the wind, but the wave of acknowledgment was clear enough.

When he turned back to Kate, she was already stomping through the fresh powder along the bank. The wind whipped her cloak around her legs, but she pushed forward with her spine straight and her chin up.

He set out with large strides to catch up with her. The last thing he needed was to lose sight of her in this thick snowfall.

The woman had nearly watched her sister drown, had felt the ice give way beneath her own boots, and now she walked through a near-blizzard like it was just another inconvenience to endure.

The snow fell heavier with each step, coating his shoulders and hat until the weight of it dragged at his neck. His boots sank into powder that came halfway up his shins in places, and each step pulled at muscles already protesting the fight in Butte and the fall on the ice. Thick flakes clung to his eyelashes and melted on his cheeks. The wind drove it sideways, stinging any exposed skin. He tugged his hat lower and squinted to make sure they were tracking alongside the river.

The bank's edge blurred into white nothingness beside him, the distinction between solid ground and open air nearly impossible to distinguish. He kept his focus split between that and Kate's form on his other side—lose sight of either and they'd be in real trouble.

Kate stumbled. He caught her elbow before she could go down, his fingers tightening through the wool. She didn't pull away this time, just nodded her thanks and kept moving.

He finally released her arm so they could both walk easier. The cold had worked its way through his coat and trousers, settling into his bones with teeth that gnawed deeper with each gust. His ribs felt like someone tightened a vise around them with every breath.

But at least he was moving. Stop now, and the cold would win.

The bank curved, and they followed it, keeping the darker shadow of the river's edge on his right.

How long had they been walking? Five minutes? Ten? Time stretched and compressed in the storm until he couldn't be sure of anything except the burn in his lungs and the way each breath sent ice down his throat.

A figure rose through the swirling snow. White and tall—twice his height. Or more.

The waterfall.

The frozen cascade rose ahead, massive and otherworldly through the swirling white. No water moved behind it—the cold had locked it solid. The wind shrieked around the formation, finding every gap in the ice fingers to strengthen its fury.

He pushed toward the figure. He'd planned to trek up the slope to the river above the falls to find a crossing. But maybe first they could rest behind it. In that hollow space where the water had carved the rock smooth over centuries, they'd have shelter from the wind. After that, could they cross to the other side behind the falls? He'd never checked to see if there was a passage all the way through.

He moved toward it, his boots punching through snow that had drifted against the base. Kate followed without question—she'd probably spotted the shelter potential too.

Smart woman. Prickly as a cactus, but smart.

He needed to check the space first—see if the shallow cave was safe to enter before he brought Kate into a potential trap. It might be too icy, or mayhap another creature had taken shelter there.

"Wait here." He had to shout to be heard over the wind's howl.

Kate turned her face toward him, snow clinging to her eyelashes and the loose strands of hair that had escaped her scarf. She looked like she might argue, but instead gave a sharp nod.

He turned to the falls, the formation rising like something from a dream—ice columns as thick as tree trunks, frozen spray fanning out in delicate sheets that caught what little light filtered through the storm. Beautiful, if he had time to appreciate it. But he didn't have energy to spare.

Ice even coated the ground where mist must have settled before the cold locked it solid. His boots found purchase on the slick surface, though each step required care.

The wind bit through his coat as he inched closer to the frozen cascade. His hand found the ice, solid beneath his glove, and he used it to steady himself as he worked his way around the formation's edge.

The hollow opened up behind the falls—deeper than he'd remembered. Maybe ten feet deep and tall enough to stand without hunching. Barely.

The roar of wind dropped to a muted howl, and the sudden loss made his ears ring. The ice covering the opening shone a translucent blue-white where the light filtered through.

He tested the ground with his boot. Slick, but manageable if they moved carefully. The back wall curved smooth where water had carved it over the years, and the space smelled of wet stone and cold—sharp and clean after the journey through the storm.

No animals. No dangerous ice waiting to break loose and crush them. Just shelter.

He let out a cloudy breath. The air even felt warmer here, protected from the wind's teeth. Not warm—nothing about this day could be considered warm—but the difference was enough that his face stopped burning.

He worked his way around the falls to where Kate waited. She'd turned her back to the wind, her shoulders hunched against the driving snow. When he touched her arm, she startled, spinning to him with wide eyes.

"It's safe." He had to lean close to be heard. "Come on."

He reached out a hand, and she took it without hesitation.

Her fingers closed around his—cold even through their gloves—and he led her around the edge of the falls. The ice beneath their boots required every bit of his attention, each step deliberate as they inched along the formation's spiky edge.

The hollow opened before them, and Kate's grip tightened on his hand as she took in the space. The wind's howl dropped to something almost peaceful, and the sudden quiet made the pounding of his pulse loud in his ears.

The cold followed them in, but without the wind, it felt almost manageable.

Almost.

He released her hand once they'd cleared the entrance, giving her room to move deeper into the shelter. She took three careful steps, then stopped, her gaze lifting to the ice masterpiece over the opening.

"We can rest here." He could talk easier now without shouting over the storm. "Wait for the snow to ease."

She turned to look at him, snowmelt already tracking down her face from where the flakes had accumulated. "How long?"

How long would a blizzard last? He'd seen storms blow through in an hour, and others that buried the ranch for three days straight. No way to know which kind this was. Reading weather in the mountains was like trying to predict which way a spooked horse would bolt—sometimes you guessed right, sometimes you ended up in the dirt.

"I don't know." He pulled off his hat and knocked the snow from it, though more would pile up the moment he stepped back outside. "But we can't cross until we can see better. Could be an hour. Could be longer."

Her jaw tightened—just a hair, but he caught it. The woman probably wanted certainty the same way he wanted his ribs to stop screaming with every breath. Neither of them would get what they wanted today.

She turned away, moving deeper into the hollow. Her boots scraped against the ice-slicked stone, the sound echoing off the frozen walls. When she reached the back, she pressed one gloved hand against the rock face, her shoulders rising and falling with a breath that looked like it took effort.

He should say something. Offer reassurance or distraction or whatever people could give in situations like this. But his mind was as frozen as the water at his back, and the cold gnawed deeper with each passing moment.

James would take care of Clara and Rose. His brother had proven himself capable in worse situations than a broken river crossing. They'd probably go on to the Walton farm, about a quarter hour's ride past the river. Or wait it out in the wagon with blankets and the supplies.

Either way, Clara McKinney wouldn't freeze today.

But standing here in this ice cave with Kate—this was a different problem entirely.

The cold bit deeper now that they'd stopped moving. His

fingers had gone numb inside his gloves, and his toes felt like blocks of ice jammed into his boots.

He needed to do something. Standing here like a useless lump while the cold worked its way deeper wouldn't help either of them.

He scanned the hollow's depths for anything that might help them survive however long this storm trapped them here. The back corners lay in shadow where the light filtering through the ice couldn't reach.

He moved toward one back corner, his boots scraping over stone. Something dark showed against the gray rock—debris of some kind. He crouched, ignoring the protest from his ribs, and fingered sticks. A small pile of them, twisted and weathered, some no thicker than his thumb.

Wind must have blown them in during warmer months. Or maybe some animal had dragged them here to build a nest.

He gathered a large handful, testing each piece. Most felt dry despite the dampness of the cave. Brittle enough to snap between his fingers. Good kindling, but they'd burn fast—maybe fifteen minutes if he was lucky.

"What are you doing?" Kate's voice carried from where she still stood at the back wall.

"Found some wood." He moved to the other corner where another small cache lay. More sticks, these longer but just as thin. He added them to his collection. "Going to try to get a fire started."

"You have a way to light it?"

He reached into his coat pocket. His benumbed fingers could barely feel the small tin case he kept there. The tinder box was old—a gift his father had sent for his thirteenth birthday—a reminder of the man he'd never really known. But the tin had proven useful countless times over the years.

He pried open the lid with stiff fingers. The char cloth he'd replenished in Butte looked intact, protected from moisture by the sealed container. He had flint and steel too, though striking a spark with frozen hands would test his patience.

He carried the tin to the center of the hollow where the ground leveled out, then arranged the thinnest pieces of wood into a small pile. His hands shook as he worked—whether from cold or exhaustion, he couldn't tell anymore. Probably both.

Before he lit the fire though, he needed to find more wood. Anything that came from outside this cave would likely be wet, and his only chance to get it to light would be for the wood to be exposed to the heat while this dry kindling burned.

He worked himself back up to his feet, the movement sending fresh fire through his ribs, and turned to the entrance. The wind's howl promised misery the moment he stepped back into it. But they needed fuel if they were to survive this blizzard without losing toes or fingers.

"I'm going to look for more wood." He stepped toward the opening, already dreading the bite of wind against his face.

"I'll come with you." Kate's voice stopped him.

He glanced back. She'd moved away from the wall, her posture rigid despite the exhaustion that showed in every line of her face. Snow still clung to her hair where it had escaped her scarf, and her lips had taken on a bluish tinge that made his chest tighten.

He shook his head. "Stay here out of the wind. I'll be back soon." Then he ducked out of the shelter before she could speak again.

CHAPTER 8

The silence pressed against Kate's ears worse than the storm's howl had.

She stood near the back of the shallow cave, wrapping her arms around herself to hold in whatever warmth remained. Blue-white light filtered through the ice over the opening, giving everything an otherworldly glow that should have been beautiful.

She couldn't appreciate it. Not with Clara on the other side of that frozen river, probably terrified and wondering if Kate had drowned.

She curled her fingers tighter around her arms. It's a good thing she hadn't forced Clara to walk across the ice.

Yet where was Clara now? Was she safe, out there in the blizzard?

Having her so far away… Being so out of control of the entire situation…

She paced the length of the hollow, counting her steps to keep from going mad. Seven steps to the ice wall. Seven steps back. The movement helped ward off the worst of the cold, but it did nothing to quiet the fear twisting in her chest.

How long had Thomas been gone? Ten minutes? Twenty? The storm still raged beyond their shelter, the wind shrieking like something alive. What if he'd gotten lost? What if he'd fallen through more unstable ice and there was no one to pull him out?

She shouldn't care. He was practically a stranger—one who'd made it clear he wanted nothing to do with the arrangement his brothers had made. Of course she didn't want him to die though.

The thought twisted in her middle.

Boots scraped against stone, and she spun toward the entrance. Thomas ducked into the hollow, his arms laden with snow-crusted branches. His hat and shoulders wore a thick layer of white, and even the dim light didn't hide the way his jaw clenched against the cold.

Relief flooded through her—sharp and unwelcome. She tamped it down.

He dumped the wood onto the cave floor, then lowered to his knees beside the pile. His movements were careful and deliberate, but that didn't hide the slight hitch in his breathing. His ribs. The ones he kept pretending weren't injured.

He picked up a branch and brushed at the snow coating the bark, his gloved fingers clumsy. The white powder clung stubbornly to the bark, packed there by wind and moisture.

The pile was substantial—enough to keep a fire going for an hour or two if they could get it lit. But the wood glistened with moisture where the snow had begun to melt.

She moved forward before she could second-guess the impulse. Her knees met the stone beside him, the cold seeping through her skirt immediately. She reached for one of the larger branches and began working the snow off with stiff fingers.

"You don't have to—" Thomas started.

"The fire won't light if the wood's wet." She kept her attention on the branch, scraping away the packed snow. Her fingers ached with the cold even through her gloves, but the work gave her something to do besides pace and worry.

He didn't argue again. Just picked up another log and worked in silence beside her.

The rhythm of it steadied something in her chest. Brush. Scrape. Set aside. Reach for another piece. Simple tasks with clear purpose—the kind of work that didn't require thinking or feeling or acknowledging the fear still churning in her gut.

Thomas set aside the branch he'd been clearing and turned to the pile of kindling and the tinderbox he'd left in the center of the cave floor. "I'll get the flame going while you finish those."

She nodded and reached for another branch while he crouched over the small sticks.

The scrape of metal on stone echoed through the hollow—once, twice. A spark flared orange in the dimness, caught on the char cloth, then died.

Thomas struck the flint again. Another spark. This one held longer, a tiny ember glowing against the blackened fabric.

He bent low, his breath forming white clouds as he blew on the ember. The char cloth began to smoke, a thin gray thread rising in the still air.

He breathed on it again, and a tiny flame lit, an orange glow of warmth in the cold.

He fed it the thinnest twigs. The orange spread to the wood, tentative at first, then with more confidence. The small flame doubled in size.

She forced her focus back on her work.

In another minute, Thomas had a bed of fire rising from the kindling and had begun to pull the snow-free logs close to circle the fire. He snapped some of the smaller branches and placed them with the dryer kindling.

The bark hissed as moisture met heat, but the wood caught. Orange light pushed back the blue-white glow from the ice, casting dancing shadows across the stone walls.

She finished clearing the last branch and moved closer to the fire. Her fingers tingled as warmth began to seep through the wet leather and fur lining. "How long do you think the fire will last?"

"I'll go out again for more wood." He sat back on his heels, finally lifting his gaze to hers. The firelight caught the bruise on his cheek and the gash that had only just begun to scab over. "I think I can find enough to last till morning."

Till morning.

The words settled in her chest with a weight she'd rather not examine. Morning meant an entire night trapped here with him. Hours of forced closeness while Clara remained on the other side of that river, probably imagining the worst.

She pulled her hands back from the fire and tucked them under her arms instead. The warmth had begun to seep through her gloves, but her core still felt frozen solid. "Your brother." She kept her voice level, businesslike. "He'll take care of Clara?"

"He will." Something in Thomas's tone softened. "James has always been the steady one. The responsible one. He'll get them safe and warm. There's a farm a few minutes up the trail where they'll likely take shelter."

The emphasis on those words—*steady, responsible*—carried an edge she couldn't quite read. As though he were drawing a comparison that didn't favor himself.

"And you?" The question slipped out before she could stop it. "What are you?"

He laughed, though the sound held little humor. "The youngest. The spare. The one they don't quite know what to do with."

"That's not an answer."

His gaze held hers across the flames, and something flicked there—surprise, maybe, or appreciation for her directness. "No." He let the word linger. "I suppose it isn't."

Silence stretched between them, broken by the crack and

hiss of the fire. Wind howled somewhere beyond their shelter, muffled by the thick ice. A reminder that the world outside remained hostile, even as this strange bubble of warmth held them suspended.

Thomas shifted, wincing as the movement pulled at his ribs. He tried to hide his pain, but anyone who watched closely enough could see it.

"Your face isn't the only thing injured."

He waved a dismissive hand. "It's nothing. Bruised ribs. They'll heal."

"And the fight that caused them?" She let the question hang. "What kind of man gets into brawls in saloons?"

His jaw tightened. "The kind who doesn't like watching women mistreated."

That brought her up short. He'd made a similar comment before but she'd discounted it. She'd assumed—what? That he was reckless? Hot-headed? Looking for trouble? Maybe he really had been protecting someone.

"There was a girl." Thomas's voice went quiet, his gaze fixed on the flames. "Couldn't have been more than sixteen. Four men kept her there—wouldn't let her leave. One of them had her around the waist, wouldn't let go." The firelight painted shadows across his features, highlighting the bruise that spread from his cheekbone to his jaw.

"So you decided to rescue her."

"I decided to give her a choice." His gaze lifted to meet hers. "Whether she took it or not was up to her."

The distinction mattered to him—she could hear it in the careful way he shaped the words. Not rescue. Choice.

"And did she?" Kate leaned forward despite herself. "Take the choice?"

"I don't know." His mouth twisted into something that wasn't quite a smile. "By the time the fight ended, she'd disappeared. I hope that means she ran...and didn't just hide in her room."

Silence settled again. He'd gotten his ribs cracked and face battered for a girl who might not have even benefited from his help.

Reckless. The word rose in her mind, but it tasted different now. Not careless or hot-headed. Just...willing to pay a price without knowing if it would matter.

She looked away, fixing her attention on the flames instead of his face. The fire had grown stronger, fed by the branches she'd cleared, but it still felt inadequate against the cold pressing in from all sides.

She should thank him for pulling her off the cracked ice. The words formed in her mind, proper and expected.

But they stuck in her throat, tangled with the memory of watching the wagon tilt, of hearing Clara scream, of feeling the ice shift beneath her boots.

He'd stopped her from going through. His hands had locked around her when every instinct screamed to reach Clara, and he'd held her back from the black water that would have swallowed her whole.

She pressed her lips together and focused on the fire. Gratitude felt dangerous—like opening a door she'd spent years learning to keep locked. Safer to maintain the distance. Suspicion. Safer to remember his family had lied to bring Clara here.

Though *he* hadn't been the one to write those letters.

The thought circled back, persistent as the wind outside. Thomas Balfour hadn't known about the arrangement. Hadn't lied. He'd been as trapped by his brothers' scheming as she and Clara were.

Almost.

"Why did they do it?" The question slipped out before she'd fully decided to ask it. "Your brothers. Why did they send for a bride without telling you?"

Thomas reached for a stick and poked at the fire, sending a shower of sparks spiraling upward. "Because they think they know what's best for me. Always have."

The bitterness in his voice made her look closer. The firelight played across his features, highlighting the set of his jaw and the dark shadows around his swollen eye. He looked tired—bone-deep exhausted in a way that had nothing to do with the day's events.

"And what do they think is best?" She pulled her knees closer to her chest, trying to trap what little warmth had begun to thaw her insides.

"They think I need settling." He tossed the stick into the flames. "That I'm too restless. Taking too many risks. That marriage would give me something to live for instead of—" He stopped himself, his mouth pressing into a thin line.

"Instead of what?"

His gaze shifted to the ice wall, then back to the fire. "Instead of leaving for California."

California. The word hung between them like smoke. He planned to leave? That's why his brothers had acted—not just to settle him, but to trap him here. Or maybe just keep him close.

"You were going to leave your family." She didn't say it as a question.

"I was going to build my own life." The distinction clearly mattered to him. "There's a difference between leaving people behind and choosing your own path."

Was there? She'd spent years planning her escape from Columbia—from her stepmother's conniving and her father's weakness. She'd dragged Clara halfway across a continent to avoid the future that had been laid out for them. Running or choosing—the destination looked the same either way.

"Is it?" Her voice held a challenge. "Choosing a path means you know where you're going. Running just means you're desperate to be anywhere but where you are."

His gaze snapped back to hers, something sharp flashing in those hazel eyes. "And which one are you doing, Miss McKinney?"

The question landed like a slap. She tightened her jaw, heat flooding her face despite the cold still clinging to her bones. He had no right to turn this back on her.

Except he did have a point, didn't he?

She looked away, focusing on the flames instead of the uncomfortable truth in his words. The fire crackled and hissed, a piece of bark curling black as it burned. Was Butte really the place she'd chosen, or just the farthest point she could reach before the money ran out?

"I'm making sure my sister has a future." The words came out defensive. "That's not running. That's protecting what matters."

"And what about *your* future?" Thomas shifted. "Or does protecting Clara mean you don't get one?"

The question dug under her skin like a splinter. She pulled her arms tighter around herself. "My future is tied to hers. It always has been."

"That's not an answer either."

Heat flared in her chest. "You don't know anything about me or my situation."

"You're right." His voice went quiet, stripped of the defensive edge. "I don't."

The admission caught her off guard. She'd expected him to push back, to defend his question or deflect with more of that easy charm he'd used when they first met. Instead he just sat there across the fire, his bruised face half in shadow, waiting.

The silence stretched. Wind howled beyond their shelter, a reminder that the world outside hadn't softened just because they'd found temporary refuge. Kate's fingers had begun to tingle as warmth crept back into them, bringing the ache that came with thawing.

She should leave it there. Let the conversation die and retreat into the careful distance she'd maintained since stepping off that stage in Butte. Safer that way. Cleaner.

But something about the firelight and the ice walls closing them in made the words rise anyway. "My stepmother wanted Clara to marry a man old enough to be her grandfather. A widower with money and connections that would elevate our family's standing in Columbia society." Bitterness coated her tongue. "Never mind that he'd buried two wives already. Never mind that Clara was terrified of him."

Thomas's gaze stayed fixed on her face, but he didn't interrupt. Didn't offer meaningless platitudes about how it would have worked out or how Clara would have adjusted. Just listened.

"Then Clara saw the advertisement your family put in the newspaper." She pulled her knees tighter to her chest. "She corresponded, and when she received the reply, she showed me. I thought it was a miracle—a way out that wouldn't destroy her." The memory of reading those letters rose unbidden. The careful words about faith and family, about building a life together in the mountains. "I never imagined your brothers had written them without your knowledge."

Thomas poked at the fire again, though it didn't need tending. "They meant well."

"Meaning well doesn't make it right." She forced herself to soften her tone. "Clara traveled more than three months to marry a man who never asked for her. Do you have any idea what that does to a person? To believe you've been chosen, that someone wants you enough to wait for you across half a continent, only to discover it was all a lie?"

He flinched.

Good. He should feel uncomfortable. His family's deception had consequences, whether he'd known about it or not.

"I can't undo what they did." His voice turned rough. "But I meant what I said in Butte. You and Clara have choices. I'll make sure of that."

The promise should reassure her. Instead it scraped raw against the trail of broken promises behind her.

"And what will you do?" She met his gaze across the fire. "You don't think your brothers will try to meddle in your life again? They must have had a good reason to start with."

Thomas's jaw worked like he was chewing on something bitter. He stared into the flames for a long moment before answering. "I'm going to California." He finally lifted his gaze back to her. "Was planning to leave in a fortnight, but I'll see that you and your sister are safely on your way first."

He was leaving. In two weeks.

She stared at the flames, at the way they bent and twisted around the wood.

Why did it matter? She'd known from the moment they arrived in Butte that this arrangement was a disaster. That Clara wouldn't be marrying Thomas Balfour. That they'd need to find another path forward.

But somehow, hearing him say it—hearing the certainty in his voice—made their situation feel more precarious. As if the ground beneath her had been unsteady all along, and she'd only just noticed.

"So you'll abandon your family." She kept her voice level. "Leave them to manage the ranch without you."

"They'll manage fine." His tone carried that same bitterness from before. "They always have. I'm just the brother who fills in where needed but isn't actually necessary."

The words should have sounded self-pitying. Instead they landed with the flat certainty of someone stating a fact they'd accepted long ago.

His profile in the firelight—the bruise spreading across his cheekbone, the set of his jaw—spoke of decisions already made. Something about the way he held himself, even battered and trapped in an ice cave, suggested a man who'd spent years being told what he was rather than getting to choose who he wanted to be.

She understood that better than she'd like to admit. "You think being the youngest makes you unnecessary."

His shoulders tensed, the defensive wall building behind his eyes even as he kept his gaze on the fire.

Still she pushed on. "But leaving won't prove you're more than that. It'll just prove them right—that you can't commit to anything difficult."

His head snapped up, and the firelight caught the flash of anger in those hazel eyes. "You don't know what you're talking about."

"Maybe I don't." She leaned forward, the heat from the fire doing nothing to cool the anger building in her chest. "But I know what it looks like when someone makes excuses for running away. You think California will be different? That you'll finally prove yourself there?" She let out a breath that wasn't quite a laugh. "You'll just be the same man in a different place, still running from whatever it is you're afraid of."

The words hung between them, sharp and cutting.

His face shifted—the anger there deepening, but something else flicked beneath it. Something that looked uncomfortably like recognition.

Then his features lost some of the expression. Turned guarded. "California has opportunities. Land for ranching. Room to build something that's mine. Not my brothers'. Not the Balfour name. Mine."

The way he said it—*mine*—carried a weight that tightened her chest.

She knew that hunger. Had felt it clawing at her own ribs since she was old enough to understand that everything in her father's house belonged to someone else. The furniture, the silver, even the roof over her head—all of it came with conditions attached. With expectations she could never quite meet.

But wanting something didn't make running toward it the right choice.

"And when you get there?" She kept her voice steady, though something uncomfortable shifted beneath her ribs. "When you've built this ranch that's all yours, who will you share it with? Or is the point to be alone?"

His jaw worked, the muscle jumping beneath the bruise. "I'll make connections. Build a life."

"With strangers." The words came out flatter than she'd intended. "People who don't know you. Don't care about your history or your family."

"Exactly." The single word carried conviction. "No expectations. No comparisons to my brothers. Just me and what I can build with my own hands."

She should understand. Should recognize the appeal of starting fresh where no one knew your failures or your family's disappointments. Wasn't that what she'd wanted when she'd dragged Clara across the continent? A place where her stepmother's poison couldn't reach, where Clara could breathe without fear of being sold to the highest bidder?

But California felt different somehow. Thomas wasn't running toward something—he was running away from people who loved him. Who'd raised him and stood by him and yes, meddled in ways they shouldn't have. But at least they cared enough to meddle.

Who would care in California?

The thought twisted in her chest, sharp enough that she had to look away from his face. The fire crackled between them, sending shadows dancing across the walls. Her fingers had finally stopped aching with cold, though her toes still felt like blocks of wood in her boots.

"Your brothers care about you." The words came out quieter

than she'd meant them to. "They interfered, yes. Overstepped in ways they shouldn't have. But they did it because they don't want to lose you."

"They have a funny way of showing it." Thomas reached for another branch and tossed it onto the fire. Sparks flew, dancing toward the ice ceiling before winking out. "Ordering me a wife like I'm some problem to be solved."

"Better than not caring at all." The words scraped her throat raw. Her father—the way he'd retreated into his study when her stepmother started planning Clara's marriage. The way he'd nodded along with every scheme, every manipulation, too weak or too indifferent to fight for his own daughters.

Thomas's gaze found hers across the flames. Something in his expression had softened, the defensive anger bleeding into something that looked almost like understanding.

"Who didn't care for you?" His voice carried across the fire, quiet enough that she almost missed it beneath the wind's howl beyond their shelter.

The question landed too close to her broken center. Her throat tightened, and she looked away, fixing her attention on the flames instead of the concern in his tone. She shouldn't have said that. Shouldn't have let her own bitterness bleed through into words.

"It doesn't matter." She forced the words out steadily and looked away from his face, back to the flames. "We were talking about your situation, not mine."

The silence stretched again, heavy with things she wouldn't say. Couldn't say. Because once she started talking about her father's weakness, her stepmother's cruelty, the way they'd both treated Clara like a commodity to be traded and Kate like she didn't deserve to be there at all—where would it stop?

She'd spent years building walls to keep those memories locked away. Opening them now, trapped in an ice cave with a man she barely knew, felt dangerous in ways she couldn't articulate.

His gaze lingered on her face, studying her the way she'd studied him since they'd met. Calculating. Measuring. Trying to understand what lay beneath the surface.

She hated it.

Finally, he shifted, the movement accompanied by a barely audible hiss of pain. "I should get more wood." His voice had returned to that careful neutral tone—the one that gave nothing away. "Fire's burning faster than I thought."

Relief slipped through her, sharp enough to make her chest ache. He was letting it go. Not pushing for answers she couldn't give. Not forcing her to examine wounds that hadn't finished scabbing over.

She nodded without looking at him, keeping her attention fixed on the fire. "The storm sounds like it's getting worse."

He stood, the movement stiff and careful. "Won't be long." As he moved toward the entrance, his shoulders hunched against the cold that already pressed in from the opening.

The blue-white light from the ice silhouetted him for a moment before he disappeared into the swirling white beyond.

CHAPTER 9

Thomas ducked back into the hollow with his final load of wood—hopefully. This third load came from a deadfall he'd found wedged against the rocks upstream.

Frost clung to his eyelashes, turning his vision crystalline at the edges, and his fingers had gone past aching into the dangerous numbness that meant frostbite wasn't far behind.

He blinked hard to clear his sight and get his bearings in the cave.

Kate had already wiped the snow from the last two loads he'd brought, and those branches stood like a wall around the fire, drying. Nice that she'd done that without him asking.

She sat huddled near the fire and started to stand as he dropped his load, but he motioned for her to stay put. "I've already knocked most of the ice off these."

Her gaze turned hesitant. She watched him another moment, then settled back to her former position—knees drawn to her chest, arms wrapped around them. The firelight caught the exhaustion in her face, the way her shoulders curved inward.

"Thought you'd gotten lost out there." Her voice carried the edge he was beginning to recognize as her defense.

"Missed me, did you?" He dropped the wood near the fire and crouched to feed the flames. "I'm touched."

She didn't take the bait. Just watched him as he knelt by the fire and shucked his wet gloves so his hands could feel the heat.

He focused on the fire—if he only fed a log at a time, this should be enough for the flame to burn slow and steady through the night.

The *night*. The word sat heavy in his chest.

He glanced around the cave. Stone walls. Stone floor. Ice on one side, casting everything in that eerie blue-white glow.

The fire helped, pushing back the worst of the cold, but the chill still seeped from the ground like water through a cracked dam.

They'd need to sleep eventually. And there was exactly one spot in this whole frozen hollow that offered any protection from the wind feeding around the edges of the waterfall and the cold radiating through the rock—the narrow strip of floor between the fire and the back wall.

One spot. Two people.

He flexed his fingers closer to the flames, their color shifting from white to mottled red as sensation crept back in painful increments. The tingling burned worse than the cold had—like a thousand needles working their way from bone to surface.

He needed to address the sleeping arrangements. Ignoring the problem wouldn't make it disappear, no matter how much he preferred to pretend they could both hover near the fire all night without collapsing from exhaustion.

He shrugged out of his coat and fought to keep from huddling against the icy breeze as he spread the garment on the flattest section of stone near the fire. The wool still held dampness from the snow, but also a bit of warmth from his body. It wasn't much, but better than bare rock.

"Here." He gestured at the makeshift bed. "You should try to sleep. I'll keep the fire going."

Kate's eyes narrowed. "And where will you sleep?"

"I'll manage." He moved to the cave wall and sank down, fighting hard against a grimace. Once he settled, he pulled his knees up and wrapped his arms around them. The stone pressed cold and hard against his back. "Done it plenty of times out with the herds. A man learns to sleep anywhere."

"Don't be ridiculous." She didn't move toward the coat. "You'll freeze."

"I'll be fine."

"You'll be dead by morning, and then I'll have to explain to your brothers how I let their youngest sibling turn into an icicle out of some misplaced sense of chivalry."

Despite everything, a laugh escaped him. "Misplaced chivalry? I think you mean common decency."

"I'm calling it foolishness." She pushed to her feet and swayed slightly—exhaustion or cold pulling at her. "I'm not taking the only warm spot while you sit there and freeze. That's not how this works."

"Then how does it work?" He kept his voice light, but something in his chest had gone tight. "Because from where I'm sitting, our options are limited."

The silence stretched between them, filled only by the crackle and hiss of the fire. Kate stood with her arms crossed, chin lifted in that stubborn way he was beginning to recognize. The firelight caught the gold in her hair, the determined set of her jaw.

She was going to fight him on this. Of course she was. Kate McKinney would rather freeze than accept help she hadn't asked for.

"We share it." Her words came out flat, matter-of-fact. "The space. It's the only practical solution."

Thomas blinked. Of all the arguments he'd expected, that wasn't one of them.

"You're sure?" He kept his voice even. "I don't want you to feel—"

"I feel cold." She cut him off, already moving toward the coat. "And tired. And if we're going to survive this night, we need to be practical. Body heat is the most efficient way to stay warm. It's simple fact."

Simple fact. Right. Because that's all this was—a matter of practicality and survival. Nothing complicated about sharing warmth with a woman who was making his pulse jump.

He rose from the wall and helped her arrange the space.

The arrangement felt awkward—the kind of necessary intimacy that came with survival—but still made his heartbeat kick harder than the cold warranted.

Kate settled onto his coat first, her movements careful as she positioned herself on her side facing the fire. Her spine stayed rigid, every line of her body radiating awareness of the space he would occupy behind her.

He lowered himself onto the makeshift bed, his ribs screaming protest at the movement. The coat beneath them did little to cushion the stone, but it blocked some of the cold seeping from the ground. He lay on his back, leaving a careful few inches between them.

The gap felt both too much and not enough.

He pulled her cloak over them both, the fabric settling over her and reaching to cover part of his chest. The wool still carried dampness but also held the heat from the fire. Better than nothing.

Her breathing had gone shallow. He could hear it even over the fire's crackle. Her shoulders stayed tense, drawn up almost to her ears.

"You can relax." He kept his voice low. "Tension makes you colder."

"I'm perfectly relaxed."

The lie was so obvious he almost laughed. Almost. But the situation felt too precarious for humor, balanced as they were between necessity and something he didn't want to examine.

"Kate." He waited until she turned her head slightly, enough that he could see the line of her jaw in the firelight. "I'm not going to…I won't do anything you don't want." The words caught in his throat. What was he even trying to say? That he was honorable? That she could trust him?

The silence stretched long enough that it seemed maybe she wouldn't respond at all. Then her shoulders lowered, not much, but enough to see the shift.

"I know." Her admission came out barely above a whisper. "If I thought otherwise, I wouldn't be here."

Something in his chest loosened. She trusted him—not fully, maybe not even mostly—but she'd made a calculation and decided he wasn't a threat. Given everything that had happened, given the way his family had lied to bring her sister here, that small concession felt like more than he deserved.

He let the quiet blanket the space. Tried to force his own body to relax.

The stone was still cold, even through the coat. Kate's teeth chattered despite her attempts to hide it. The fire crackled, but its warmth only reached so far.

He forced himself to focus on the blaze. The flames had settled into a steady burn now, fed by the wood he'd gathered. If he was careful, it would last through the night. He'd need to add another log soon though. Maybe in an hour.

"This isn't working." Kate's voice came out tight. "It's still too cold."

She was right. The gap between them might as well have been a canyon, letting the chill pour through.

Thomas stared at the ice curtain, watching the firelight

dance across its surface. Would she allow him to...? The only way to find out was to ask.

"I'm going to..." He motioned between them. "I'll block the cold from behind."

A pause. "All right."

He inched closer, then curled around her, not quite touching but close enough that her warmth seeped through their clothes. His arm hovered for a moment before resting on her waist—the most natural position, the one that would share the most heat.

Kate went rigid. Every muscle in her body seemed to lock up, and for a moment it felt like she'd pull away, demand he move, remind him exactly how little she trusted him.

Then, slowly, she exhaled. Her shoulders dropped. She let herself lean back, just slightly, into the warmth he offered.

"Better?" His voice came out rough, and she could probably feel his breath on her ear.

"Better." Barely a whisper.

The fire popped and calmed. Wind howled somewhere beyond their shelter, muffled by ice and stone but still audible—a reminder of the storm that had trapped them here.

He focused on keeping his breathing steady, on not noticing how perfectly she fit against him, on not thinking about the fact that this was the closest he'd been to a woman in longer than he could remember.

"I hate this." Kate's voice broke the silence, so quiet he almost missed it.

He tensed. Being so near to him? He should pull back. But maybe he should make sure of her meaning. "The cold?"

"The helplessness." She shifted a tiny bit, and he felt the tension still coiled in her frame. "Clara is out there somewhere, and I can't do anything. I can't protect her. I can't even get to her."

The raw edge in her voice cut through the distance he'd kept between them. He'd heard her sharp and defensive, seen her angry and suspicious. But this—this was something else.

Something true.

"James will take care of her." He kept his voice low. "He's the most responsible man I know. Probably already has her warm and fed at that farmhouse up the trail."

"You don't understand." Her body tensed even more, as tight as her voice. "Clara is all I have. She's the only one who's ever..."

She stopped. The silence that followed felt fragile, like ice too thin to bear weight.

"Ever what?" But part of him already knew the answer. Had seen it in the way she positioned herself between Clara and every potential threat, in the fierce protectiveness that colored her every move.

"Seen me." The words came out cracked. "Really seen me. Not the disappointing stepdaughter. Not the common girl with the dead mother. Just...me." And then her voice grew strength again. "Every decision I've made, every plan I've laid—it's all been about keeping her safe. And now she's across that river and I can't—"

The words cut off. Her whole body was rigid.

"You can't protect her from everything." The truth tasted bitter even as he said it. "No matter how hard you try."

"Watch me."

The fierce certainty in those two words made something tighten in his chest. He'd heard that same tone in his own voice when his brothers tried to tell him California was too risky, too uncertain. The stubborn refusal to accept limitations that other people tried to place on you.

Except Kate's stubbornness came from love, not restlessness. From wanting to shield someone else rather than escape. Her protectiveness wasn't weakness—it was the only form of love she'd been allowed to give. The only relationship where she'd been needed, wanted, chosen.

"And what about you?" The question slipped out before he could stop it. "Who watches out for you?"

Her breath hitched—just for a moment, but he felt it through the layers of wool between them. "That's not the point."

"Isn't it?" He adjusted his arm slightly, giving her room to pull away if she wanted. She didn't. "You've spent so long protecting Clara that you've made yourself invisible. Who looks out for Kate McKinney?"

"I don't need looking out for."

The automatic response wasn't a surprise. He'd used the same deflection countless times when his brothers tried to involve themselves in his plans. The difference was his brothers kept trying anyway, kept pushing until he wanted to punch something. Or leave for California.

Kate had no one pushing. Just her, carrying the weight of keeping Clara safe, keeping them both fed, keeping everything together through sheer force of will.

The realization settled in his chest like a stone.

"Everyone needs someone." He spoke the words to the back of her head as firelight danced across the dark strands that had escaped her chignon. "Even you."

She didn't answer.

The silence stretched until it seemed almost like she'd fallen asleep. Then her voice came again, so quiet he had to strain to hear it over the fire's crackle.

"My mother died when I was four. Father promised he'd protect me."

He kept himself motionless, barely breathing. Anything to keep from ruining whatever had loosened enough for her to offer this piece of herself.

"My father remarried within the year, said it would be good for me to have a mother. Clara was born a year later. I thought..." She paused, and he felt her swallow. "I thought I'd have a family again. A mother and a sister. That the house wouldn't feel so empty anymore."

The wind howled beyond their shelter, but inside the hollow, everything had gone quiet except for the fire and Kate's voice.

"But my stepmother made it clear from the start that I was an obligation. An inconvenience to be tolerated." A bitter edge crept into her words. "I was the reminder that my father had loved someone else first…perhaps more."

Thomas's chest tightened. He wanted to say something, anything, but the words stuck in his throat. What could he offer that wouldn't sound like empty platitudes?

"When I was eight, I overheard them." Her voice had gone flat, stripped of the emotion that colored her earlier words. "My stepmother and father, in his study. The door wasn't closed all the way."

She stopped again. With his arm still draped over her waist, he could feel the rapid thump of her pulse where his hand rested near her ribs.

"She told him I was common. Like my mother had been. That I'd never be a proper lady, no matter how much money he spent on tutors and deportment lessons." The words came out emotionless, as if she'd rehearsed them so many times, they'd lost their power to wound. "She said I embarrassed them in company. That Clara would be tainted by association if they weren't careful. And then, Clara wouldn't be able to marry well enough. Like even Clara was a prized filly."

His jaw clenched. He forced himself not to speak, not to interrupt with the anger building hot in his chest.

"My father said nothing." Those four words carried more weight than everything that had come before. "Not a single word in defense of me or my mother. He just...sat there. Let her say those things. Agreement in his silence."

The fire popped, and Kate flinched against him.

And then she breathed out. "Clara was different though. She never saw me as competition or a burden. She just..." Her voice softened. "She just wanted a sister. And I wanted someone to belong to. So we held onto each other while my stepmother poisoned my father against me. At one point, he told me that if I didn't accept a marriage, he would trade Clara to the highest bidder. I agreed for her sake. But then I heard about their plans for her and I couldn't…"

His throat tightened so it was hard to breathe. Her walls made sense now, the suspicion she wielded like armor. She'd learned early that the people who should protect you would turn their backs without a second thought.

His own family wasn't perfect—far from it. But even when his brothers drove him to the edge of sanity with their meddling, even when he felt invisible as the youngest son, he never doubted they loved him. That they'd fight for him if it mattered.

Kate had grown up with a father who wouldn't defend her when his new wife belittled her.

"I'm sorry." The words felt inadequate, but he said them anyway. "You deserved better than that."

"Deserving has nothing to do with it." Her voice regained some of its edge, the vulnerability closing like a wound stitching itself shut. "Life doesn't care what we deserve. It just keeps moving, and we either adapt or get crushed." A pause. "Clara was the only one who ever told me different. Who made me feel like I was worth something beyond what I could do for other people."

"She's right." The words came out before he could stop them. "Your stepmother was wrong."

Kate's ribs expanded against his arm, a slight hitch in the rhythm of her breath. "You don't know me well enough to say that."

"I know you dragged your sister across a continent to save

her from a marriage she didn't want. I know you walked into a situation you knew was dangerous because the alternative was worse. I know you haven't complained once about being trapped in an ice cave with a man you don't trust, even though you have every right to complain." He tightened his arm around her, just slightly. "That's not common. That's extraordinary."

The silence that followed felt different than the ones before —charged with something he couldn't quite name. His body became acutely aware of every place they touched. Her back against his chest. Her hair brushing his chin. The warmth building between them that had nothing to do with survival.

CHAPTER 10

"Why are you really going to California?"

Thomas fought to keep from cringing at Kate's question as he lay beside her on the cave floor. She'd just told him so many personal details. Let down her walls enough for him to peer into her thoughts and fears. He couldn't brush off her question now.

But there were so many ways to answer. How much was he willing to tell? About the valet who'd died during his "heroic" rescue in Fort Benton—the man whose face still haunted his dreams? The knighthood that felt like a brand marking him as a fraud? The desperate need to start over somewhere no one knew his shame?

"Because I need to prove I can be more than what they expect." The half-truth tasted bitter. "Because staying here means being the spare brother forever. Because—"

Because running was easier than facing the truth about what he had done.

He didn't say it. Couldn't say it. But something in the way Kate shifted against him suggested she heard it anyway.

"Running doesn't change who you are." Her voice had gone soft, almost gentle. "It just changes the scenery."

"Speaking from experience?"

"Maybe." She was quiet a moment. "I thought bringing Clara here would fix everything. New place, new start, new life. But I'm still the same person I was in Columbia. Still afraid. Still trying to control everything because I don't know how to trust anyone else."

The confession hung between them, vulnerable and raw. She'd built so many walls, used sharp edges to keep people at a distance. And here, in the dark, with nothing but firelight and ice and the howling wind, she'd let him see behind them.

His pulse kicked against his ribs. The honesty in her words stripped away something he'd been holding onto, some pretense that this was just about survival. Just about waiting out a storm.

"I don't know how to trust either." His voice scraped. "My brothers—they love me. I know that. But they also see me as someone who needs managing. Someone who can't be trusted to make his own choices."

He shifted, searching for words for something he'd never said aloud. "I was knighted a few months ago. In Fort Benton, for saving the queen's cousin. Everyone thinks I'm a hero. But I'm not. What no one talks about is that another man died because I made a stupid decision, and somehow, I'm the one who got rewarded for it."

Kate turned in his arms—not pulling away, just shifting so she could see his face in the firelight. Her hazel eyes caught the orange glow, searching his features with an intensity that made his breath catch. In this light, her skin looked like porcelain. Flawless. Breathtaking.

"What happened?"

Her words pulled him from the distraction of her face. Back to the story he never should have begun.

He should deflect. Change the subject. Use that easy charm

to smooth over the raw edges of truth. But something about the way she looked at him—like she actually wanted to know, not just to judge but to understand—made the words rise anyway.

"The queen's cousin came to the Montana territory on a hunting expedition." He forced the words past the tightness in his throat. "Our father asked that at least one of us go to honor the royal party. Represent the family."

Kate's brow furrowed. "Your father asked? Why...?"

The confusion in her voice made him realize what he'd assumed—that she knew about his family's background. But why would she? The letters his brothers had written probably hadn't mentioned titles or nobility. Just ranch life and faith and building a future in Montana.

"I—" He swallowed, suddenly aware of how this would sound. "My father is the Duke of Clarence. In England."

Her eyes went wide, the firelight catching in them as her whole body went still against his. "Duke. As in—"

"English nobility, yes." Heat crept up his neck despite the cold. "We were sent to Montana as boys and have lived here ever since." He pushed on before she could ask more questions. He and his brothers had spent years keeping that information quiet, building reputations based on their own merit rather than bloodlines that meant nothing in the Montana Territory.

But Kate wasn't letting him move on that easily. "Sent to Montana as boys." Her voice carried that quiet tenacity he was learning to recognize—the tone that meant she'd spotted a loose thread and intended to pull it. "Dukes don't usually send their sons to the frontier. What happened?"

He should have kept his mouth shut. Should have deflected or changed the subject. But Kate's hand found his where it rested against her waist. Her fingers curled around his, warm and steady.

"My father has a cousin. Reginald Balfour." Even the name tasted foul. "He wanted Father's title—the dukedom—and he didn't care how he got it. First he tried to discredit our mother. Attacked her Scottish heritage, her Catholic faith. Claimed it made her and her sons unfit heirs."

Kate's fingers tightened against his. She said nothing, but the tension in her hand told him she was listening with every fiber.

"When that didn't work, Reginald had my oldest brother kidnapped. Will was just a boy." He kept the words flat, stripped of the emotion that still churned beneath whenever he thought of it. "Father's men found him within a day, but that was enough. Our father sent us here with our mother and the Wangs—our housekeeper and her husband—to keep us safe. An ocean between us and Reginald."

"Where is your mother now?"

His throat tightened. "She died two years later. By the time Father considered bringing us home, we'd all grown to love this place more than we ever loved England."

The silence that followed held a different quality than before—not the sharp-edged tension of their earlier exchanges, but something heavier. Sadder. Kate's thumb moved once across his knuckles, a small gesture she might not even realize she'd done.

"So the Balfour name didn't just give you a title," she said quietly. "It cost you a mother and a homeland."

The words landed somewhere deep in his chest, in a place he usually kept locked. He swallowed against the ache and forced himself back to the story he'd been telling—the one that mattered more right now than old wounds from childhood.

"ANYWAY, I went to Fort Benton to meet Lord Weldon's party. They'd set up camp outside the fort—wanted the frontier experience." He didn't succeed at keeping the bitterness from his voice. "We were three days into the hunting expedition when a grizzly wandered into camp."

Kate's breathing went shallow, her attention fixed on his face.

"It was dusk. Most of the party had gathered near the fire for dinner. I was checking my horse when I heard the screaming." The memory rose sharp—the raw terror in those voices, the way his pulse kicked into his throat. "The bear went straight for Lord Weldon. Just charged through the camp like the rest weren't even there."

His hands had started to shake. He pressed them against Kate's side, using her warmth to anchor himself in the present.

"Lord Weldon's valet—a man named Charles—he tried to stop it. Threw himself between the bear and his lord." Thomas's throat tightened. "I grabbed my rifle. But my hands shook so badly I nearly dropped it. The bear swiped at Charles, sent him flying. Then it turned toward Weldon again."

The fire crackled, and somewhere beyond their shelter the wind shrieked. Yet the echo of that grizzly's roar still vibrated through his body.

"I fired. Hit it in the shoulder. Should have aimed for the head or the heart, but I panicked. The bear turned on me instead." His chest clenched so hard, he had to remind himself to draw breath. "It charged, and I—I froze. Just stood there like a simpleton while death came at me on four legs."

He could still feel the paralyzing fear, but something about the dark and the cold and the way her hand still rested in his made it easier to break through.

"Charles threw himself at the bear again. Gave me time to get another shot off. This one hit the heart." He'd managed to make his voice flat now. Feeling these emotions would make him too raw. "The bear went down. Everyone cheered. Called me a hero. Said I'd saved Lord Weldon's life."

"But Charles?"

"Died three hours later from his wounds." Thomas couldn't make himself meet her gaze. "While I sat in a tent drinking brandy with Lord Weldon, being congratulated for my bravery. They gave me a knighthood. Threw a ceremony in Fort Benton with the territorial governor in attendance. Made speeches about courage and honor."

He forced air out through the rock on his chest. "The whole time, all I could think about was Charles's face. The way he looked at me before he threw himself at that bear the second time. Like he knew. Like he'd accepted he was going to die so I wouldn't have to."

"Your brothers don't know?"

"They know Charles died. They know I was knighted. They think..." He had to stop and breathe through the pressure building in his chest. "I guess they were hoping it would settle me down. Then when it only made it worse…"

Kate's fingers tightened around his, and he finally made himself look at her face.

He expected disgust. Judgment. Confirmation of what he already knew—that he was a fraud wearing a title he hadn't earned.

Instead, her eyes held something that looked almost like understanding.

"You think you don't deserve the knighthood because someone else died." Her voice carried no accusation, just simple observation. "You think going to California will let you escape the guilt."

"I think staying here means living with everyone believing I'm something I'm not." It was hard to speak through the lump in his throat. "My brothers look at me like I finally did something worthwhile. Like the knighthood proves I'm not just the reckless youngest anymore. But they're wrong. I'm the same person who froze when it mattered. Charles was the brave one, and he's dead while I get to wear a title and pretend I earned it."

"And now you're trying to earn what you think you didn't deserve."

The words landed like a fist to his already-bruised ribs. They'd known each other less than two days, spent most of that time arguing or trapped by circumstances. Yet somehow she'd looked past his easy smiles and deflections straight to the rot underneath.

"I froze. When it mattered most, I froze. And a good man died because of it."

"A good man died protecting someone he'd sworn to serve." Kate's voice carried quiet conviction. "That was his choice, Thomas. Not yours."

"I should have been faster. Should have aimed better the first time. Should have—"

"Should have what? Been perfect?" Her hand squeezed his harder. "You were facing a charging grizzly. Most men would have run."

"I wanted to run." The words burned worse than the cold had. "Every instinct screamed at me to drop the rifle and bolt. I stayed because my legs wouldn't move, not because I was brave."

"But you stayed." She shifted slightly, and the movement brought them closer together. "You fired. You stopped the bear. Lord Weldon lived because of your actions."

"Charles died because of them."

"Charles died doing his duty." Her voice turned fierce. "You can't take that from him by claiming responsibility for his choice. He saw his lord in danger and acted. That's who he was —not a victim of your mistakes, but a man who made a decision."

The words should have brought comfort. Instead they scraped against everything he'd been telling himself for months. His failure...he'd been using it to justify leaving Montana, running to California, where no one would know about the knighthood or Charles or the way his hands had shaken.

He'd prayed about it—once, twice, a hundred times—always

circling back to the same bargain. *If I work hard enough, if I prove myself enough, You'll let me forget.*

But God didn't bargain like that.

The guilt stayed. The title stayed. And the hollow ache stayed too, because no amount of sweat on a California range would turn him into the man Charles had been.

"My brothers think the knighthood changed me." He let his gaze roam up to the darkness shielding the stone ceiling above them. "They see me taking more risks with the horses, talking about California, and they think I'm being reckless. But really, I'm just trying to prove I'm not the coward I've already shown myself to be."

Her thumb began tracing circles on his hand again. "Anyone paying attention can already see you're not. When you pulled that girl away from those men in the saloon. When you pulled me off the ice today. When you went into that storm three times to gather wood, even though your ribs were burning and you probably couldn't feel your fingers." She paused. "Those aren't the actions of a coward."

He wanted to argue. Wanted to point out that helping a girl in a saloon and gathering firewood weren't the same as facing down a charging grizzly. But the conviction in her voice made the protests die in his throat.

"You're not running from cowardice." Kate's words came softer now, almost gentle. "You're running from the weight of everyone's expectations. From having to be the hero they think you are."

The accuracy of it stole his breath. That was exactly it—the suffocating pressure of living up to a reputation built on one terrible moment. The way his brothers looked at him now, like he'd finally become someone worthy of the Balfour name. The settlers in Walnut Springs who'd heard about the knighthood and treated him with new deference he hadn't earned.

"California won't fix that." She said it so matter-of-factly, like stating the obvious. "You'll just carry it with you. The guilt. The doubt. All of it."

"At least there I can fail on my own terms." He'd not thought about those words before they came out, but they were true. "Not as the Duke of Clarence's disappointing youngest son. Not as the knight who let a man die. Just...me."

"Just you." She repeated the words, and the hint of a smile touched her mouth. A pretty mouth. "And who is that, exactly?"

The question hung between them, simple and impossible. Who was Thomas Balfour when you stripped away the title, the family name, the expectations?

He didn't know. That was the terrifying part—he'd spent so long defining himself in opposition to what others wanted that he'd never stopped to figure out what he actually wanted for himself.

"I don't know," he admitted. "But I thought maybe in California I could find out."

Kate was quiet for a long moment. The fire had burned lower, casting longer shadows across the ice walls. The cold pressed closer now, seeping through their makeshift bed despite their shared warmth.

"You know what I think?" Her voice carried a thoughtful quality he hadn't heard before. "I think you already know who you are. You're just afraid you won't be enough."

The words struck something deep in his chest, resonating like a bell. *Afraid you won't be enough.*

Wasn't that the heart of it? The fear that without the title, without his family's name, without some grand achievement to point to, he'd just be...ordinary.

Forgettable.

The spare brother who never quite measured up.

Kate's expression shifted, something in her features softening. "Maybe you should take some time to figure out who you want to be. Not in California. Not by running away from people who care about you. But here. Where it's hard."

"You sound like James."

The corners of her mouth curved. "Your brother sounds wise."

A laugh escaped him despite everything. "Don't let him hear you say that. His head's big enough already."

A sparkle lit her eyes, and the sight of it did something strange to his pulse. When had she gotten so close? He could count her lashes in the firelight, see the exact place where gold met green in her irises.

"You should sleep." He rose on his elbow and leaned forward just enough to toss two more logs on the fire. Then he sank back down to the cave floor beside her.

This time, when he closed his eyes, his mind didn't churn with all the worries. He could breathe a little deeper. And the luxurious feeling of Kate's warmth beside him was his last thought before sleep pulled him in.

CHAPTER 11

Sunlight.

Kate blinked against the golden glow of morning streaming through the ice wall, so bright after the blue-gray dimness from before. The storm had passed sometime in the night, leaving behind a world transformed—the frozen waterfall no longer a prison but a glittering cathedral, light penetrating through the ice in a thousand tiny rainbows.

She lay still for a moment, letting her eyes adjust. Warmth pressed against her back, solid and steady, and it took her sleep-fogged mind a long moment to remember why.

Thomas.

His arm was draped over her waist, heavy with sleep. His breath stirred the hair at the nape of her neck in a slow, even rhythm. At some point in the night, they'd shifted—or she had—and now she lay on her side, snuggled back against him like a child seeking comfort from a nightmare.

She should move. Should pull away before he awoke and realized how tangled they'd become.

Instead, she turned her head. Just enough to see his face.

In sleep, Thomas Balfour looked younger than his twenty

years. The tension she'd grown accustomed to seeing in his jaw smoothed away, leaving something almost vulnerable in its place. The bruise on his cheekbone still smudged a dark purple, and the gash above it had scabbed into an angry red line. But even battered, even exhausted, there was a handsomeness to his features that made her chest ache in ways she'd never let herself feel.

His copper-brown hair had fallen across his forehead, and before she could stop herself, her fingers twitched with the urge to brush it back.

What was wrong with her?

She knew better than this. She'd spent years learning not to want things she couldn't have, not to trust in promises that people would only break.

But lying here, watching Thomas sleep, the familiar warning felt hollow. Like words repeated so often they'd lost their meaning.

He'd kept her warm through the night. Had shared pieces of himself she suspected he didn't show many people. Had looked at her across the fire and called her extraordinary.

For one moment, she let herself want. Not just the warmth of his body or the safety of his arms—but him. This frustrating, charming, reckless man, who was planning to move to California and leave his entire life behind.

Then Thomas stirred, and the moment shattered like thin ice.

She squeezed her eyes shut to pretend she still slept.

His breathing changed—the slow, even rhythm shifting to something more conscious. The arm around her waist tensed, then carefully withdrew.

She kept her eyes closed, her own breathing deliberately steady while every nerve in her body tracked his movements. The rustle of fabric as he sat up. The soft hiss of pain that escaped when the motion must have pulled at his ribs. The scrape of his boots against stone as he moved toward the fire.

The cold rushed in where his warmth had been, sharp enough to make her want to pull him back.

She didn't.

Only when she heard him feeding wood to the flames did she allow herself to pretend to wake.

She stretched, making the movement slow and deliberate—as though she'd been deeply asleep and hadn't felt every moment of his withdrawal. Her muscles protested the hard ground, her hip aching where she'd lain on the stone despite the coat beneath her.

"Morning." His voice came from near the fire, his tone flat.

She pushed herself upright, wincing as her body reminded her of yesterday's ordeal. Every joint stiff, every muscle sore. She must look a disaster—hair falling from its pins, dress wrinkled and stained, face probably smudged with smoke and dirt.

She couldn't let herself care.

"The storm stopped." She kept her tone as level as his, as though they hadn't spent the night wrapped around each other. As though she hadn't lain beside him while he shared about Charles and the grizzly.

"Hours ago, from the looks of it." Thomas crouched by the fire, poking at the flames with a stick. He didn't look at her. "Sun's been up a while."

She moved to join him, her legs unsteady as blood flow returned to her feet. "How long do you think it will take to find the others?"

"Less than an hour probably. We should be able to cross above the waterfall, then it's just a matter of getting back to the main trail. I suspect they all spent the night at the Walton place, about a quarter hour from the river."

The Walton place. She didn't know who Walton was—probably some rancher or settler who'd carved out a life in these mountains. But knowing Clara had shelter made the knot in her chest loosen a little.

"We should go then." She moved toward her cloak, now piled beside their makeshift bed. The fabric had dried stiff, but it would be better than nothing.

Thomas finally looked at her, and something flickered in his expression before his features went guarded again. "You should eat something first. I have jerky in my coat pocket."

Her stomach clenched—hunger she'd been ignoring. But the thought of sitting here, drawing out this strange intimacy while pretending last night hadn't happened, made her want to bolt into the snow.

"I'm fine." She fastened her cloak with fingers that fumbled more than they should. "Clara's been alone all night. I need to get to her."

"She hasn't been alone." His voice carried an edge now, frustration bleeding through the careful tone. "Rose and James were with her. She's probably had a hot meal and a warm bed while we've been freezing in a cave."

The words stung more than they should have. She tightened her jaw as she finished with the clasp. "I'm aware your family is taking care of her. That doesn't change the fact that she's probably terrified something happened to me."

Thomas stood, the movement stiff despite his attempt to hide it. "You're right." The fight drained from his voice as quickly as it had appeared. "Let me put out the fire, and we'll go."

He kicked snow over the flames, the hiss and steam rising between them like a wall. The silence felt different than it had last night—heavier now, weighted with all the things they'd said and couldn't unsay.

He gathered his coat from the ground and shrugged into it, his face tightening as the movement pulled at his ribs. She looked away before he could catch her watching.

They left the hollow without speaking, stepping between the ice curtain and the rocky cliff. Ahead, the blinding white of sun on snow glared so sharp, she had to raise a hand to shield her eyes.

The snow crunched beneath their boots as they rounded the frozen cascade. Thomas moved ahead of her, his shoulders hunched against the cold, breath forming white clouds in the crisp morning air.

The world had transformed overnight. Snow blanketed everything in pristine white, unmarred except for the tracks of some small animal that had ventured out at dawn. The river stretched ahead, its surface a solid sheet of white where yesterday's break had already been covered by fresh snowfall.

A horse's whinny cut through the stillness.

She snapped her head toward the sound. There—at the river's edge, perhaps twenty strides downstream—sat a man on horseback. Dark coat. Expensive by the cut of it, even from this distance. The horse beneath him was a fine bay gelding, the kind that cost more than most families earned in a year.

Recognition slammed into her chest.

Edmund Hartwell.

"Who is that?" Thomas had stopped beside her, his attention following her gaze.

She couldn't answer. Her throat had closed around the words as Mr. Hartwell turned his horse toward them. Even across the distance, she could see the moment he recognized her—the way his posture shifted from casual observation to rigid attention.

The horse picked its way through the snow, each step deliberate as they came closer.

Kate's pulse hammered against her ribs. What was he doing out here?

Mr. Hartwell reined his horse to a stop a few strides away, his gaze sweeping from Kate to Thomas and back again. His silver hair caught the morning light, perfectly styled despite the weather, and his dark coat showed barely a wrinkle. Even his gloves looked pristine—expensive leather that had probably never seen a day of real work.

"Miss McKinney." His voice carried the same cultured tone it had when he spoke during the stage ride. But underneath it ran something cold. "I must say, this is quite unexpected."

She forced herself to stand straighter, to meet his gaze without flinching. "Mr. Hartwell. What brings you out in this weather?"

"I might ask you the same question." His attention shifted to Thomas, lingering on the bruised face and rumpled clothes with obvious distaste. "Though I believe I'm beginning to understand the situation."

The implication in his words made her stomach dip. She opened her mouth to explain—the storm, the broken ice, the cave—but the expression on Mr. Hartwell's face stopped her cold. Their wrinkled clothing. The cave behind them. The complete absence of any chaperone.

He'd already decided what this looked like.

"Mr. Balfour and I were caught in the storm," she said anyway, keeping her voice level. "The river ice broke. The rest of our party made it across, but the blizzard grew worse. We took shelter until it passed."

"I see." Mr. Hartwell's mouth curved into something that wasn't quite a smile. "And this gentleman is...?"

"Thomas Balfour." Thomas stepped forward, extending his hand. "Of the Balfour Ranch, about a day's ride north of here."

Mr. Hartwell made no move to take the offered hand. His gaze traveled over Thomas again. "The Balfour Ranch. Yes, I've heard of it." His tone suggested he'd heard nothing favorable. "And you were escorting Miss McKinney to this ranch?"

"Her sister is traveling there." Thomas's tone had gone flat. "Miss McKinney was accompanying her."

"Her sister." Mr. Hartwell repeated the words slowly, as though tasting them. His attention shifted back to Kate, and something in his expression made her skin crawl. "The young woman who was to be married, I believe? The mail-order bride?"

Heat flooded Kate's face. He'd heard their conversation on the stage—of course he had. She'd been foolish to discuss Clara's situation so openly, but exhaustion and worry had loosened her tongue.

"My sister, Clara, yes." She lifted her chin, refusing to show the shame burning through her. "She's engaged to Mr. Balfour's brother."

The lie came out smooth, automatic. Better to let him believe the arrangement still stood than try to explain the tangled mess of Thomas's brothers' deception.

"Is she?" Mr. Hartwell's eyebrow climbed. "How convenient. And you spent the night...where, exactly?"

Her mind scrambled for an acceptable explanation—trapped overnight in a cave with an unmarried man, no chaperone, their bodies pressed together for warmth. It didn't matter that nothing improper had happened. Society didn't care about truth when scandal made a better story.

And Edmund Hartwell moved in the exact society she needed to build her seamstress business.

"In a cave behind the waterfall." Thomas gestured behind them toward the frozen cascade. "It was the only shelter available. Miss McKinney's safety was my main concern."

"Your main concern." Mr. Hartwell's tone dripped with skepticism. "How very noble of you, Mr. Balfour." He shifted in his saddle, the leather creaking.

She tried again. "We were caught in the storm. There was no impropriety. We simply—"

"You spent the night together." Each word fell like a stone into still water. "Alone. Unchaperoned. In a cave."

Thomas shifted into a wider stance, his presence like a wall at her side. "Mr. Hartwell, we were traveling with my brother and sister-in-law to my family's ranch when the accident occurred. I assure you, nothing untoward—"

"I know the Balfour family by reputation." Mr. Hartwell's gaze didn't soften. "Respectable ranchers. Your brother James, if I recall, recently married. But that doesn't change what I've witnessed here."

His hand moved to his coat pocket, and he rubbed something between his fingers—a nervous habit, perhaps, or a way of steadying himself for what came next.

"My wife had arrangements with Miss McKinney." He spoke slowly, as though the words pained him. "Business arrangements. She was quite taken with the young lady's needlework on the stage from Fort Benton."

Hope flickered in her chest—irrational, desperate hope that maybe he would understand. That the connection with his wife might count for something.

"Mr. Hartwell, please." She hated the pleading note in her voice but couldn't quite suppress it. "If you would just let me explain to Mrs. Hartwell—"

"Miss McKinney." His tone gentled, but his expression remained fixed. "I am a businessman. I deal in facts and appearances. The fact is that you spent the night unchaperoned with a man who is not your husband. The appearance..."

He spread his hands, letting the implication hang in the frozen air. "Butte society may be rougher than what you knew in the East, but it is no less unforgiving. If word spread that Audrey had taken on a seamstress of questionable reputation—" He shook his head. "She would never recover from the shame. Nor would I ask her to."

The words landed like a shovel-full of dirt on the coffin of her plans—the business arrangement, gone. The independence she'd planned to build, gone. The backup plan if the ranch didn't work out, the security of knowing she could support herself and Clara, all of it crumbling to dust.

"There was nothing improper." Thomas's voice went hard. "Miss McKinney behaved with perfect propriety under dangerous and impossible circumstances. Any man with sense would see that."

Mr. Hartwell's gaze flicked to Thomas with something that might have been sympathy. "Perhaps. But sense has little to do with society, young man. You would do well to learn that."

He gathered his reins, preparing to leave, and the last of her hope drained away. This was really happening. Her reputation —the only thing of value she possessed in this new land—was being stripped away by a chance encounter and the rigid rules of propriety she'd spent her whole life trying to escape.

"I am sorry." Mr. Hartwell met her eyes, and what looked like genuine regret pooled in his gaze. "Truly. You seemed a capable young woman, and Audrey was looking forward to your work. To helping you succeed with your plans. But you must understand—reputation is the only currency that matters out here. Once lost, it cannot be recovered."

He tipped his hat—still maintaining the form of civility even as he destroyed her future—and turned his horse toward the trail.

Then he was gone, picking his way down the ridge, leaving Kate standing in the snow with her ruined reputation and the man who had inadvertently destroyed it.

CHAPTER 12

The Walton cabin sat squat and solid against the white landscape, just as Thomas remembered it. The smoke curling from its chimney held the promise of warmth.

The door flew open before he and Kate had crossed half the yard. Clara burst through it like a shot from a cannon, skirts clutched in her fists, her honey-blonde braid streaming behind her. "Kate! Oh, thank God—Kate!"

She collided with her sister hard enough to make Kate stumble, arms wrapping around her in a grip that looked almost painful.

Thomas hung back, taking it all in as Kate's composure finally cracked—her face crumpling as she buried it in Clara's shoulder, her hands fisting in the back of her sister's coat.

Neither of them spoke. They didn't need to. The raw relief pouring off them both said everything words couldn't.

Something twisted in his chest. This was what Kate had meant in the cave, when she'd talked about Clara being the only one who truly saw her. This fierce, desperate love between them —it was a bond he recognized. The kind he had with his own brothers, even when they drove him mad with their meddling.

James appeared in the doorway, his shoulders filling the frame. His eyes swept over Thomas with the assessing gaze of an older brother who'd spent too many years worrying. "You're all right?"

Thomas nodded, but something in his expression must have given him away. James's eyes narrowed. At least he didn't voice his question. Not yet.

"Come inside." Rose poked her head around James. "There's food and a fire. You both look half-frozen."

He'd never been inside the Walton place, though he'd stood in the yard getting to know the family a few times. As he followed the women inside, he had to squint against the dimness.

The interior matched most of the other cabins in this wilderness—a single large room that served as kitchen, eating space, and parlor all at once. A fire crackled in the stone hearth along one wall, and the smell of something savory made his stomach clench with sudden, desperate hunger.

Mrs. Walton stood at the stove, a woman in her middle years with graying brown hair tucked under a simple cap. She turned as they entered, her weathered face creasing into a smile. "Come and warm yourself by the fire. There's plenty of hot porridge ready for you."

He let himself be ushered to a ladder-back chair near the hearth, his body sinking into it with relief he didn't want to show. Kate took the chair beside him, Clara hovering close like she feared her sister might vanish if she moved too far away.

Mrs. Walton pressed a bowl of porridge into his hands, steam rising from the thick mush.

The first bite scalded his tongue, but he didn't slow. After a night of nothing but jerky and cold, the warmth spreading through his chest felt like salvation.

James moved to stand against the wall nearest Thomas, his arms folded across his chest in that way he had when he was working through a problem. Rose stepped to Kate's other side and rested her hand briefly on the younger woman's shoulder—a gesture of comfort Kate didn't quite flinch away from.

"We waited at the river as long as we could." James's voice carried the weight of a man who'd spent the night second-guessing every decision. "But the storm was getting worse, and the horses were panicking. I had to get Rose and Miss Clara to safety."

"You did the right thing." He swallowed his bite. "We took shelter in the cave behind the waterfall. Made it through fine."

James nodded. "I figured you had." He slid a glance to the sisters. "It's the only reason I didn't go back out after you." He pushed off from the wall. "We were praying for you both. Thankful God brought you through. I'm going out to check on the horses. Once you two get warm and your bellies full, we'll head out." He clapped a hand on Thomas's shoulder as he passed toward the door.

Thomas did his best not to let his mind wander through the last day as he spooned his final bite of mush.

Clara kept up a steady stream of chatter—how worried she'd been, how James had assured her they'd find shelter, how she'd barely slept for fear of what the morning would bring.

Kate listened and nodded and made soothing sounds, but she didn't offer much about their night. Didn't mention the cave or the fire or the conversations that had stretched into the dark hours.

Didn't mention waking up tangled together.

He forced his attention to his bowl. Every time he looked up, Kate was carefully *not* looking at him. As if by unspoken agreement, they'd decided to pretend the intimacy of those hours hadn't happened. That they were still the same strangers who'd snipped at each other in that Butte café, suspicious and defensive and miles apart.

Except they weren't. And pretending otherwise felt like a lie.

The memory surfaced unbidden—Kate's voice in the darkness, cracked with vulnerability she'd never have shown in daylight. His arm around her waist, pulling her close against the cold. The moment he'd called her extraordinary and watched something shift in her eyes.

He shoved another bite of stew into his mouth and tried to think about California.

They set out within the hour, pushing on to the ranch while the weather held. The wagon had survived intact, the horses were rested, and no one wanted to impose on the Waltons' hospitality longer than necessary.

The miles passed in near silence. Thomas sat up on the bench beside James again as the familiar landmarks slid by—the split pine where lightning had struck three summers back, the outcropping of granite that marked the turn off the main road toward home, the valley opening up ahead where herds of elk and deer always grazed.

Home. The word sat strange in his mind now, weighted with complications it hadn't carried two days ago.

James cast sideways glances at him, the kind that said he had questions but was waiting for the right moment to ask them. Thomas kept his attention fixed on the trail ahead.

Behind them in the wagon bed, the women's voices rose and fell—Clara's bright chatter punctuated by Kate's quieter responses and Rose's gentle additions. Normal conversation. Safe conversation. Nothing about caves or storms or the way two people could share their darkest truths in the night and then pretend it never happened in the daylight.

His ribs ached with every jolt of the wagon. His face throbbed where the bruises had deepened overnight. But those pains felt distant compared to the hollow sensation spreading through his chest every time Hartwell's words resurfaced.

I believe I'm beginning to understand the situation. The way his face had hardened when Kate hesitated. The careful, devastating way he'd explained exactly what her ruined reputation would cost her.

He gripped the edge of the bench seat. Nothing improper had happened. He'd kept her alive through a blizzard—that was all. Any decent man would have done the same.

But Hartwell hadn't cared about decency. Hadn't cared about survival or necessity or the simple fact that Kate McKinney had done nothing wrong. All he'd seen was a woman emerging from a cave with a man who wasn't her husband, and he'd rendered judgment accordingly.

The injustice of it burned in his chest.

Kate had plans. Dreams.

A future she'd been building with nothing but her own two hands and a talent for needlework. And now, because of a blizzard and a broken wagon and Thomas's presence at the wrong moment, all of it might be gone.

The sun had climbed a little past the midday mark by the time James pulled the wagon off the trail into a clearing sheltered by tall pines. The spot caught the light in a way that made the snow sparkle like scattered diamonds, and the trees blocked the worst of the wind still gusting down from the peaks. "We'll stop here. Let the horses rest."

Thomas climbed down from the bench, his boots sinking into snow that had already begun to soften in the midday warmth. In the wagon, the women were already gathering food from the crate where Rose had packed supplies for the journey.

He and James helped the women down, then James moved to check the horses' hooves for ice, leaving Thomas standing uselessly in the snow.

He should help. Should do something with his hands besides curl them into fists every time his mind circled back to Hartwell's insinuations.

"Thomas."

He turned. James had straightened from examining the lead

mare's front hoof, his expression unreadable in the dappled sunlight filtering through the pines.

"Walk with me." It wasn't a request.

Thomas followed his brother away from the wagon, their boots crunching through the crusted snow until the voices of the women faded to a distant murmur. When James finally stopped, they stood at the clearing's edge where the ground dropped away into a shallow ravine.

"What happened?" James kept his voice low, but the weight behind it pressed hard on Thomas's shoulders.

"I told you. Storm got worse. We took shelter."

"And?"

Thomas met his brother's gaze. James had always been able to read him—a talent that had saved Thomas from consequences more times than he could count growing up...and gotten him lectured just as often. No point in trying to hide what his brother would fish out anyway.

"We had a visitor this morning. As we were leaving the cave." He tried not to growl the words. "Edmund Hartwell. The copper baron from Butte."

James's expression sharpened. "Hartwell found you?"

"Found us coming out from behind the frozen waterfall, looking exactly like two people who'd spent the night together in a cave." He bit out a laugh. "He drew his own conclusions."

"Which were?"

"That Kate's reputation is ruined. That his wife can't possibly associate with a woman of questionable character, or recommend her services." The bitterness in his voice came out stronger than he meant. But honestly. The gall of the man. "He was decently polite about it. Very regretful. Made sure we understood that reputation is the only currency that matters out here."

James stood quiet a moment. The silence stretched between

them, broken only by the whisper of wind through pine branches and the distant sound of Rose's laughter.

His brother's jaw worked, the muscle jumping beneath the skin. James had that look—the one he got when he was calculating possibilities, weighing options against each other with the careful precision he brought to everything.

"Did you tell him nothing improper happened?"

"Of course I did." Thomas kicked at a clump of snow, sending it tumbling down into the ravine. "Might as well have been talking to a fence post. He'd already made up his mind."

"And Kate? How did she take it?"

The memory of her face—the way all color had drained from it as Hartwell delivered his verdict—tightened his chest all over again. She'd stood there in the snow, spine straight despite the blow, chin lifted even as everything she'd planned crumbled around her. Determined to the last.

"She didn't say much." He forced the words past the knot in his throat. "What could she? The man wasn't wrong about how it looked."

"But he was wrong about what happened."

"Doesn't matter." He turned to face his brother fully. "You know how this works. Truth doesn't count for much when scandal makes a better story. And Kate was counting on Mrs. Hartwell's patronage to establish her seamstress business in Butte. That's gone now."

"We'll need to do something." James's voice had shifted into that practical mode. The older brother identifying a problem, preparing to solve it. "Something to protect them both."

"What kind of something?" The question felt hollow. He already knew the answer. Had known it since Hartwell rode away, leaving devastation in his wake.

"When we get to the ranch, we'll all sit down. Talk about what the right thing is." James met his gaze. "All of us. Including you."

The right thing.

"Maybe both women should plan to stay at the ranch." James shrugged.

"She won't want to."

"Wanting and having choices are different things." His brother's tone carried that practical edge Thomas had always both admired and resented. "You said yourself she has nowhere else to go."

The truth of it sat like a stone in his gut. Kate McKinney, who'd spent her whole life fighting for independence, who'd dragged her sister across half a continent to escape being trapped. She'd have no choice now but to accept the charity of strangers. The very thing she'd been so determined to avoid.

And it was his fault. If he'd been faster crossing that river. If he'd found different shelter. If he'd made her stay in the wagon with James and the others instead of—

"This isn't on you." James's voice cut through the spiral of his thoughts.

Thomas glared at him. "It is though. If I hadn't—"

"If you hadn't what? Kept her alive through a blizzard?" James's expression hardened. "The ice broke. The storm came. Those were circumstances neither of you controlled. You did what any decent man would do—you made sure she didn't freeze to death."

"And destroyed her reputation in the process."

James shook his head. "Hartwell destroyed her reputation. By choosing to see scandal instead of survival. By valuing appearance over truth. Don't take that burden on yourself."

Thomas nodded and shifted his focus back over the landscape. In truth, none of this was what really bothered him.

Maybe it was time he admit the reality aloud. Maybe James would stop pushing so hard.

He swallowed. "I don't know if I can—" His voice almost

cracked, so he stopped. Tried again. "I don't know if I can give her what she needs."

James stayed quiet a long moment. When he spoke, his tone had softened. "None of us know that when we start. We just choose to try."

The knot in his throat had pulled tight enough to keep him from answering, even if he'd had the words. So he nodded.

After another moment, James braced a hand on Thomas's shoulder—the same gesture he'd used a thousand times over the years. "We should get moving. Still have a few hours to the ranch."

They walked back to the others in silence. Kate looked up as they approached, and for just a moment, her eyes met his.

A question lingered there. The fear she was trying to hide behind that careful, guarded expression. She knew something was coming. Could probably guess what it would ask of her, of them both.

He had to look away first.

He wasn't ready to face what he saw in her eyes. Wasn't ready to face what stirred in his own heart when he looked at her.

Stay or go. Run or commit. Keep pretending he was fine, or admit that something changed in that frozen cave—something that couldn't be unchanged.

The decision waiting at the ranch felt close enough to touch.

And for the first time in his life, he had no idea which way he would—or should—choose.

CHAPTER 13

The Balfour ranch house rose from the darkness like something out of a dream—lamplight spilling golden from every window, smoke curling from the massive stone chimney into the pitch-black sky.

Kate's chest tightened as the wagon rolled to a stop in the yard. After two days of cold and fear and uncertainty, the sight of that solid log structure felt almost too good to be real. Like it might dissolve if she blinked too hard.

The front door burst open before James had even set the brake. An older woman emerged—petite, dark-haired, moving with the kind of quickness that spoke of years managing a household. Behind her came two men, both tall and broad-shouldered—Balfour brothers for sure.

"Thank the Lord." The woman's voice carried across the yard, rich with relief and something that might have been a slight accent. "We watch for you since the storm cleared. Come, come—inside, all of you. There's hot food and warm fires."

Kate let one of the men help her down from the wagon, her legs unsteady after hours of sitting. Clara pressed close to her side, and having her there helped settle the racing in Kate's chest. Something solid to anchor to while the world tilted and re-shaped around them.

The older woman descended the porch steps with surprising speed for someone of her years, her dark eyes sweeping over both sisters with an assessing warmth that tightened Kate's throat.

"You must be frozen through." She took Kate's arm on one side and Clara's on the other. "I am Mrs. Wang—Bea. I keep house for these boys since they were small. Come now. Inside with you both."

They were shepherded up the porch steps before Kate could form a protest.

The warmth hit the moment they crossed the threshold, wrapping around her like a blanket. She squinted as her eyes adjusted from the darkness outside to the golden lamplight filling the great room.

Polished wood floors. A massive stone fireplace with flames crackling behind an iron screen. Furniture that looked both sturdy and somehow refined—not the rough-hewn pieces she'd expected in a frontier ranch house, but something that spoke of care and taste.

Movement near the fireplace caught her attention. A young woman rose from a rocking chair, a bundle of blankets cradled in her arms. Dark hair pinned up in a simple style. A face that carried a delicate, almost ethereal beauty despite the shadows of exhaustion beneath her eyes.

"You made it." Relief laced her voice. She moved closer, and Kate caught a glimpse of the infant's face—tiny features slack with sleep, a tuft of dark hair visible beneath the blanket's edge. "We've been so worried. I'm Mandie—Enoch's wife."

Enoch. That would be the oldest brother Thomas mentioned.

Mandie offered a tired smile. "I'm so glad you're all safe. When the storm came through yesterday, we feared the worst."

Kate managed a nod, though exhaustion made her mind sluggish. This room held so much warmth and light and so many people suddenly surrounding them. She'd expected...what? A cold reception? Suspicion? Instead, these strangers looked at her and Clara with something like genuine concern.

One of the men who'd helped them from the wagon stepped forward—taller than Thomas, with darker hair and gentle brown eyes. "I'm Robert Balfour. The middle brother." His gaze moved between Kate and Clara. "You've had quite an ordeal."

"That's putting it mildly." Thomas's voice came from behind them as he and the other brother entered, carrying the trunks. His tone held that same careful lightness she'd come to recognize as his usual cover.

Robert's attention fixed on his youngest brother, and something passed between them—a question in Robert's expression that Thomas didn't quite answer.

Instead, Thomas set down the trunk and moved toward the fire, his movements stiff enough that his ribs were probably bothering him more than he'd admit.

Mrs. Wang clucked her tongue, her sharp gaze taking in Thomas's bruised face and careful movements. "You look like you wrestle bear. Sit. I bring food."

"I'm fine, Mrs. Wang—"

"Sit." The command left no room for argument. She pointed at a chair near the fire. "Get warm. No one argue with me tonight."

Kate almost smiled. This feisty housekeeper didn't seem daunted by anything.

Clara's hand found Kate's, and Kate gave a gentle squeeze as she slid a look at her sister. Exhaustion was written in every line of Clara's face. How much sleep had she gotten last night because she'd been worrying?

The man who'd carried in the other trunk stepped forward now. His bearing held a quiet authority that set him apart from his brothers, something in the set of his shoulders that spoke of a responsibility carried long.

"I'm Enoch." His voice was deeper than Thomas's, steadier than Robert's. His blue eyes moved from Kate to Clara with careful assessment. Not cold but measuring. "Welcome to our home."

Our home. The words settled strangely in Kate's chest. She'd expected this place to feel foreign, hostile even. Instead, the warmth and genuine concern radiating from these people made something ache behind her ribs.

"Thank you." She gave a slight nod. "We're grateful for your hospitality."

"Let me show you to your room." Mandie appeared at Kate's elbow. "Then you can decide whether you want to come down to eat, or I can bring up a tray. You both need rest more than anything, I'd wager."

She should protest—to insist she was fine. But maybe Clara did need the rest.

And besides, her body felt like it weighed twice what it should, every muscle protesting the hours of sitting in the cold wagon after a night on stone.

"This way." Mandie moved toward the stairs, and Kate followed, with Clara still pressed close to her side.

The staircase rose along the far wall, wide enough for two people to walk abreast. Kate's hand found the smooth banister, worn from years of use but well-maintained. Everything in this house spoke of that same care—nothing ostentatious, but nothing neglected either.

They reached the landing, and Mandie led them down a hallway lit by oil lamps in brass sconces. The baby stirred in her arms, making a small sound before settling again. "We didn't know you were both coming, so I only had one room ready. I can ready another easily though."

"One room is perfect." Clara spoke up before Kate could respond. "We'd prefer it, actually."

Mandie's expression softened. "Then you'll be comfortable here." She stopped before a door near the end of the hall and pushed it open.

The room beyond was smaller than Kate expected, but somehow that made it feel cozier rather than cramped. A large bed dominated one wall, covered in a lovely quilt—intricate stitching in shades of blue and cream that caught the lamplight. A washstand and chest of drawers stood near the window, and a braided rug covered most of the floor.

But the window itself drew her attention more than anything else. Even in the darkness, the outlines of mountains rose against the star-scattered sky. Vast and solid and somehow reassuring in their solidness.

"There's fresh water in the pitcher." Mandie moved to light the lamp on the small table beside the bed. "Clean towels on the stand and extra blankets in the chest. Your trunks will be up soon."

Kate's throat tightened at the simple kindness in the woman's voice. "Thank you. You've been very thoughtful."

"It's no trouble." Mandie adjusted the baby in her arms. "One of us will bring up some food and hot water for washing. Unless you'd rather come down?"

"Here would be better," Clara said. "If it's not too much trouble."

"None at all." Mandie moved toward the door, then paused. "I'm glad you're both safe. When the storm came through yesterday..." She trailed off as she shook her head. "Well. The Lord was watching over you."

The door closed softly behind her, leaving Kate and Clara alone in the quiet room.

Clara moved to the bed and sank onto it with a sigh that rose up from her bones. "I thought you were dead." Her voice came out small, stripped of the cheerfulness she'd managed all day. "When the ice broke, and you couldn't come across with us, I thought—"

"I'm here." Kate crossed to her sister and eased down beside her, then slipped her arm around Clara's waist as she had so many hundreds of times before. "I'm fine. We're both fine."

Clara leaned into her, resting her head against Kate's. The strength of Clara's inhale pressed against her, then Clara's body trembled as she released a long breath.

Kate allowed her eyes to drift shut as she breathed in the familiar scent of Clara's hair—a tiny remnant of lavender soap and something indefinably Clara. For a moment, she let herself simply hold on, let the fear of the last day drain away in the solid warmth of her sister beside her.

"What happened out there?" Clara's question came softly, curiosity mixed with lingering worry.

Kate opened her eyes and stared at the far wall, at the way lamplight played across the simple wooden planks. Where did she even start? The cave? The fire? The hours pressed against Thomas while the storm raged outside?

The way he'd looked at her in the darkness and called her extraordinary?

"We found shelter behind the waterfall." She kept her voice steady. Matter-of-fact. "Thomas built a fire. We stayed as warm as we could."

Clara pulled back just enough to study Kate's face. Her hazel eyes—so like their father's, so unlike Clara's mother's calculating gaze—searched for something Kate couldn't let her find.

"That's all?"

"What else would there be?"

But Clara knew her too well. Had spent too many years reading the things Kate wouldn't say aloud. Her sister's expression shifted as understanding dawned in her eyes, along with something that looked almost like concern. "Kate—"

A knock interrupted whatever Clara had been about to say. A relief.

Kate stood and moved to the door. When she opened it, Mrs. Wang held a laden tray.

"Hot stew. Fresh bread. Tea." The older woman bustled into the room without waiting for invitation, then set the tray on the bedside table. "You eat. Then sleep. Tomorrow we talk about what comes next."

What comes next. The words settled in Kate's stomach like stones. "Thank you, Mrs. Wang." She did her best to inject warmth into her voice despite the tightness in her chest. "This is very kind."

The older woman paused at the door, her dark eyes sharp as they swept over both of them. "You are safe here. Remember that." Then she was gone, the door clicking shut behind her with a finality that made Kate's pulse kick harder.

Clara moved to the tray, lifting a bowl of stew and breathing in the steam. "She's right, you know. We are safe here."

Safe. The word felt slippery, hard to hold onto.

Safe from what? The storm, yes. Starvation and cold, certainly.

But safe from the consequences of a night spent unchaperoned in a cave with Thomas Balfour?

She moved to the window and pressed her palm against the cool glass. Somewhere out there in the darkness lay Butte. Soon, Edmund Hartwell would spread word of what he'd seen. Or what he thought he'd seen.

Mrs. Hartwell would be the first to know. By next week, half of Butte society would be whispering about the seamstress with questionable morals. Her carefully laid plans, the future she'd been building—all of it crumbling before she'd even had a chance to begin.

"You should eat something." Clara's voice pulled her back from the darkness of her thoughts.

Kate turned. Her sister had already started on the bread, tearing off pieces with fingers that still trembled a little. Her bowl of stew sat beside her, steam still rising in lazy curls.

Kate forced herself to move away from the window, to cross the room, to take up the second bowl, and sink onto the bed beside Clara. The stew's warmth spread through her hands, and she lifted a spoonful to her lips. Rich beef broth, vegetables that had been preserved, herbs she couldn't quite identify. It tasted like comfort. Like home, though she'd never had a home that felt quite like this.

The weight of Clara's gaze was strong, though Kate didn't acknowledge it.

"What aren't you telling me?"

Kate took another bite. Then another.

"Kate." Clara set down her bread, fixing her full attention on Kate now. "What happened?"

The spoon in her hand weighed as much as a log. She set it in the bowl, then placed the bowl on the tray. Her fingers wanted to shake, so she pressed them flat against her thighs. "We had a visitor this morning."

Clara's expression shifted—wariness creeping into her features. "A visitor?"

"Edmund Hartwell." The name tasted bitter. "The copper baron from the stage. Audrey Hartwell's husband. He was riding near the river when we left the cave."

Understanding dawned across Clara's features, followed by something that looked like dread. "Oh no."

"He drew his own conclusions about what we'd been doing all night." Kate worked for a casual tone, though her chest felt tight enough to crack. "Made it clear that his wife can no longer associate with me. That recommending my services to Butte society would damage her own reputation."

Clara's hand flew to her mouth. "Kate, no."

"So the seamstress business is gone." She tried to keep her

voice matter-of-fact, tried to sound like this was just another setback to be managed. But the words came out hollow.

Clara's eyes filled with tears. "That's not fair. You didn't do anything wrong."

"Fair has nothing to do with it." Kate reached for her bowl again, though the thought of eating made her stomach turn. "You know that as well as I do. Reputation is all that matters to people like the Hartwells. And mine is ruined."

"Then we'll go somewhere else." Clara's voice took on that determined edge—the stubborn streak that ran through both of them, inherited from a father too weak to use it properly. "We'll leave Montana Territory entirely. Travel on to California or Oregon or—"

California. Where Thomas planned to go. She shoved that thought aside.

"With what money?" The question came out too sharp, so she softened her tone. "The stage fare to Butte already took most of what we had. And we'd need funds to establish ourselves wherever we went. To rent a room, buy supplies, eat while I built up a client base."

Clara's face crumpled. "So we're trapped."

The word landed between them like a stone dropped into still water, sending ripples through everything Kate had been trying not to think about since Hartwell rode away.

Trapped. Just like they'd been in Columbia, only now the cage was made of circumstance rather than their stepmother's machinations. And the key to escape—Kate's skill with a needle, her ability to support them both—had been snatched away before she could even use it.

Clara straightened, her eyes brightening. "You know what could be a solution for us..." Her voice carried a note Kate couldn't quite identify—not hope exactly, but something close to it.

"What?" Even as she said the word, she braced for whatever Clara might suggest.

"You could marry Mr. Balfour. Thomas." Clara said his name like she'd been practicing it. "That would solve everything."

Her middle dropped. "Clara—"

"No, listen." Her sister shifted to face her fully, tucking one leg beneath her on the bed. "He's the one who was with you in the cave. If anyone's reputation is damaged, his would be too. And marriage would restore both your honors."

"That's not how it works." Kate set her bowl down before she could drop it. "Men don't suffer the same consequences women do. You know that."

"Maybe not in Columbia. But this is Montana Territory." The excitement in Clara's voice rose with each word. "Things are different here. And the Balfours seem like good people—people who care about doing right."

Kate's throat tightened.

The memory of Thomas in the firelight, his voice raw as he confessed about Charles and the grizzly… The way his arm had tightened around her waist when she'd told him about her stepmother's meanness…

But then the careful distance he'd maintained all day, as though he too was trying to pretend those hours hadn't happened…

"He doesn't want to marry me. He made that clear from the beginning. He's planning to leave for California."

"Plans change." Clara reached for Kate's hand. "And even if he doesn't love you now, there's no way he can keep from it when he gets to know you."

She couldn't help a small smile at her sister's innocence. Clara believed the best in people, no matter how many times life showed her otherwise. Yet her words lodged in Kate's throat like broken glass.

Love. As if that had anything to do with their situation. As if

Thomas Balfour would look at her—prickly, defensive, undesirable Kate McKinney—and see something worth loving.

"This isn't a fairy tale, Clara." She pulled her hand free and stood, anything to get distance from her sister's hopeful expression. "Marriage should be built on more than just solving a scandal."

"But you like him." Clara's voice carried quiet certainty. "I can see it in the way you won't look at me when you talk about him."

Heat flooded Kate's face. "That's absurd."

"Is it?" Clara rose too, moving to stand beside her at the window. Their reflections ghosted in the dark glass—two sisters who'd protected each other their whole lives, now facing a choice neither of them wanted to make. "Kate, you've spent years watching over me. Let someone take care of you for once."

The tenderness in her sister's voice made Kate's chest ache. "Thomas Balfour doesn't want to take care of me. He wants to escape to California and build a life that has nothing to do with family expectations or—"

"Or what?" Clara pressed. "Kate, what are you so afraid of?"

Everything.

The word was too honest to speak aloud. She was afraid of wanting something she couldn't have. Afraid of trusting someone who would leave. Afraid of the way her chest had tightened when Thomas called her extraordinary, like some long-dead part of her had woken at his words and refused to go back to sleep.

"I'm afraid of making another mistake." The truth scraped her throat raw. "Of choosing wrong and dragging you down with me. We should never have come here."

"You've never dragged me anywhere I didn't want to go." Clara rested a hand on her shoulder, the touch stronger than usual. "And this isn't just about me anymore. It's about you too. About what *you* need."

What she needed.

She stared at their reflections in the window glass—two women far from home, their futures hanging by threads that could snap at any moment.

What she needed was security. Independence. The ability to support herself and Clara without relying on anyone else's goodwill or charity.

What she needed was exactly what Edmund Hartwell had destroyed with his assumptions and his rigid morality.

"You should at least think about it," Clara murmured. "About staying here. Both of us. The Balfours seem like good people. And Thomas—"

"He's leaving for California." She forced the words out, as though repetition could make it hurt less.

"Then maybe he needs a reason to stay."

CHAPTER 14

The remnants of supper had been cleared away, but no one moved to leave the table.

Thomas sat in his usual chair, between Mandie and Mrs. Wang. The weight of expectation pressed down from every direction. At the head of the table, Enoch's steady blue gaze tracked him with that particular brand of patience that had always made Thomas want to bolt.

James sat to Enoch's right, Rose beside him, both wearing expressions that said they'd already discussed what needed to happen here. Robert leaned back in his chair across from Thomas, arms folded, watching with the kind of quiet assessment that meant he was calculating details.

Kate and Clara had been shown to their room an hour ago. Mrs. Wang carried up their supper herself, insisting they needed rest more than company. The absence of the sisters should have made the coming conversation easier. Instead, it amplified the weight of what had happened. Proof this was something his family needed to face without witnesses.

Mrs. Wang broke the silence first, as she so often did. "We talk now about what must be done." Her accent thickened a little, the way it always did when she was being particularly direct. "No more pretending. No more waiting."

His ribs ached. His face throbbed. But neither of those pains compared to the heaviness settling in his chest as every eye in the room fixed on him.

"I know what you're going to say." He forced the words out before anyone else could speak. Before Enoch could use that reasonable tone, or James could lay out the practical arguments, or Mrs. Wang could cut straight to the bone with her knife-edged truth.

"Do you?" Enoch's question carried no challenge, just genuine curiosity.

Thomas met his eldest brother's gaze. "You're going to tell me I need to marry her. That it's the honorable thing to do. That her reputation is ruined, and marriage is the only way to fix it."

"And is it?" Robert's voice came quiet from across the table. "The honorable thing?"

The question landed differently than Thomas expected. Not an accusation, but an actual inquiry—as if Robert genuinely wanted to know what Thomas thought, rather than simply telling him what to do.

He looked down at his hands, at the calluses from ranch work and the cuts that hadn't quite healed from gathering wood in the storm. "I don't know."

"You don't know if it's honorable?" James leaned forward, his expression intent. "Or you don't know if you want to do it?"

Both. Neither.

His throat tightened around words he couldn't quite shape. How did he explain that marrying Kate felt simultaneously like the right choice and a trap closing around him? That the thought of her leaving made his chest ache, but the thought of staying at the ranch made him feel like he couldn't breathe?

"She deserves better than being trapped in marriage because of circumstances." He forced himself to meet Enoch's gaze again. "She came here with plans. Dreams of building something that was hers. And now those are gone because I—"

"Because Edmund Hartwell is a fool who looks at appearance over truth." Mrs. Wang's sharp tone cut through his wallowing. "You keep her alive in the storm. You do what any good man do. The shame is his, not yours."

"She's right." Rose's voice carried that gentle strength he'd always appreciated about her. "You protected Kate when she needed it. What Hartwell chose to see says more about him than about either of you."

Thomas shook his head. "But the damage is done. Her seamstress business—everything she was counting on—it's finished before it started."

"So we give her another option." Mandie tipped her head as her expression turned thoughtful. "Both sisters could stay here. We have the room. Kate could still do her needlework—there are plenty of Walnut Springs families in these mountains who'd pay for quality work. She wouldn't have Butte society, but she'd have independence."

"Would she though?" He caught the frustration in his tone and reined it in, but not before Enoch sent a glare. "Or would she be trapped here, dependent on our charity? That's exactly what she was trying to escape."

"There's a difference between charity and hospitality." Enoch's voice carried that steady authority Thomas had grown up both respecting and resenting. "Between offering help and forcing dependence."

"Is there?" Thomas met his brother's gaze. "Because from where Kate's standing, it probably looks the same."

Another group of people telling her what's best. Another situation where her choices have been taken away.

"Then give her a choice." James's quiet words carried across the room. "A real one."

James was right. Kate deserved the choice. But giving her

that choice—actually asking her to marry him—meant he'd have to be willing to set aside his own dreams.

He stared at the grain of the wooden table, tracing the knots with his eyes while his mind churned. California had been his escape plan for months now—the promise of something that was entirely his, untainted by family expectations or the weight of a title he hadn't earned.

But the image that rose in his mind wasn't golden hills or a herd of horses grazing free on open range. It was Kate's face in the firelight, the way she'd looked at him when he told her about Charles. The way she'd called him brave when he'd felt like anything but.

He had to do the right thing for her. The honorable thing.

"What are you thinking, little brother?" James leaned forward, elbows braced on the table. "When you go quiet like this, it's usually a sign you're about to do something either foolhardy or heroic."

He sent a glare James's way. That was another rub in this whole situation. If he married Kate—did the noble deed—his brothers would get what they'd wanted to begin with. What they'd lied and schemed to accomplish.

He slouched back in his chair and blew out a hard breath.

This was about Kate, not his brothers. Not even really about him, unless he wanted to be a selfish pig.

He'd talk to her in the morning. Give her a full proposal so she'd know he was all in. Let her decide from there.

He scanned the gazes around the table once more—Enoch's steady patience, James's concerned intensity, Robert's quiet calculation, Mrs. Wang's sharp assessment. Even Mandie and Rose watched him with that feminine intuition that said they'd already guessed which way this would fall.

"Well." He pushed his chair back and stood, ignoring the protest from his ribs. "This has been a delightful evening of everyone staring at me like I'm a horse they might purchase. But I think I'll retire before you start checking my teeth."

"Thomas—" Enoch started.

"I'll tell you in the morning." He kept his tone light despite the weight pressing on his chest. "After I've had a chance to sleep on something that isn't frozen stone and think about more than how to keep from dying in a blizzard."

Mrs. Wang's eyes narrowed, but the corner of her mouth twitched. "You think sleeping make choice easier?"

"No. But it'll make me less likely to say something I'll regret." He offered her a slight bow—the kind that always made her swat at him. "Good night, all. Try not to plan my entire life while I'm gone."

He didn't wait for a response. Just turned and headed for the stairs as their eyes tracked him across the room. He kept his head high, showing every ounce of the fortitude his brothers assumed he lacked.

CHAPTER 15

Something about the light was all wrong. Kate squinted at the unfamiliar ceiling as she struggled to clear her sleep-fogged mind. Like a wave crashing on rocks, the memories surged in.

Montana. The Balfour ranch. The cave. Thomas.

She closed her eyes and sucked in a breath, then let it out. Today was a new day. With a good night's rest, she could face it all with more strength than she had before.

She turned her head on the pillow. Clara slept beside her, honey-blonde hair spilling from her braid across the white pillowcase, her breathing deep and even. The worry lines that had etched themselves around her sister's mouth yesterday smoothed away in sleep, leaving her looking younger than her nineteen years.

Kate eased herself upright, doing her best not to disturb the bed. Morning light streamed through the window—brilliant and clean, the kind of light that came after storms had scrubbed the world raw. The mountains beyond the glass stood sharp against a sky so blue it almost hurt to look at.

Everything deceptively perfect. As though yesterday hadn't happened at all.

Except it had. And Edmund Hartwell's words still echoed in her mind with the clarity of a death knell: *Reputation is the only currency that matters out here. Once lost, it cannot be recovered.*

The seamstress business that had come together so easily that she'd dared to cling to real hope for the first time—gone. The future she'd planned—shattered. The independence she'd fought so hard to claim—stripped away by circumstances and one person's rigid judgment. The same way her stepmother had judged her common and worthless all those years ago.

She pressed her fingers against her eyes, willing back the pressure building behind them. Crying wouldn't change anything. It never had.

As she stood, the floorboards held the morning chill beneath her stockinged feet. She'd slept in her chemise and petticoat, too exhausted to change into anything clean. Now the wrinkled fabric clung to her skin, a reminder of how far she'd fallen from the careful standards she'd maintained her whole life.

Clara stirred but didn't wake. Good.

Kate needed time to think before her sister started in again about marriage and Thomas Balfour and how staying here could solve everything.

As if marriage fixed anything. As if binding herself to a man she barely knew—a man planning to leave for California—would do anything but trap her in a different kind of cage.

She pulled a dress from the trunk. None of their clothing was clean after the journey, but the one she'd worn during the storm had tears and spots she'd need to spend time repairing. This emerald taffeta bore plenty of wrinkles, but it would have to do. She dressed quickly, her fingers fumbling with buttons and laces she could normally fasten in her sleep. Her hands weren't quite steady this morning.

The mirror above the washstand showed a woman she

barely recognized. Hair disheveled from sleep and shadows beneath her eyes that spoke of too little rest and too much worry. The fading remnants of dirt she must have missed last night still smudged along her jawline.

She scrubbed at her face and neck, the cold cloth bringing some clarity even as it raised gooseflesh along her arms. Then she worked at her hair, pulling it back into something resembling order. The chignon she managed looked severe, but at least it was neat. Controlled.

She needed control right now. Needed something she could manage when everything else kept slipping through her fingers like water.

She paused at the door to glance back at Clara's sleeping form. Part of her wanted to wake her sister, to have a familiar presence at her side when she faced whatever waited downstairs. But Clara needed rest more than Kate needed comfort.

The hallway was quiet, and as she descended the stairs, she couldn't quite gauge the time. Not early morning, for daylight streamed in through the windows. But not mid-morning yet. Maybe the family had already begun their daily business, whatever that was. What did a duke's sons raised as ranchers do all day? Ranching work?

The great room below looked different in daylight—larger somehow, the details she'd missed in last night's exhaustion now visible. Books lined the shelves near the massive fireplace. A painting hung above the mantel, mountains rendered in oils that caught the morning light. Everything spoke of permanence, of roots sunk deep into this wild place.

She'd made it halfway across the room when Thomas emerged from what must be the dining room.

He stopped short when he saw her. His copper-brown hair was damp, as though he'd recently washed. The bruise on his cheek had faded a little, shifting into a greenish-brown color.

For a moment, they simply stared at each other across the

expanse of polished floor. The silence stretched between them, weighted with everything they'd shared in the cave and everything left unsaid since.

He cleared his throat. "Hungry? There's food on the stove. We've each been eating as we wanted, but I can prepare you a plate."

"I'm not—" She pressed a hand to her middle. Her nerves had knotted so tight the thought of food made her queasy. "Tea would be good. Or coffee, if there is any."

"Both." He gestured the way he'd entered. "Come on."

She followed him through the dining room, past a long table surrounded by chairs, into a kitchen that smelled of bacon grease and fresh bread. A large cast-iron stove dominated one wall. Dishes sat drying beside a deep basin, evidence of the morning meal she'd missed.

Thomas moved to the stove with an easy familiarity that suggested he'd done this a thousand times. "Mrs. Wang keeps a pot going most of the day." He lifted a kettle, testing its weight. "Still warm. Tea's in the canister if you want it later."

"Thank you."

He poured a cup and handed it to her, their fingers brushing in the exchange. The contact lasted only a second, but it was enough to send heat crawling up her neck.

She took a step back and cradled the cup between her palms. The warmth seeped through the ceramic, anchoring her to something solid and real.

Thomas leaned against the counter, his own cup in hand, and watched her with an expression she couldn't quite read. Not wariness. Curiosity maybe?

She met his gaze squarely. This usually made a person either back away or say what they meant.

The corners of Thomas's mouth twitched. "I was hoping to catch you this morning."

Her pulse kicked against her ribs. "Oh?"

"There's something we need to discuss." He glanced toward the dining room, then back at her. "Privately, if you're willing."

The formality in his tone made her stomach clench. This was it, then. The conversation Clara had predicted. The one she'd been dreading since Hartwell rode away yesterday morning.

She could refuse. Could insist on having Clara present, or Mrs. Wang, or anyone else who might serve as a distraction.

But running from this conversation wouldn't change what needed to be said. And Kate McKinney had never been a coward, even when cowardice might have served her better.

"All right." She kept her voice steady despite the way her heart hammered. "Where?"

He pushed off from the counter. "The study. It's quiet there, and we won't be interrupted."

She followed him back through the dining room, through the great room. He opened a door on the far wall and stood aside to let her enter first.

The room was smaller than the great room but no less carefully appointed. A desk sat before a window that looked out toward the mountains. Bookshelves lined two walls, filled with volumes that ranged from leather-bound classics to what looked like ranch ledgers. Opposite the desk, a pair of chairs faced each other with a small table in between.

Thomas closed the door behind them, and the soft click made her pulse jump.

Alone again.

Just the two of them, like in the cave. Except this time, there was no storm. A different kind of survival required this intimacy.

He moved to one of the chairs and gestured for her to take the other. "Please."

She sat, then adjusted her skirts with the hand not gripping her mug. Anything to avoid looking at him directly. To delay whatever was coming next.

Thomas lowered himself into the opposite chair, his movements still carrying that careful quality that spoke of ribs not quite healed. He set his cup on the small table between them.

"I've been thinking about your situation." His voice had lost its usual lightness. "About what Hartwell said. What it means for your plans. It seems to me you have three options." She finally met his eyes, and something in his expression made her chest tighten. "I want to lay them all out. Let you choose what's best for you and Clara."

Choose. The word should have brought relief. Instead, it made the knot in her stomach pull tighter. She most likely knew what those options would be, and none of them felt like real choices at all.

"Number one." Thomas leaned forward, elbows braced on his knees. "If you and Clara want to return to South Carolina, I'll pay the fare. Whatever you need for the journey—funds, supplies, accommodations along the way. You'd arrive home with enough to establish yourselves comfortably."

Home. Columbia wasn't home. It was the place where her stepmother's designs waited like a spider in its web, where her father's weakness had failed her and Clara again and again. The place where they would both be forced back into the marriage they'd fled across a continent to escape.

Going backward had never been part of the plan.

"And the second option?" She kept her voice steady.

Thomas's hand dropped to his side. "You stay here. Both of you. My family would be honored to have you—not as guests, but as...as family, I suppose. You could run your seamstress business from the ranch. Walnut Springs families would pay for quality work. It's not Butte society, but you could make a living."

The offer was generous—more generous than she had any

right to expect. But the word that caught in her throat was the same one that had haunted her since they'd arrived.

Charity.

Even if she paid for her and Clara's board from her earnings, this would simply be another cage with nicer walls. The two of them wouldn't actually be part of the Balfour family. Just guests.

She'd spent her whole life trying to escape dependence on people who could withdraw their goodwill at any moment, and here was Thomas Balfour offering her exactly that—wrapped in kindness, yes, but dependence all the same.

"And the third?" Her voice came out smaller this time. Too small.

Thomas straightened. Just a slight movement—shoulders squaring, chin lifting—but she couldn't miss it for what it was. This was the hard one.

"The third option is different." He paused, and his gaze held hers with an intensity that made her pulse skip. "It would be my honor if you would consider marrying me."

Marry. He'd actually said it. Not danced around it or implied it, but stated the act plainly.

She'd known it was coming—Clara had predicted it, his family had probably discussed it over their evening meal. But hearing Thomas actually say the words made it feel as though she'd stepped outside her body.

"I know this was never your plan." He continued when she didn't speak. "It certainly wasn't mine. But I've come to respect you, Kate. More than respect you. The way you fight to protect your sister. The way you faced that storm without complaining. The way you see through people's pretenses straight to the truth underneath." He leaned forward a little. "You're the strongest woman I've ever met."

Not the most extraordinary. The strongest.

The distinction shouldn't have mattered, but it did. Extraordinary could be dismissed as flattery spoken in the heat of a moment. Strong was something else—something that suggested he'd been watching her, seeing her in ways she hadn't realized.

Her throat tightened. She forced herself to breathe through it, to think past the way his words warmed all through her.

Clara's voice from last night echoed back. *Let someone care for you for once.*

The thought, the possible idea of giving over control, made fear surge in her throat. Clawing.

She forced it back. Forced herself to think. What questions should she ask? What details did she need to know to make the best decision?

Only one rose up. She swallowed so she could form the word. "Why?"

Thomas blinked. "Why what?"

"Why would you do this?"

His brow furrowed. "Because it's the right thing to do."

The right thing. The statement landed hard, though his tone held no cruelty. Just honesty—the same bare honesty he'd shown in the cave when he told her about Charles and the grizzly.

"The right thing." She worked to keep emotion from her voice. "So this is about honor? About fixing the damage to my reputation?"

"Partly." He didn't look away, didn't soften the truth with pretty words. "I won't lie to you, Kate. What Hartwell saw—what he'll say—it matters. Marriage would restore your reputation. Give you and Clara security. But that's not the only reason."

"Then what is?"

He stayed quiet a long moment, and his gaze dropped to his hands. When he looked up again, something raw flicked in his hazel eyes. "Because when I think about you leaving—going back to Columbia or even just staying here as a guest—something in my chest feels wrong. And when I think about you marrying me, about building a life together..." He trailed off, shaking his head. "I don't know how to explain it. But it doesn't feel like a trap. It feels like maybe—maybe it could be real."

The confession hung between them, vulnerable in a way she wouldn't have expected from Thomas Balfour. This man, who sometimes used charm like armor, who deflected with easy humor whenever conversations grew too serious—he'd just stripped that away and shown her his true self. A part of him anyway.

Her hands trembled around the coffee cup. She set it on the table before she spilled the drink.

"You're still planning to go to California." It took everything in her to keep her emotions controlled as she spoke.

His jaw tightened. "I was. But plans can change."

That should have brought relief. Instead, everything inside her pulled tighter, coiling like a spring wound too hard.

"Can they?" She held his gaze. Locked into his so he would hear her next words. "I won't be your obligation, Thomas. I won't be the weight that drags you down from your dreams just because you feel guilty about a storm neither of us could control."

"That's not—" He ran a hand through his hair, frustration bleeding through his composure. "You think this is guilt?"

"Isn't it?"

"No." His voice came out fierce. Then softer. "It's not guilt."

"Then what is it?"

He hesitated a long moment. Outside, a bird called—bright and sharp in the cold morning air. "I don't know how to explain it." He turned to look toward the window, his profile sharp against the morning light. "I've spent months planning my escape. California was supposed to be freedom—a place where no one knew about the title I didn't earn or the man who died because I froze when I should have acted. A fresh start where I could build a life that was mine alone."

Her insides knotted tighter. The last thing she wanted was to take that fresh start away from him.

"But then there was you." He looked back at her, and the intensity in his expression made her forget how to breathe. "Prickly and stubborn and so determined to protect your sister, you'd cross the entire country to give her a better chance. You looked at me in that cave and called me brave when I felt like anything but."

He turned to face her fully. "I'm not offering this out of guilt, Kate. I'm offering it because I've come to respect you, and I think we could build a good life together. I can't promise you love." His eyes nearly shimmered with the earnestness in his voice. As though he wanted her to hear the nuance of every word. "Not yet. I don't know if I even know what that looks like. But I can promise you partnership. Respect. A home that's yours as much as mine, not charity or dependence but something we build together."

The tightness in her throat made it almost impossible to swallow.

Everything in her should want to pull back, to protect herself from wanting something good that could be taken away. But she couldn't bring herself to turn away.

She drew in a shaky breath, then another. The walls she'd spent years building—stone by careful stone—trembled under the weight of what he was offering.

Partnership. Not rescue. Not obligation. Something they would forge together.

Thomas Balfour had proven himself a good man. He didn't hold back the truth, even when it was hard. But he didn't intentionally hurt with his words. He'd protected her over and over since that first meeting in the cafeteria. From the way he'd given the hard truth, to every one of his actions in the storm. Even this offer of marriage now proved his integrity.

If she were going to trust a man, the deepest part of her said Thomas Balfour might just be trustworthy.

"All right." She pushed the words out before she could press them down again.

His brows shot up. "All right?" The shock on his face showed he'd expected that answer even less than she had.

She should clarify. Maybe give him a chance to take back his offer. Perhaps it had only been a kindness. A request he never expected her to accept.

A muffled thud sounded from the main room, jerking Thomas's attention toward the door.

Voices rose from beyond the study door, or maybe outside? One end of this room likely bordered the front of the house. Was that Enoch speaking?

Thomas was on his feet before she could make out any words. He opened the study door, and she stood to follow him.

The front door was just opening, and Enoch strode in with James just behind.

"—had to be from last night," Enoch was saying. His measured voice hummed with tension. "The ashes were cold, but the ground underneath still held some warmth."

Thomas moved toward his brothers, and Kate followed. "What are you talking about?"

Enoch's gaze flicked to her, then back to Thomas. "Someone camped near the house last night. Just inside the tree line where they could watch us."

CHAPTER 16

The tracks circled the house like a predator sizing up prey.

Thomas crouched beside the imprints in the half-frozen mud. Single horse. Single rider, as far as they could tell.

The campsite sat just inside the tree line—close enough to watch the house, far enough to avoid easy detection. Then the man had stayed just out of sight as he rode past the house, down the road that led to Walnut Springs. That's where they lost him. The frozen path was too hard to hold any imprints. They searched for a quarter hour, but finally turned back toward the house.

"Could be a drifter." Robert voiced what Thomas had wondered about more than once. "Reached the house too late to knock. Decided to wait out the cold rather than risk disturbing us in the middle of the night."

"Polite drifter." James's tone carried skepticism. "Most would've knocked anyway. Risked waking us rather than freeze. Or slept in the barn at least."

"Maybe he caught a rabbit and needed to cook it."

Enoch's jaw tightened. "I don't like it."

Thomas straightened, pushing past the burn in his ribs. Something about this felt wrong—the deliberate positioning of the camp, the careful tracks that skirted the house before heading toward town. A drifter would have approached directly, would have asked for shelter or moved on entirely.

"I'll ride toward Walnut Springs." Enoch's voice carried the weight of a decision already made. "See if I can catch up with him. At least get a look at who we're dealing with."

"You want company?" James asked.

"No. Stay here and keep an eye on things." Enoch's gaze shifted to Thomas and Robert. "All of you. I should be back before dark, even if I have to go all the way to town." Enoch turned toward the barn, and something inside Thomas scrambled to stop him.

He needed to tell them now. While they were all together.

"Wait."

His eldest brother paused and looked back, brows raised in question.

The words stuck in Thomas's throat. He glanced at James and Robert, both watching him with expressions that matched Enoch's. Better to get it over with.

He swallowed down the knot and forced the news out. "Kate agreed to marry me."

Silence weighted the air, thick enough to cut. All three of his brothers stared at him. Practically gaping. As though he'd just announced he planned to move to England instead of California.

He shifted his weight and offered them his most irreverent grin. "Try not to look so shocked. I'm not completely without charm."

Robert recovered first, his expression slipping to something that might have been amusement. "Congratulations are in order then."

"When did this happen?" James's voice held genuine curiosity rather than judgment. "You only just got back."

"This morning. In the study." Thomas shoved his hands in his pockets. Why did all three of them have to stand there studying him like he'd sprouted a second head? "I laid out her options. She chose marriage."

"Her options." Enoch's tone had gone stoic—the one he used when he thought he had to work carefully around a problem. "You gave her a choice?"

"Three of them, actually." Thomas met his eldest brother's gaze. "Return to South Carolina with funds for the journey. Stay here as a guest and run her seamstress business from the ranch. Or marry me." He shrugged. "She picked the third."

"Just like that?" Robert's skepticism bled through, despite his possible attempt to sound supportive.

"Just like that." He quirked up one side of his mouth and did his best to keep his voice light, though his chest had gone tight.

"You're sure about this?" Enoch's blue eyes searched his face with that particular intensity that had always made him feel like his brother could see straight through any pretense. "Marriage isn't something to enter lightly."

Thomas threw up his hands. Honestly. "What do you all want from me? First you scheme and lie behind my back to order me a bride. And now that I'm willing to actually marry her, you're questioning whether I'm sure?" He shook his head, aiming for exasperation rather than the defensiveness rising in his throat. "Make up your minds."

James had the grace to wince. "That's fair."

"We were wrong to do that." Enoch's voice carried the weight of genuine regret. "I'm sorry. We all are. But this—Thomas, this is your life we're talking about. I need to know you're not just doing this because you feel obligated."

The concern in his brother's tone stripped away a layer of Thomas's irritation. Enoch wasn't trying to control him. This was protection—the way he'd always tried to protect all of them, sometimes to the point of suffocation.

"I'm not." Thomas forced himself to meet each of his brothers' gazes in turn. "I won't pretend it's a love match. We barely know each other. But I respect her. And I think we can build a good life."

"Respect is a solid foundation." James's expression softened. "It builds a great friendship, which can lead to a wonderful marriage."

"That turned out well for you and Rose." Robert's dry tone carried a hint of warmth beneath it. "You're disgustingly happy."

A smile tugged at James's mouth despite his obvious attempt to stay serious. "My point is that Thomas could do worse than marrying a woman he respects. Especially one as capable as Miss McKinney appears to be."

"She is capable." Maybe he sounded defensive, but it didn't matter. "She's one of the strongest people I've ever met. And she deserves better than having her reputation destroyed because we were caught in a storm."

"Then you're doing the right thing." Enoch's shoulders relaxed, though his expression remained serious. "When?"

"When what?"

"When do you want to have the ceremony?" Enoch glanced toward the house, then back at Thomas. "The sooner the better, I'd think. Given the circumstances with Hartwell."

His insides knotted. He hadn't thought that far ahead—hadn't let himself picture standing before a preacher with Kate beside him, speaking vows that would bind them together for life. The image formed now, and his chest twisted.

Not unpleasant. Just...significant.

"I suppose you're right." He cleared his throat. "Maybe see if the sheriff can come out tomorrow?" That would give Kate and the other women a day to prepare.

"I'll ask when I'm in town." Enoch turned toward the barn

again. "Try not to let anyone else camp in our woods while I'm gone."

Robert snorted. "Sure."

After Enoch disappeared into the barn, Thomas glanced at James and Robert, who were both still watching him.

"What?" He shifted his weight. He should just go in the house and leave these jokesters outside.

"Nothing." James's mouth twitched. "Just never thought I'd see the day you willingly chose to settle down."

He glared. "I'm not exactly entering my dotage."

Robert clapped a hand on his shoulder—hard enough to jar loose his ribs again. "For what it's worth, I think you made the right choice. Miss McKinney strikes me as the sort of woman who won't let you get away with your usual nonsense."

"That's supposed to be encouraging?"

"Extremely." Robert's rare smile appeared. "You need someone who'll call you on your foolishness. God knows the rest of us are tired of doing it."

Thomas aimed a half-hearted shove at Robert's arm and turned toward the house. Behind him, his brothers' laughter carried on the cold air, but he didn't look back. They could enjoy their amusement all they wanted—he had more important matters to attend to.

Like telling Kate the sheriff would come tomorrow.

Like facing the reality that in one day, he'd be a married man.

The thought should have made him want to bolt for the barn and saddle his horse for California. Instead, what rose in his chest felt closer to anticipation.

He found them in the dining room—Kate, Clara, and Rose gathered around the table with plates of what looked like Mrs. Wang's apple cake and steaming cups of tea. The three women looked up as he entered, their conversation dying mid-sentence.

Kate's hazel eyes met his across the space. Something flicked in her expression—awareness, maybe, or the same strange expectancy that had been building in his own chest since she'd said yes.

"Thomas." Rose gestured to an empty chair—Enoch's chair at the head of the table, but also the one nearest Kate. "Join us. Mrs. Wang just brought out fresh cake."

"I'm fine." But he took the seat.

"What did you all learn about the campfire?" Rose leaned forward, her expression turning serious.

He glanced at Kate and Clara. The last thing he wanted was to worry them, but they deserved to know the details as much as anyone. Hiding the truth wouldn't help them learn to live in this mountain wilderness.

"Not much." He accepted the plate Mrs. Wang placed in front of him and sent her a grateful smile, though his appetite had vanished somewhere between finding those tracks and announcing his engagement to his brothers. "Single rider. Made camp in the trees last night where he could watch the house." He kept his voice matter-of-fact. "Tracks lead toward Walnut Springs, but we lost them once the ground froze. Enoch's gone to see if he can catch up."

Clara's hand went to her throat. "Someone was watching us?"

"Could be nothing," he added quickly. "Maybe just a drifter who arrived too late to knock. Decided to wait out the cold rather than disturb us."

"But you don't think so." Kate's words weren't a question. She'd already read the truth in his expression.

He met her gaze. "I don't know what to think. But Enoch will find out."

The silence that followed pressed heavy. Rose reached a hand to stroke Clara's back. She would make a great mother one day, with that ever-present calm she resonated.

But Kate's expression had gone nearly blank—the same

guarded look she'd worn when they'd first met in Butte.

Maybe she needed a distraction. "While Enoch's in town..." He forced himself to continue, to push past the sudden tightness in his throat. "He'll ask Sheriff Hawkins to come out tomorrow. For the ceremony."

Kate's eyes went wide. "Tomorrow?"

"If that works for you." He kept his voice steady, though something in his chest twisted at the flash of panic crossing her features. "I know it's fast. I figured you'd want to move quickly, given what Hartwell will likely say once he returns to Butte. But we can hold off if you'd rather."

Her face had gone pale—close to the gray of storm clouds. Her hands gripped the edge of the table, knuckles white.

Clara's expression shifted from worry to something that looked almost like joy. "Oh, Kate." Her voice held a bit of wonder. "You said yes?"

Kate's gaze didn't leave Thomas's face. "I did."

Clara's squeal of delight cut through the tension. She launched herself at Kate, wrapping her arms around her sister's shoulders hard enough to make Kate's chair scrape backward. "I'm so happy for you. For both of you."

Kate's arms came up to return the embrace, but her eyes stayed locked on Thomas's. Something moved in those hazel depths—fear and determination tangled together in a way that made his ribs ache worse than any bruise.

He'd moved too fast. Pushed too hard. She'd agreed to the marriage in theory, but facing the reality of it happening tomorrow—that was something else entirely.

But then she spoke. "Tomorrow then." Her voice sounded steady. Determined. And the hint of a smile she gifted him felt like maybe she might be looking forward to the event. Or at least not dreading it.

Rose stood, her smile warm despite the worry Thomas could

see flickering at its edges. "Then we have work to do. We'll all help you prepare. Everything will be perfect."

"I don't need perfect." Kate finally looked away from Thomas, focusing on Rose instead. "Just...simple."

"Simple can still be lovely." Rose wrapped an arm around Kate's shoulders. "Trust me. We'll take care of everything."

CHAPTER 17

The dress fit like it had been made for Kate, though it hadn't of course. This particular gown had been commissioned by Madame Gautier in Columbia.

She stood before the mirror in the upstairs bedroom, smoothing her hands down the jade silk that Clara had packed so carefully to be her own wedding dress. Now Kate would wear it instead.

She'd spent several hours altering the seams yesterday afternoon—taking in the waist, adjusting the shoulders, hemming the skirt until it brushed the floor at exactly the right length. The color brought out the green in Kate's hazel eyes, made her skin look less pale than it had these past few days.

"You're beautiful." Emotion clouded Clara's voice behind her.

Kate met her sister's gaze in the mirror. Clara wore another of her best dresses—a soft rose muslin that made her honey-blonde hair glow in the morning light streaming through the window. Tears already pooled in her eyes, threatening to spill over.

Kate swallowed down the lump in her throat. "Don't cry yet."

She turned from the mirror and reached for Clara's hands. "Save it for the ceremony at least."

"I can't help it." Clara squeezed her fingers. "You're getting married. My sister is getting married."

The words settled strange in Kate's chest—heavy and light all at once. Married to Thomas Balfour. A man she'd known less than a week. A man who'd kept her alive through a blizzard and seemed to see past all the defenses she kept raised. Who seemed to truly enjoy her company. Even to respect her.

And tonight would be her wedding night.

The thought sent warmth creeping up her neck. By evening's end, she would become his wife in truth—give herself to a man she barely knew.

She trusted him. That much had settled into certainty somewhere between the cave and the study. Thomas Balfour would not be cruel or careless with her. Probably.

But trust didn't erase the vulnerability of what lay ahead.

She drew a slow breath and steadied herself. This was the path most women walked—binding themselves to husbands they'd known only through the careful choreography of courtship. Maybe she'd not been given that opportunity, but she'd seen Thomas stripped of pretense, exhausted and fighting for their survival. Perhaps that was worth more than months of parlor visits and chaperoned strolls.

It would still be hard. But she would face it the way she faced everything else—head high and spine straight.

A soft knock interrupted the moment, and Rose's voice drifted through the door. "May we come in?"

"Of course." Kate released Clara's hands and turned as the door opened.

Rose stepped inside, her dark hair pinned up in an elegant chignon, and Mandie entered just behind her, carrying a small bundle wrapped in brown paper. "We brought you something."

Both women stopped just inside the doorway and stared at

her. The heat from their gazes crept up her neck, but she straightened her shoulders and met their eyes.

"Oh, Kate." Rose's hand flew to her mouth. "You look absolutely stunning."

Mandie nodded, her eyes bright. "Thomas won't be able to look away."

Her pulse kicked harder. *Thomas.*

"Here." Mandie crossed the room and placed the wrapped bundle on the bed. She opened the paper to reveal a small bouquet of dried wildflowers—mountain asters and Indian paintbrush, if she wasn't mistaken. Someone had tied them with a pale green ribbon that matched Kate's dress perfectly.

"Mrs. Wang saved them." Mandie lifted the bouquet. "She has a whole collection from last summer."

Kate's throat tightened as she accepted the flowers. The gesture was so simple, so thoughtful. These women barely knew her, yet they were treating her wedding like it mattered. Like *she* mattered.

"Thank you." Her voice rasped, so she worked to clear it. "They're perfect."

Rose moved to Kate's side, reaching up to adjust a few loose strands of hair that had escaped her simple chignon. "You're nervous."

It wasn't a question.

She would usually deny it—being nervous was a weakness.

But something about Rose's gentle tone, the understanding in her eyes, made the truth slip out.

"Terrified."

Rose's hands stilled for a moment, and her gaze met Kate's. "May I pray for you?"

Her insides clenched. There were a dozen reasons to refuse—old reflexes, old wounds, the sour memory of her stepmother's polished prayers spoken for an audience.

But Rose's eyes weren't sharp or expectant. They held a kindness Margaret McKinney's never had.

Kate managed a nod. "If you wish."

Rose didn't make a show of it. She didn't even take Kate's hands. She just bowed her head slightly, like she was speaking to someone close enough to hear a whisper.

"Father, thank You for bringing Kate and Clara safely here. Thank You for the way You've carried Kate through all these challenges. Please give her peace this morning. Give her courage for what comes next, and let her know she isn't alone. Bless Thomas and Kate's marriage, Lord. In Jesus' name, amen."

The word amen followed by Clara in a hiccupy voice.

Kate didn't say it. She couldn't. But something in her chest eased anyway.

Then Rose lifted her head and smiled, as though such a prayer was typical in any conversation. "Being terrified on your wedding day is perfectly normal. I was shaking so badly on my wedding day, James had to hold both my hands through the vows to keep me steady."

Clara chuckled. "Really?"

"Really." Rose stepped back to examine her work, then nodded in satisfaction. "Marriage is a leap of faith, even when you've known someone for years. When it happens quickly like this..." She met Kate's gaze in the mirror. "It's natural to be afraid."

"But Thomas is a good man." Mandie settled onto the edge of the bed. "He drives his brothers half-mad sometimes with his restlessness, but his heart is true. He'll honor his vows to you."

Kate's fingers tightened around the bouquet. "I know."

And she did know it, somewhere deep in her bones. Thomas Balfour might be reckless and charming and a smooth talker, but he was honorable. He wouldn't lie to her or make promises he didn't plan to keep.

That wasn't what terrified her.

What terrified her was the way her chest tightened when she thought about standing beside him. The way her pulse jumped when their eyes met across a room. The way something in her had shifted in that cave, cracked open despite every wall she'd built to keep herself safe.

She'd spent her whole life learning not to want things. Not to trust promises that could be broken. And now she was about to bind herself to a man who made her *want* despite every lesson she'd learned.

A knock sounded at the door—firmer this time. Mrs. Wang's voice carried through the wood. "Time to come down. Everyone is waiting."

Kate's stomach dropped. This was it. The moment when everything changed.

Rose reached for her hand and squeezed. "Remember—you're not alone."

The words settled deep in Kate's chest, both foreign and achingly welcome. She drew a steadying breath, lifted her chin, and nodded. "Let's go."

Clara stepped to her side, looping their arms together as Rose opened the door.

Mrs. Wang's beaming smile met them in the hallway. "You are beautiful bride, child." Her eyes glistened as she scanned all the way down Kate's dress. "Come. Your young man waits."

She followed the woman down the hallway, then down the staircase.

The great room stretched out below, transformed from the comfortable space it had been just that morning. Someone had hung garlands of evergreen boughs along the rough-hewn mantel above the massive stone fireplace where a fire crackled and popped, filling the room with warmth. The rugs had been pushed aside to clear a space before the hearth, and simple wooden benches had been arranged to face it.

And there, standing in the midst of his brothers, was Thomas.

Her heart nearly stopped.

He'd tamed his copper-brown hair—or tried to, at least. It still held that slight wave that made it fall across his forehead, catching the firelight in shades of bronze and gold. He wore a dark suit perfectly tailored to his tall frame, with a crisp white shirt and a simple cravat.

His eyes tracked her from the moment she appeared at the top of the stairs, and the expression that crossed his face made her breath catch. Not just appreciation—though that was there too. Something deeper. Something that looked almost like wonder.

As she reached the bottom landing, he met her there.

"You look..." He trailed off, his gaze sweeping from the jade silk to her face and back again. "I don't have the words."

Heat climbed her neck. "Thank you." She managed to keep her tone steady despite the way her pulse hammered. "You clean up rather well yourself."

A smile tugged at his mouth—that easy, charming grin she'd grown to love. But underneath it lay something more genuine. More vulnerable.

He offered his arm, and she took it. The solid strength beneath the fine wool of his jacket steadied her trembling.

She let him guide her toward the fireplace, where the sheriff stood waiting. The man was younger than she'd expected—perhaps thirty, with sandy hair and a kind face that spoke of someone who took his responsibilities seriously without becoming rigid about them.

As she and Thomas took their place before the man, the others settled onto the benches.

She glanced over to search out Clara. Her sister sat beside Mrs. Wang, and when their eyes met, Clara smiled—a real smile, full of hope and joy that lit her face.

James sat on Clara's other side, with Rose tucked against him. Robert claimed the bench behind them, his quiet presence somehow reassuring in its steadiness. Enoch stood near the back with Mandie, the baby sleeping peacefully in his arms.

Thomas's family. Soon to be her family too.

Sheriff Hawkins cleared his throat, drawing her attention back. "Dearly beloved, we are gathered here today in the sight of God and these witnesses to join together Thomas William Balfour and Katherine Anne McKinney in holy matrimony."

The words washed over her—familiar phrases she'd heard at other weddings, back in Columbia when her stepmother had dragged them to society events.

But hearing them now, with the strength of Thomas's arm beneath her hand and his warmth radiating through the scant inches between them, made everything feel so real.

"Marriage is not to be entered into lightly." The sheriff's voice carried easily through the quiet room. "But reverently, deliberately, and in accordance with the purposes for which it was instituted by God."

Her fingers tightened on the bouquet. The dried flowers crackled a little under the pressure, releasing a faint sweet scent that mingled with the woodsmoke from the fireplace.

The sheriff's gaze moved between them. "If any person can show just cause why they may not be joined together, let them speak now or forever hold their peace."

The silence that followed stretched long enough for her heart to hammer against her ribs. What if someone objected? What if Thomas changed his mind? What if—

"Thomas." Sheriff Hawkins turned to him. "Do you take this woman to be your lawfully wedded wife, to have and to hold from this day forward, for better or for worse, for richer or for poorer, in sickness and in health, to love and to cherish, till death do you part?"

Thomas's hand covered hers, where it rested on his arm. The

touch spread warmth through her, despite the trembling in her limbs.

"I do." His voice rang clear and steady, no hesitation coloring the words.

The sheriff shifted his attention to Kate. "Katherine, do you take this man to be your lawfully wedded husband, to have and to hold from this day forward, for better or for worse, for richer or for poorer, in sickness and in health, to love and to cherish, till death do you part?"

Her throat closed around the words. Every instinct screamed at her to run—to protect herself from the vulnerability of binding her life to another person who could hurt her, leave her, fail her the way her father had.

But then Thomas's thumb traced a gentle circle against the back of her hand. The small gesture anchored her, reminded her that he'd already proven himself in a dozen small ways. That he'd chosen honesty when lies would have been easier. That he'd called her strong when everyone else had called her difficult.

That he'd looked at her across a fire in a frozen cave and seen her—really seen her—in a way no one but Clara ever had.

She drew a breath. "I do."

Relief flickered across Thomas's face, so quick she might have imagined it. But his hand tightened on hers, solid and real.

The sheriff smiled and produced a simple gold band. She hadn't thought about a ring—hadn't expected one, given how quickly everything had happened.

Thomas took the ring with fingers that weren't quite steady. He held her left hand and slid the band onto her finger, fumbling only a little.

Then he repeated the words the sheriff gave him. "With this ring, I thee wed." His voice was low, meant only for her. "And with all my worldly goods, I thee endow."

The metal sat cool against her skin, foreign and strange. She could only stare at it—this small circle that symbolized how much everything had changed.

"By the power vested in me by the Territory of Montana and in the presence of these witnesses," the sheriff declared, "I now pronounce you husband and wife."

Husband and wife.

The words echoed in the sudden stillness.

"Thomas, you may kiss your bride."

Thomas turned to face her fully, and his eyes met hers, a question flickering in their depths.

Permission. He was asking for permission even now, when tradition and propriety gave him every right to claim the kiss without hesitation.

The consideration in that silent question made something crack open in her chest.

She gave a tiny nod.

One palm came up to cup her face, and the gentleness in his touch made her throat ache. He brushed his thumb across her cheekbone. The knot at his throat worked.

He leaned in slowly, giving her time to pull away if she wanted. She didn't.

His kiss was soft. Careful. The barest brush of his mouth against hers.

But heat bloomed through her like a match struck in darkness—unexpected, undeniable, *terrifying*. Her hands rose to rest on the lapels of his jacket without her permission.

He made a small sound against her lips, almost surprised, and deepened the kiss just a fraction—just enough for her to taste the promise of more.

Her pulse thundered in her ears. Every wall she'd built, every defense she'd erected, trembled at its foundations.

Then he drew back.

His eyes had darkened, the brown overtaken by deeper green. His chest rose and fell with a quickened breath. For a single moment, he wore everything on his face—wonder and want and something that looked almost like fear.

This was real. Her heart pounded even harder. This was far more than real.

The room behind them erupted into applause and well-wishes, shattering the moment. Thomas's expression shifted back into that easy smile, though the heat in his eyes remained.

Kate turned to the others as her own face burned.

Clara reached them first, pulling her into a hug that nearly toppled them both. "You're married," she whispered against Kate's ear. "You're really married."

Kate could only cling to her, burying her face in Clara's hair as she squeezed her eyes shut and breathed in. All the familiar scents—Clara's lavender soap, the hint of rose water she'd sprinkled on her collar that morning.

And underneath it all, simply Clara. Her sister. Her constant through every storm.

Clara was safe now. They both were.

She glanced at Thomas, who was nearly surrounded by his brothers. Yet even with James speaking to him, Thomas was watching her.

His eyes locked with hers, and one corner of his mouth lifted in that half-smile that made her stomach flip.

She'd made this choice. They both had. And whatever came next, they'd face it together.

For better or for worse.

CHAPTER 18

The wedding breakfast had stretched into early afternoon, a blur of laughter and stories and Mrs. Wang's seemingly endless supply of food. Thomas smiled through all of it, playing the part of the happy groom—which wasn't difficult, really. He *was* happy.

He just didn't quite know what to do about it.

Now that the celebration had finally wound down, he needed to find Kate. She'd slipped away sometime between Mrs. Wang's third course and Enoch's surprisingly heartfelt speech about their family growing stronger.

As the jade silk of her dress had disappeared around the corner, something had tightened in his chest.

His wife.

The words still felt foreign, like wearing a new pair of boots that hadn't quite broken in yet.

Kate Balfour. Lady Balfour, technically, though she might not want to use the title any more than he did his own.

She'd slipped away from the great room perhaps a half hour ago, Clara following close behind. Probably needing a moment to breathe after all the attention.

He knew that need well—the desire to escape when too many eyes watched, too many voices offered congratulations he didn't really deserve.

Now he finally had a chance to spend time with his bride. Maybe do some proper courting, even if they'd gotten the order backward by marrying first.

He'd been thinking about tonight too. About what she might expect. What he should say.

He'd decided not to push. Not to assume.

They'd married to protect her reputation, yes, but also because they'd both felt something worth exploring. That deserved time. Deserved the chance to grow without the pressure of obligations neither of them was ready for. Well…an obligation she might not be ready for anyway.

He'd tell her that. Make sure she knew he didn't expect her to share his bed until they were both ready.

He checked the great room first, then the kitchen, where Mrs. Wang shooed him away with a wooden spoon and a knowing smile that made heat climb the back of his neck. Not in the parlor. Not on the porch.

He climbed the stairs two at a time. Kate had been sharing Clara's room since they'd arrived at the ranch—the same guest chamber their mother had once kept for visiting relatives.

He paused outside the door and ran a hand through his hair. Then knocked.

Footsteps approached, lighter than Kate's purposeful stride. The door opened to reveal Clara, her honey-blonde hair slightly mussed and her warm hazel eyes widening at the sight of him.

"Thomas." She glanced over her shoulder, then back at him. "If you're looking for Kate, she's not here."

"Do you know where she went?"

A small smile played at Clara's lips—the same knowing expression Mrs. Wang had worn. Did all women share some secret language?

"She's taken her things to your room." Clara's grin widened at whatever she saw on his face. "About twenty minutes ago."

Thomas blinked. "She—*my* room?"

"Your room." Clara tilted her head, studying him a bit too much like her older sister did. "I suppose it's her room now too."

Of course she had. Because he hadn't talked to her yet about his plan.

"Right." He cleared his throat. "Thank you."

He turned and strode toward his own chamber. She'd moved her things without discussion. Without waiting for him to offer or even ask. She'd simply done what she believed was expected, because that's who Kate was. Someone who faced hard things head-on, chin lifted.

The door to his room stood slightly ajar.

He tapped on the wood as he eased it open. "Kate?"

She stood by the window, her back to him, still wearing the green silk dress that made her blonde hair shimmer. Her trunk sat at the foot of his bed, and a smaller valise rested on the chair near the wardrobe.

She turned at his voice. The way the soft afternoon light framed her figure made his mouth go dry. She was stunning.

His *wife* was stunning.

A few rich blonde strands had escaped her chignon to curl against her neck. The sight made his fingers itch to touch, to trace the line of her throat, to—

He swallowed hard and forced himself to focus. "I didn't expect you to move your things so quickly."

"It seemed the logical step." Her voice carried that practical edge, the one she used when she was nervous but refused to show it. "We're married after all."

He stepped inside and closed the door behind him. The click of the latch sounded too loud in the quiet room. "I wanted to talk to you about...arrangements."

Something flickered across her face—too quick to read. She folded her hands in front of her. Braced. Ready.

It made his chest ache.

"Kate." He moved closer, stopping when three strides still separated them. "We don't have to—that is, I don't expect—" He blew out a breath. Usually words came easily. Usually he could charm his way through any awkward situation.

But this mattered too much.

Her chin lifted. "I'm aware of my duties as a wife, Thomas. You don't need to—"

"That's not what I mean." He held up a hand. "Kate, I'm not going to push myself on you. I won't even ask you to share my bed until we've had time to know each other better."

Her brows drew together. "But we're married."

"We are." He took another step closer, searching her face for any sign she understood. "And I plan on being married to you for the rest of my life. That's a long time. You deserve the chance to get to know me before we..." He nodded toward the bed and did his best to fight down the heat climbing up his neck. "Before we do anything more."

Confusion flashed through her eyes. And was that…hurt? Her hands smoothed down the front of her dress. A nervous gesture, no doubt. He was making a muddle of this.

"I committed to this marriage." That determined edge returned to her voice. "I'll fulfill my obligations."

Obligations. The word twisted a knot in his gut.

"Kate, I'm not asking you to fulfill obligations. I'm asking you to let this develop naturally. Without pressure. Without feeling like you owe me something just because we spoke vows."

Her jaw tightened, and the elegant lines of her neck flexed. "You're saying you don't want—" She stopped as her cheeks turned pink. "You don't want me in your bed."

"That's not—" He dragged a hand through his hair. Surely

she didn't actually think that. "Kate, of course I want you. That's not what I mean."

Her jaw tightened. "Then what else do you want?"

The question hung between them, raw and honest in a way that stripped away every easy answer he might have given.

What did he want?

He wanted her to look at him the way she had in the cave—like he was someone worth trusting.

He wanted to earn the right to touch her, to hold her, to make her his in truth.

He wanted her to choose him, not because circumstances forced her hand, but because she wanted to.

He swallowed. Could he say all that? Would it overwhelm her? Instead of taking the pressure off, would it simply add more?

He focused on the easiest part of it. "I want you willing, not dutiful. I want you to come to me because you choose to, not because you think it's expected."

She stared at him, her hazel eyes searching his face with an intensity that saw everything. "I don't understand you." Or maybe not everything.

He almost smiled, though his pulse hammered against his ribs. "That's exactly my point. We barely know each other. You don't understand me, and I certainly don't understand you yet. But I'd like to. I'd like us to have the chance to build something real before we..."

"Consummate the marriage." She said it flatly, like stating a business transaction.

His chest tightened. "Yes."

She pulled back. Maybe not in physical distance. But a wall dropped over her eyes, shuttering her feelings away from him. "I'll move my things back to Clara's room then."

He'd hurt her. In trying to be noble, once again, he'd messed up.

He had to fix it. Now.

He stepped sideways to block her from moving around him. "Kate, I would be honored—truly honored—if you would share this room with me. I won't touch you until we're both ready, but I'd love your company."

She paused and eyed him. He held his breath, praying she could see his sincerity. For a long moment, she simply stared at him.

Then it came—just a flicker, there and gone. A shadow of relief passing through her eyes before she hid it.

He'd made the right choice.

"You mean that." It wasn't quite a question.

"I do." He allowed a small smile. "Seems I'm saying that a lot today."

The corner of her mouth twitched—not quite a grin, but close enough. Some of the tension eased from her shoulders.

"Very well." She inclined her head in that formal way she had, like a queen accepting the terms of a treaty. "I appreciate your...consideration."

It wasn't consideration—it was simple decency, the bare minimum any man should offer his wife. But Kate had likely known too little of decency in her life to recognize it as standard rather than unusual.

So instead, he just nodded. "I'll leave you to settle in. Take whatever space you need in the wardrobe. Just move my clothes over or set them aside."

He escaped before he could say anything else foolish. Before he could tell her how beautiful she'd looked walking down the stairs. Before he could admit that the taste of her lips during their wedding kiss had kept him distracted through the entire breakfast.

Time. They both needed time.

A few hours later, he stood in the hallway outside his own

bedchamber door again. He'd become like a stranger in his own home.

He'd given Kate time to prepare for bed, staying overlong in the great room to sit by the dying fire and pretend to read. James had given him an odd look. Robert raised an eyebrow. Mrs. Wang had pressed a cup of warm milk into his hands with a sympathetic pat that somehow made everything worse.

Now the house had settled into nighttime quiet—just the creak of old timbers and the distant howl of wind across the mountains. The strip of light beneath his door had dimmed, suggesting Kate already extinguished most of the lamps.

He was regretting his noble promise.

Not because he intended to break it—he'd meant every word. But standing here in the cold hallway, knowing his wife waited on the other side of that door, knowing he would lie beside her all night without touching her...

God had a sense of humor, clearly.

He raised his hand and knocked on his own door.

"Come in." The wood muffled Kate's voice.

He turned the handle and stepped inside.

The room was dim, lit only by a single lamp on the bedside table turned down to its lowest setting. Kate already lay in bed, the quilts pulled up to her chin, her honey blonde hair in a much looser braid than her usual tight style.

She looked...

What was the right word? Beautiful, yes. But more than that. Soft in a way Kate almost never allowed herself to appear. Younger. More vulnerable.

The sight hit him somewhere beneath his sore ribs.

Thank you. The prayer rose from a little-used part of him. *I don't deserve her, but thank you for this woman.*

His bed was positioned against the wall—had been since he was a boy, when he'd liked having something solid on one side so he didn't roll off. Kate had scooted all the way over to that wall, leaving as much space between her and his side as the double mattress allowed.

He should say something charming. Something to ease the tension that hung thick as woodsmoke in the air.

In his mind, he'd imagined making some kind of show of preparing for bed—removing his cravat with exaggerated flourish, perhaps, or commenting on the quality of Mrs. Wang's quilting. Something to prove he was perfectly comfortable, perfectly at ease, perfectly unbothered by the presence of a beautiful woman in his bed.

But looking at Kate now—at the way her fingers clenched the edge of the quilt, at the careful blankness of her expression that didn't quite hide the wariness beneath—he couldn't bring himself to perform.

She looked more vulnerable than he'd ever seen Kate McKinney—Kate *Balfour*—look.

So he simply moved to the other side of the bed. Removed his boots. Shrugged off his jacket and hung it on the chair. Kept his shirt and trousers on, though he normally changed into a nightshirt.

"Do you want me to turn out the lamp?" he asked quietly.

"Please."

He blew out the flame. Darkness swallowed the room, broken only by thin moonlight seeping through the window curtains. The bed ropes creaked as he lowered himself onto the tick, staying carefully on his side, leaving space between them.

The quilts smelled a little like lavender. Kate's doing, perhaps, or Mrs. Wang's thoughtfulness.

Silence settled over them like snow.

He stared at the far wall he couldn't see. Behind him, Kate's breathing barely sounded—far too controlled to be natural.

He should let her rest. Should keep his mouth shut and his eyes closed and pray that exhaustion eventually claimed them both.

Instead, he said, "You know, you're Lady Balfour now."

A pause.

"What?"

"Lady Balfour." He turned his head toward her, though he could barely make out her shape in the darkness. "That's your title. Since we're married."

More silence. When she spoke again, her voice held a note of confusion. "I...hadn't considered that."

"It's true." He couldn't quite keep the smile from his voice. "You're a viscountess now. Married into the English peerage."

The blanket rustled as she shifted. "That feels...strange."

"Welcome to the madness." He kept the words light, no matter how much truth lay beneath them. The absurdity of titles and bloodlines had chafed at him for years. "Though I have to say, Lady Katherine Balfour has a rather nice ring to it."

"Kate." She spoke almost automatically. "Just Kate."

"Kate." He let her name settle on his tongue, simple and strong. Like the woman herself. "Just Kate. Viscountess of these Montana mountains."

A sound escaped her—something that might have been a laugh, quickly suppressed. "You're ridiculous."

"I've been told."

The darkness didn't weigh as much now. Some of the tension had eased from the air between them, replaced by a sense of companionship.

"Go to sleep, Thomas." Kate's voice had softened.

"Yes, my lady."

This time, the sound she made was definitely a laugh.

He smiled into the darkness and closed his eyes. This wasn't how he'd imagined his wedding night. But lying here beside Kate—the warmth of her presence drifting across the distance between them, hearing the quiet rhythm of her breathing—he didn't mind at all.

They had time.

CHAPTER 19

Kate had never known a household could feel like this.

She sat at the round work table in the kitchen, afternoon light streaming through the window as she worked her needle through the worn cuff of a flannel shirt. Around her, the comfortable sounds of women at work filled the space—the rhythmic thump of Mandie kneading bread dough, the soft scrapings of Rose's knife as she peeled potatoes, and through the open door down to the cellar, Clara's bright laugh at something Mrs. Wang said.

Or rather, *Bea*. The older woman had insisted all the women call her by her Christian name. Her dark eyes had warmed as she'd pressed Kate's hands between her own. "You are family now. My girls call me Bea."

Family. The word still felt so foreign, like a language she was only beginning to learn.

Two days. Kate had been married for two days, and already the rhythm of the Balfour household had begun to seep into her bones. Breakfast at dawn with the whole family crowded around the massive dining table, voices overlapping in easy conversation. Then the men would disappear to the barn and pastures, leaving the house to settle into its own quieter industry.

And Kate had found her place in it.

She'd discovered the mending basket on her first morning—overflowing with shirts missing buttons, trousers with torn seams, stockings worn thin at the heels and toes. A ranching household of four brothers generated no small amount of work for a needle, and from the state of the pile, it had been neglected for some time.

Now the mending pile had shrunk by half, and Kate moved on to washing—scrubbing work shirts clean, then reinforcing seams and patching worn spots before they became holes.

"Kate." Mandie's voice pulled her from her work. The woman stood at her shoulder, flour dusting her apron, examining the shirt in Kate's hands. "Is that Enoch's old work shirt? The one with the tear along the shoulder?"

Kate lifted the garment so Mandie could see the repair. "I added an extra layer of fabric underneath, then reinforced the seam with a double stitch. It should hold through another season at least."

Mandie's eyes widened. "I was going to use that for rags. I thought the fabric was too frayed."

"I think it can go through the spring." Kate smoothed her hand over the nearly invisible stitches. Good work, even if she wasn't objective.

"You're wasted on simple mending." Rose leaned forward to peer over the pile of potatoes. "These repairs are works of art."

Heat climbed Kate's neck. "They're just practical. No sense throwing away something that can be fixed."

Bea appeared at Kate's other side, wiping her hands on her apron. "Practical and beautiful can live in same." She lifted one of the finished shirts from the stack beside Kate's elbow—one of Thomas's, the blue cotton she'd washed and mended that morning. "Look at this buttonhole. Perfect. And this elbow—I can barely see where the hole was."

"It's what I was trained to do." Kate set down Enoch's shirt and reached for the next item in the basket—another of Thomas's shirts, if she wasn't mistaken. He'd worn this green flannel the first morning after they reached the ranch, when he gave her the three choices, and she chose marriage.

The fabric held the faint scent she was coming to know as his—horse and leather and something uniquely him. Something that made her pulse quicken.

She worked her needle quickly through the worn cuff, her fingers coaxing the fraying threads back into order. This, at least, she understood. Fabric and thread—problems with clear solutions.

So much simpler than the complicated tangle of emotions whenever she thought about her husband.

Her husband. Two words that still didn't quite fit together in her mind.

Last night had been their second night sharing a bed. Like the first, Thomas had kept carefully to his side, maintaining the space between them. But this time, that distance had felt smaller somehow. A foot instead of two. Close enough that she could feel the warmth radiating from him in the darkness, could hear each shift of his breathing.

And in that darkness, they'd talked again.

It seemed to be their ritual—this strange intimacy that only existed when they couldn't see each other's faces. In the night, with the covers pulled up, and the world reduced to darkness and murmured words, she said things to him she'd never told anyone.

And Thomas... He listened in a way no one ever had. Not even Clara. Not waiting for his turn to speak. Not judging. Just...listening.

He told her about the first horse he'd ever trained on his

own—a half-wild mare everyone else had given up on. How he'd spent weeks just sitting with her, letting her come to him, earning her trust inch by inch. The triumph he'd felt when she finally let him touch her.

"That's what I felt like," Kate admitted into the darkness. "After my mother died. After Father remarried so soon. And his choice seemed to hate me so. I felt like a wild thing everyone had given up on. Only there was no one patient enough to sit with me."

"But later you had Clara," Thomas said quietly.

"Yes." Kate swallowed against the thickness in her throat. "Clara became the one person."

A pause. Then, "And now you have me too."

She hadn't known how to respond to that. Hadn't trusted herself to speak around the pressure in her chest.

But somehow, in the silence that followed, her hand had found his across the space between them. Just the lightest brush of fingers. A connection as fragile as spider silk.

They'd fallen asleep like that, barely touching. And when she awoke at dawn to find her hand still resting near his on the mattress, something had budded inside her.

Something terrifying. Something that felt almost like hope.

Now, in the bright light of midday, that midnight vulnerability felt distant. Unreal. She was Lady Katherine Balfour—the title still sat awkwardly on her shoulders—wife of a viscount, sister-in-law to three English lords turned Montana ranchers. She had a place in this household, work to do, people who seemed to value her presence.

It was more than she'd ever dared imagine for herself. It should be enough.

It *was* enough.

So why did some traitorous part of her keep wanting more?

The sound of boots on the porch scattered her thoughts. In the great room, the front door opened, followed by male voices—James and Robert, from the sound of it. Maybe Enoch too.

But no Thomas.

Kate's hands stilled on the fabric, her ears straining even as she told herself not to. She'd become too attuned to the particular cadence of her husband's voice, the way it carried differently than his brothers'.

Lower. Warmer.

The other women had slipped into action, gathering coffee cups and food they'd already prepared.

Kate set aside her work and stood to help. Mrs. Wang placed a tray of mugs in her hand and nodded toward the open door to the dining room. Kate followed Rose, who carried twin plates of sliced bread.

James entered the dining room first, stamping snow from his boots, followed by Robert and Enoch. They moved with the easy coordination of men who'd worked together their whole lives, unfastening coats and settling around the table while the rest of them laid out the simple meal—thick slices of bread, cheese, cold meat from last night's supper, and a heaping pot of coffee.

She'd just started to turn back to the kitchen when Thomas stepped through the doorway.

He looked...different in the daylight. His copper-brown hair tousled from the wind, his cheeks flushed from the cold. He moved with that easy grace that was his own, all loose-limbed confidence, as though the world had been built specifically to accommodate him.

His eyes found hers across the crowded dining room, and warmth flickered in their depths.

Heat crept through her. This man. This incredibly handsome, far-too-charming man was *hers*.

Thomas broke the moment first, offering her that easy half-smile of his—the one she was beginning to realize hid more than it revealed. He crossed to the table and took a seat beside James, accepting a cup of coffee from Mandie with murmured thanks.

But his gaze kept drifting back to her.

And she didn't return to the kitchen. Instead, poured coffee while Mandie laid out plates. Thomas's gaze tracked her progress, the weight of it like a physical touch. She had to work to keep her hands from trembling.

"How are the new horses settling in?" Mandie laid a dish in front of her husband.

Enoch smiled his thanks. "Well enough. The bay mare's still skittish, but Thomas has been working with her."

"She just needs patience." Thomas leaned back in his chair. "She'll come around."

James snorted. "You always say that. Hopefully she won't turn out like that stallion."

"She won't." Thomas's tone was light, but there was a slight tightening around his eyes. She was learning to read the small signs—the places where his easy charm was a mask rather than a mirror.

The conversation continued as they all sat to eat, ranch talk she only half followed—something about feed stores and the condition of the north pasture and whether the early March thaw would hold.

She watched Thomas more than listening. The way his hands moved as he spoke, the play of light through the windows across his features. The way his eyes crinkled at the corners when Robert said something dry and clever.

As Rose started collecting used plates, the rumble of approaching hooves outside made them all lift their heads.

A rider coming fast at midday couldn't be normal. Not in this remote place with the nearest neighbor an hour's ride away.

James rose from his chair and moved to the window.

"Single rider from the south. I think that's Mary Jenkins."

The young family Thomas had mentioned, the one with the baby less than a year old.

Enoch was already moving toward the door, Thomas and Robert close behind. Kate followed them all into the great room, then slipped outside with them.

The cold air sliced through her, and she wrapped her arms around herself. She should have grabbed her coat.

A brown mare stood heaving in the yard, sides lathered white despite the chill. Mary Jenkins sat slumped in the saddle, exhaustion etched into every line of her young face. She clutched a bundle against her chest—the baby, wrapped in what looked like every blanket they owned.

"Mrs. Jenkins." Enoch reached the horse first, his hand steadying the mare's bridle. "What's happened?"

"Samuel." Mary's voice cracked. "There's been an avalanche. The cattle—they're trapped in the canyon."

Thomas moved to her side, reaching up to help her down. "Easy now. Take a breath."

But Mrs. Jenkins was already sliding from the saddle, clutching her baby tightly as her boots hit the snow. "Samuel's watching them, but there's nothing he can do. They're trapped, and there's another storm coming, and we can't—we don't—"

A hearty wail loosed from the babe, muffled by the pile of blankets.

Rose was there in an instant, wrapping her arm around the younger woman's shoulders. "Come inside and get warm. Tell us everything."

The next few minutes were a blur of motion. Rose guided Mrs. Jenkins to a chair by the fire. Bea pressed a cup of hot tea into her trembling hands. Mandie took the baby—a round-cheeked infant with dark eyes and a surprisingly powerful wail—and began walking the room, bouncing gently until the crying subsided.

Kate hung back with Clara. Everyone seemed to know what to do in this crisis. What more was needed?

"Start from the beginning." Enoch perched on a chair near the woman. "What happened?"

Mrs. Jenkins drew a shaky breath. "We wintered the herd in Coldwater Canyon, like always. The shelter's good there, and the spring doesn't freeze. Except the grass has been eaten for days, and Samuel was planning to move them. Then two days ago, that warming spell started, and then—" She broke off, swallowing hard. "Yesterday morning, the whole north slope came down. Blocked the canyon entrance. Twenty feet of snow and rock and broken trees."

Kate drew a sharp breath. Twenty feet.

"Samuel tried to dig through." Mrs. Jenkins curled in around her teacup. "Worked all day and barely made a dent. And the cattle—" Her voice wavered. "They're still alive, we can hear them, but they're trapped on the other side with no food and barely any water. If we can't get them out before the next storm hits..."

She didn't finish the sentence. She didn't need to.

"How many head?" James asked.

"Eighteen. It's everything we have."

The weight of that settled over the room. Kate didn't know much about ranching, but she understood enough. Eighteen cattle might not sound like many compared to the Balfour herds, but for a young couple just starting out, it must be everything. Their entire future, trapped behind a wall of snow.

The brothers exchanged glances. Communicating in that wordless way siblings did—the way she and Clara could.

"We'll need shovels," Enoch said finally. "Picks. The draft horses might be able to help move the larger debris."

"It'll take days." Robert frowned. "Even with all of us working in shifts—"

"We don't have days." Mrs. Jenkins's voice held an edge of

desperation. "The next storm is coming. Two days at most, Samuel thinks. Maybe less. If the snow gets deeper before we get them out..."

"Then we work faster." James was already buttoning his coat. "We've dug through worse."

"Wait." Robert held up a hand. "If we could rig some kind of pulley system—use leverage instead of brute force—"

"That would take time to set up." Enoch stood. "Time we don't have."

"What about the back trail?"

Thomas's voice cut through the discussion, drawing every head toward him.

He stood slightly apart from his brothers, arms crossed over his chest, his expression thoughtful. "The north ridge route. It comes down into the canyon from above. If we went in that way, we wouldn't need to dig at all—just drive the cattle up that back slope and loop around on the old trapper's path."

A moment of silence.

"I—" Mrs. Jenkins's face had drained of color. "Samuel won't take that trail." She spoke quietly, but her tone made the words sound absolute. Final in a way that closed off discussion.

Thomas frowned. "Why not? I know it's narrow in places, but with the ice melting, it won't be slick—"

"He *won't*." Mrs. Jenkins's voice cracked. Her hands had started trembling again, sending ripples through her tea. "When we first moved west, he tried that trail. Early spring, just like now. He thought it was safe."

She stopped. Drew a breath that made her shoulders shudder.

"The ground gave way beneath his horse. He fell... I don't know how far. He's never told me everything. But I know he nearly died. I know he spent weeks recovering, and I know he still has nightmares about it." She looked up at Thomas, her eyes bright and glassy. "He made me a promise. He would never take that trail again. Ever. I can't ask him to break that promise. I *won't*."

The weight of her words pressed down on the room.

A shimmer of understanding touched Thomas's gaze. Clearly, the Jenkins' fear ran bone-deep, the kind that couldn't be reasoned away.

But he must have realized his suggestion could make the difference in this situation. "Mrs. Jenkins, I understand he's afraid. I do. But the conditions are different now—the snow's had time to settle. Samuel doesn't need to come with us. I could lead the way, check every foot of the path before we—"

"Thomas." James's voice was gentle but firm. "You heard her."

"I'm just saying that if we—"

"We're not going to force a man to face his worst nightmare." Enoch cut him off, the words landing like stones. "Not when there's another option."

"An option that might not work in time." Thomas's jaw tightened. "They might lose some of those cattle."

"Then we work faster." James clapped his brother on the shoulder—maybe a touch meant to be reassuring, she could almost feel the frustration flaring from Thomas like heat from a fire. "We'll dig through. All of us working together, around the clock if we have to. We'll get those cattle out."

Robert nodded. "I'll start gathering the tools. We should take the draft horses—"

"I pack food." Mrs. Wang marched toward the kitchen.

Thomas's posture had changed. Closed off. Locked down. His face wore that easy half-smile she was coming to recognize as armor—the look that meant he was feeling something he didn't want anyone to see.

She knew that feeling well. Had tried to hide it herself more times than she could count. The expression of someone whose voice didn't matter. Whose ideas were dismissed before they could fully form.

The injustice of it burned in her chest.

"I'll get the horses ready." Thomas's voice came out flat. He turned to the door without waiting for a response.

As the rest of the group dispersed to make preparations, she watched through the window as he descended the porch steps and crossed the yard toward the barn, his shoulders straight, his stride just a little too controlled.

I see you. Even if they don't.

And when, exactly, had *seeing* Thomas Balfour started to matter so much?

CHAPTER 20

Five days.

Five days that could have been a single day if his brothers would have just listened to him.

Thomas shifted in his saddle as the ranch house came into view, every muscle in his body screaming for rest. His hands ached from wielding picks and shovels. His shoulders burned from hauling rock and ice. And his ribs—the ones that had only just begun to heal—throbbed with each breath, a constant reminder of every wrong move he'd made over the past week.

Behind him, James and Enoch rode in similar silence, their horses plodding through the churned mud of the trail. Robert had stayed behind a few more hours at the Jenkins' place to help Samuel move the surviving cattle to fresh pasture.

Fifteen head. That's how many they'd saved.

Three dead when they finally broke through the wall of snow and debris. Three animals that might have lived if they'd taken the back trail like Thomas had suggested. If his brothers had trusted him enough to consider his plan instead of dismissing it outright.

The familiar bitterness rose in his throat, sharp as bile.

He'd worked alongside them without complaint. Dug until his hands bled through his gloves. Taken the night shifts when the cold cut deepest.

And through it all, not one of them had acknowledged that maybe—just maybe—he'd been right.

The ranch yard spread before them now, smoke curling from the main house chimney in lazy spirals against the gray afternoon sky. Home. Though the word felt hollow in his chest.

"I'll take the horses." James's voice came out rough with exhaustion. "You two go on inside."

Thomas dismounted without answering, his boots hitting the packed earth with a jolt that traveled up through his knees. He handed his reins to James and headed for the house, not trusting himself to speak.

Enoch fell into step beside him. "You did good work out there."

"Did I?" The words came out a bit too sharp. "Didn't feel like it mattered much."

His brother's jaw tightened, but he didn't respond. Just climbed the porch steps and pushed through the front door, letting a wave of warm air wash over them both.

The great room stood empty save for the fire crackling in the hearth. The familiar scent of Mrs. Wang's cooking drifted from somewhere deeper in the house—beef stew, maybe, with that hint of ginger she always added. His stomach clenched with hunger, but the rest of him didn't care about food right now.

He needed to find Kate. Needed to tell her what he'd decided during those long, cold nights of digging through snow while his brothers pretended his ideas didn't exist.

California.

The name had become a drumbeat in his mind. Constant. He was done waiting. Done hoping things would change. Done being the youngest brother whose voice didn't matter.

He needed to talk to Kate about the plan. Should he go ahead to California now, get things established, then come back for her and Clara in the summer? Or would they want to go with him right away?

Either way, he couldn't stay here. Not as an afterthought. Not as someone whose judgment would never be trusted simply because he'd had the misfortune of being born last.

"You're back." Mrs. Wang stepped from the dining room with a tray in her arms, but halted when she saw him and Enoch. Her sharp gaze swept over them both. "Go wash. Both of you. Then come and eat. Where are James and Robert?"

"Robert stayed to help Samuel." Enoch pulled off his gloves and tucked them into his coat pocket. "James is seeing to the horses."

Her expression softened. "The cattle?"

"Three lost. Fifteen saved." Enoch's voice carried the weight of those numbers—the cost of decisions made and time wasted.

She nodded, then turned to Thomas. Something in her gaze made him want to look away—that particular knowing she'd perfected over the years of raising them all. "You need rest more than food, I think."

"I'm fine."

"Hmm." She didn't believe him, of course. But she simply gestured toward the stairs. "Your wife is in her sister's room. Clara is not well."

The words cut through his fog of exhaustion and frustration. "Not feeling well? What's wrong?"

"A fever. Started yesterday." Mrs. Wang's tone had gone matter-of-fact, though concern flickered beneath it. "Nothing serious yet, but Kate has stayed with her."

He started toward the stairs.

"Take this to her." Mrs. Wang held out the tray she'd been carrying.

But when he shifted his direction to take it from her, she frowned. "Do not make dirty."

Despite it all, he managed a tip of his mouth. "Yes, ma'am."

The tray felt heavier than it should have as he dragged himself up the stairs, each step an effort that made his ribs protest.

As he moved down the hallway, the door to Clara's room opened. He slowed when Kate stepped out.

She pulled up short when she saw him, her hazel eyes widening. He let himself take in the sight of her.

She looked tired. Dark circles shadowed her hazel eyes, and her hair—usually pinned in that neat chignon she favored—had come loose in places, dark strands falling around her face. Her dress was wrinkled, as though she'd been sitting in the same position for hours.

His insides twisted.

"Thomas." Her voice carried relief and something else he couldn't quite name. "You're back."

"Just now." He stopped a few feet from her. He should have washed before he came upstairs. What with the dirt ground into his clothes, the week's worth of stubble on his jaw, and his stench...she probably wanted to back away from him.

Too late to change that now.

He held out the tray. "Mrs. Wang sent this up. Is Clara all right?"

"She's sleeping. The fever seems to be holding steady." She reached for the tray, her fingers brushing his as she took it. Even that brief contact sent warmth up his arms. "I was just going to get more blankets. I can't seem to get her warm."

Her eyes swept over him again—taking in the mud caked on his boots, the exhaustion weighing down every part of him. "You look terrible."

A laugh slipped out. "I've been told."

But she didn't smile. Instead, she stepped closer, and her hand rose as though she might touch his face. Then she caught herself and let it fall. "Did it go well? The rescue?"

A new rush of frustration surged. "We saved fifteen head. Lost three."

"Oh." Something flicked across her expression. Understanding, maybe. Or sympathy. "I'm sorry."

"Not your fault." He tried to keep his voice light, but bitterness crept in anyway. "Might have saved them all if we'd taken them out the back way. But what do I know?"

Kate's eyes sharpened. That look she got when she was reading past his words to the truth underneath. "Thomas—

"I need to talk to you, Kate."

Her brows rose. "About?"

He inhaled a breath to rein in his words. "About California."

Her face went pale. "What about it?"

"I'm going." Maybe he shouldn't have been so abrupt.

He worked to soften his tone. "I can't stay here anymore. Not like this. Not when they—" He broke off, swallowing back the tide that rose too strong. "I'm done being treated like I don't know anything. Like my ideas don't matter because I'm the youngest."

Kate's lips parted, but no sound emerged.

"We lost three cattle out there." He couldn't get the edge in his voice to ease. "Three animals that might have lived if they'd just listened to me about that trail. But no. Thomas is reckless. Thomas takes too many risks." He laughed, the sound harsh in the quiet hallway. "I'm so tired of proving myself to people who've already decided I'm not worth hearing."

"Thomas—"

"I want you and Clara to come with me." He refocused on her face...one that seemed to be going paler with each breath.

She took a step back. "You want us to leave? Now?"

"Not necessarily now." He dragged a hand through his filthy hair. "I could go ahead—get things established, find us a place, come back for you both in the summer. Or..." He paused. "Or you could come with me when I leave. We could all go together. Start fresh somewhere new."

The color had drained from her face entirely. "Thomas, Clara is sick."

He was making a muddle of this. "I know. I'm not saying we'd leave tomorrow." Though part of him wanted exactly that —to saddle his horse and ride until Montana was nothing but a memory behind him. "But soon. As soon as she's well enough to travel."

Kate shook her head. "I don't—I need time to think about this."

Time. The word landed wrong, scratching against his already raw nerves. How much more time did she need? They'd talked about California before. She'd known this was something he wanted.

Though maybe she hadn't realized how much he needed it.

He studied her face, doing his best to read what she wasn't saying. Her knuckles had gone white where she gripped the tray. Her jaw was set in that stubborn line.

"How much time?" He tried to keep the frustration from his voice. Hopefully he mostly succeeded.

"I don't know." Her voice had gone brittle. "But Clara is sick. I can't—" She shook her head, and he caught the shimmer of something in her eyes that might have been tears. "I need time to think about it. I can't make a decision like this right now, Thomas. Not with Clara lying in there, unable to keep down anything more than tea."

He was a heel. The grandest of heels.

He shook his head to clear out the cobwebs from his half-witted mind. "I'm sorry. You're right." He glanced toward the closed door. "What can I do to help?"

"You can rest." Her voice softened, though tension still held her shoulders rigid. "You look like you're about to fall over."

"I'm fine."

Her eyes narrowed—that look that said she saw right through him. "When was the last time you slept? Really slept, not just collapsed for a few hours between shifts?"

He couldn't remember. The days had blurred together into an endless cycle of digging and hauling and trying to prove something that apparently couldn't be proven.

"Thomas." She shifted the tray to one hip. "Go wash. Eat something. Sleep in an actual bed instead of frozen ground. Once Clara's better, we can talk about...everything else...when you're not dead on your feet."

The practicality in her tone should have irritated him. Should have felt like another person dismissing what he needed.

But something in the way she said it—the concern beneath the brusque words—made the fight drain out of him.

Maybe she was right. Maybe he was too exhausted to have this conversation properly. Too raw to explain without letting bitterness poison every word.

"All right." He took a step back. "But come find me if I can do anything to help."

She nodded. "I will." Though whether that was a promise or just a way to end the conversation, he couldn't tell.

He turned toward his room—their room—but paused at the door. When he looked back, Kate still stood in the hallway, watching him with an expression he couldn't quite read.

Worry, maybe. Or a deeper emotion that his exhausted mind couldn't process.

He wanted to go back to her. Wanted to pull her close and bury his face in her hair and let the solid warmth of her presence chase away the cold that had settled into his bones over the past five days.

But Clara needed her. And he had to wash off a week's worth of grime before he could think about anything else.

So he just offered her a tired nod and slipped into their room.

CHAPTER 21

Clara's forehead burned like Kate was holding her hand to a cookstove.

Kate's middle clenched tighter as she dipped the cloth back into the basin of cool water on the bedside table, wrung some of the liquid out, then laid it back over Clara's brow.

Her sister stirred but didn't wake—hadn't truly woken in the last couple hours. Not since the fever spiked.

Kate had been dozing beside her in the bed, but a moan from Clara made her jerk awake. Her sister's skin had been hot enough to make her gasp.

And then she'd seen the rash.

Red splotches scattered across Clara's chest and arms like angry fingerprints. Now they'd spread up her neck. Probably other places Kate hadn't checked yet too.

The bedroom door opened, and Bea slipped inside. One hand carried a water pitcher, and the other a cloth tied in a bundle.

Her dark eyes moved immediately to Clara, then to Kate. "Any change?"

Kate shook her head. "The rash is spreading. And she's

hotter than before." She didn't even try to keep the worry from her voice. Bea would see through whatever she managed.

The older woman set down her supplies and moved to the bedside. Her wrinkled hand pressed against Clara's forehead, then her cheek, then the side of her neck where the pulse beat too fast beneath such pale skin.

"Is not good." Bea's tone carried no false comfort. "I have seen this before. In England, and here too. It is either measles or scarlet fever."

No.

Both could kill—she knew that much. Had heard the stories of entire families wiped out by such illnesses, children buried in small graves while their parents wept.

"Which one?" She forced the question past the tightness in her throat. "Which do you think?"

"Cannot know for certain." Bea straightened and turned back to the cloth bundle. "Enoch will come soon with doctor. For now, ice to make her cool."

She pulled back the fabric to reveal packed snow—clean white crystals that must have been gathered from a drift near the house. Steam rose where the cold met the room's warmth.

Bea divided the snow into smaller portions and wrapped each in strips of cloth. "Under her arms. Behind her neck. Along her sides." She demonstrated with the first bundle, tucking it against Clara's reddened neck. "The cold will draw out some of the heat."

Kate took one of the wrapped bundles and positioned it on the other side of Clara's neck. The contrast between the ice and her sister's burning skin made her stomach turn. How could a body generate this much heat and still work as it should?

Clara whimpered at the cold, turning her head on the pillow, but didn't wake.

"Good." Bea lifted the quilts and placed another bundle

under Clara's arm. "We change them when they melt. Keep her cool until doctor comes."

Kate arranged the remaining bundles along Clara's sides. Measles or scarlet fever. Either one could be deadly. Either one could—

She wouldn't let herself finish that thought.

Bea stood and moved to the door. "We must be careful now. Very careful."

Kate jerked her head up to catch Bea's expression. "What do you mean?"

The older woman turned back. "If this is scarlet fever—or even measles—it spreads easy. Like fire through dry grass." She motioned toward the hallway beyond. "We keep everyone away from this room. Only you and me with Clara. No one else come in."

Her insides churned anew. She couldn't risk Bea with this sickness either. Not more than she'd already been exposed.

She swallowed to clear the lump from her throat. "You'd better stay out too. Just leave what we'll need at the door. I'll take care of it."

Bea's expression softened with something like approval. "You are wise." She gave a single firm nod. "I will bring more snow. You call if you need anything."

Then she was gone, the door clicking shut with a finality that made the room feel smaller.

She sank onto the edge of the bed, then reached for Clara's hand where it lay limp against the quilts. The palm was hot, but the fingertips icy.

"You're going to be fine." Her whisper cracked, but she didn't stop. Like saying this aloud could make it true. "The doctor will come and tell us what to do, and you'll be fine."

Clara's breathing came shallow and quick, each exhale carrying a faint rasp that hadn't been there before.

Kate's vision blurred, but she blinked hard against the moisture. Crying wouldn't help. Wouldn't bring the doctor faster or cool Clara's fever or make the rash disappear.

She needed to keep busy.

She adjusted the ice packs around Clara until they melted to only damp fabric. Mrs. Wang brought another bundle of snow and a cup of tea for Kate that she couldn't bring herself to drink.

At some point, someone—Rose, maybe, or Mandie—tapped on the door and asked if there was anything they could do. She'd been able to think of nothing, and they said everyone was praying below.

Praying. Kate had been doing little else, though she wasn't sure God was listening. The words felt hollow in her mind, desperate pleas that seemed to dissolve before they could reach heaven.

Please. Not Clara. Take me, not her.

The rash had spread farther—down Clara's arms now, angry red patches that seemed to pulse with the fever burning beneath her skin. Her breathing had grown more labored too, each inhale a visible effort that made Kate's own chest burn.

A sound drifted from outside. Hoofbeats, approaching fast.

Hope surged through her so quickly it almost hurt. She crossed to the window, pushing aside the curtain to peer down at the yard below.

A single rider emerged from the tree line. Kate's heart leaped—

But no. She knew the set of the shoulders, the dark hair beneath the hat.

Robert. Not the doctor.

He dismounted and handed his reins to someone—James, probably, emerging from the barn. They exchanged words she couldn't hear, and Robert's posture went rigid. Even from this distance, she could see the alarm that crossed his features.

A moment later, he strode to the house with a kind of urgent purpose. Had James told him about Clara?

Kate turned back to the bed, to her sister's flushed face and rasping breaths. Robert's arrival meant nothing had changed.

They were still waiting. Still hoping.

Still watching Clara slip further away with each passing hour.

The doctor arrived perhaps ten minutes after Robert. Voices sounded downstairs, then boot thuds coming upward. Then Mrs. Wang tapped on the door of Clara's chamber and opened it.

Dr. Morrison had the weathered look of someone who'd spent decades practicing medicine on the frontier—deep lines carved around his eyes and mouth and a serious focus as he approached the bed.

Thomas stood in the hallway behind him, and she caught his gaze. That look. The support he was trying to offer her…

But he could do nothing. Nothing that would make a difference to Clara's condition. If there was, she would have already done it.

Bea stepped inside and pulled the door closed, and Kate forced herself to turn and focus on the doctor.

"How long has she had the fever?" Dr. Morrison's voice was brisk as he set down his black bag and bent over Clara.

"It started yesterday morning." Kate moved closer, toward Clara's feet, where she could see but be out of the way. "Just a slight warmth at first. But it spiked this afternoon."

"And the rash? When did it come?" The doctor's hands moved over Clara's neck, pressing as they traveled.

"A few hours ago. It started on her chest but has spread." She gripped her hands together. "What is it? What's wrong with her?"

Dr. Morrison didn't answer immediately. He pulled back the quilts and adjusted Clara's nightdress to examine the red marks that now covered most of her upper body.

His jaw tightened as he worked—pressing here, listening

there with a long cylinder he'd pulled from his bag. His expression remained blank as he examined the splotches, but something in the set of his jaw made her middle twist even tighter.

Finally, he straightened. "It looks like scarlet fever."

No. Her knees threatened to buckle, but she forced herself to stay upright. "What...what do we do?"

"Keep her cool. The ice packs are good—continue those. Garlic poultices. I'll leave medicine." He straightened and turned to Kate, then glanced over at Bea, who still stood at the door. His expression had gone grave. "Have either of you had scarlet fever? Or any of the family?"

Kate's throat tightened. "I haven't."

Bea spoke from behind them. "Only Robert, when he was a boy. I remember the rash—we almost lose him."

Dr. Morrison nodded. "Then Robert is the only one who should enter this room. Anyone who hasn't had scarlet fever risks infection."

"No." The word burst out before she could stop it. "I'm staying with her."

"Mrs. Balfour." The doctor's expression softened a tiny bit. "Scarlet fever is extremely contagious. If you stay in this room, you will almost certainly contract it yourself."

"I don't care."

"You should care." His tone sharpened. "If it spreads beyond this room, the entire household could fall ill. Your husband. His brothers. The women. The baby." He paused, letting the weight of those words settle. "I've seen whole families wiped out by scarlet fever. Every last one of them dead within a fortnight because they didn't take proper precautions."

The image rose unbidden—Thomas lying fevered and rasping like Clara. Mandie's tiny babe—that terrible red rash spreading across her skin.

All because she'd been selfish enough to stay with her sister.

Her fingernails bit into her palms. "But Clara needs me."

"Clara needs someone who can care for her without risking the lives of everyone else in this house." Dr. Morrison's voice gentled slightly. "I understand your desire to stay. But you must think of the greater good here."

"Robert can tend her." Bea moved closer, her hand finding Kate's shoulder. "He will do what is needed."

Kate shook her head, even as her eyes burned. Robert was capable—she didn't doubt that. But he was practically a stranger to Clara. And a man at that. How would he know exactly what to do when Clara was too miserable to voice her needs?

"Please." Kate's voice cracked. "She's my sister. I'm all she has."

The doctor's gaze held hers. Uncompromising. "You'll be no good to her if you fall ill yourself. In fact, you may already have been exposed. We need to quarantine you separately until we know whether you've contracted the disease."

"Quarantine?" The word tasted bitter on her tongue. "You want to lock me away while Clara—"

"I want to keep you alive." The doctor's voice never wavered. "Both of you, if possible. But I cannot do that if you insist on remaining in this room."

Kate looked at Clara—at her flushed face and labored breathing, at the rash spreading like wildfire across her skin. Her sister. The one person in this world she would do anything to protect.

And now they were telling her she had to walk away.

The doctor was already moving, gathering items from his bag and setting them on the small table beside the bed. Glass bottles clinked together—medicines probably. "I'll show Robert what needs to be done. The fever must be kept down. She'll need fluids—broth if she can take it, water if not. The garlic poultices every few hours."

Kate's vision swam. This couldn't be happening. She'd crossed an entire continent to keep Clara safe, and now—

A soft moan escaped Clara's lips. Her head turned on the pillow.

Kate moved to her side, taking her burning hand. "I'm here, Clary. I'm right here."

Clara's eyelids fluttered but didn't open. Her lips moved, forming words too quiet to hear.

"What is it?" Kate leaned closer. "What do you need?"

"Robert… Let him…" Her sister's voice rasped, yet the words came clear enough.

Kate had to swallow back the tears. Everything in her screamed to stay here. Yet she had to stay alive to protect Clara.

She turned back to Bea. "He'll let me know everything that's happening? If she changes at all?"

Bea nodded, her dark eyes shimmering. "Every hour, one of us will come tell you. And if she wakes, if she asks for you, Robert will send for you right away."

"I promise." Robert's voice came from the doorway.

There he stood, flanked by Thomas and others.

Robert—the quiet brother, the one who kept the ranch's books and rarely spoke unless he had something important to say. His blue eyes met hers with a steadiness that reminded her of Enoch.

"I'll take care of her, Kate." He moved into the room with that same careful deliberation he brought to everything. "You have my word."

Her throat closed around any response she might have given. She looked down at Clara one more time—at her too-pale face and the angry rash.

She forced herself to lean down, then pressed a kiss to her sister's burning forehead. "I love you. Fight this. Please fight this."

Clara's only response was another shallow breath.

Dr. Morrison touched Kate's elbow. "Come. We need to get

you settled in another room. Away from everyone else until we know whether you've been infected."

She let him guide her toward the door, though every step felt like tearing away a piece of herself. At the threshold, she turned back one last time.

Robert had already taken her place, standing at Clara's bedside. His large hands were surprisingly gentle as he adjusted the ice pack at her neck. He looked up and met Kate's gaze with a single, firm nod.

She turned away before the tears could fall.

CHAPTER 22

Thomas sat in the hallway with his back against the wall, a worn copy of *The Count of Monte Cristo* open across his knees. They'd had three long days of this so far. The door to Kate's room stood cracked just enough to carry his voice through—close enough to feel like a presence, far enough to honor the doctor's strict instructions.

"'All human wisdom is contained in these two words—Wait and Hope.'" He let the final line settle before closing the book. "That's where Dumas ends it. Though I've always thought it was a bit convenient, wrapping everything up so neatly."

"You don't believe in hope?" Kate's voice drifted through the gap.

"I believe in it." He traced the book's worn spine with his thumb. "I just think hope works better when you're doing something while you wait. Sitting still never suited me much."

A soft sound came from the other side—almost a laugh. "I've noticed."

The afternoon light slanted through the window at the end of the hall, casting long shadows across the floorboards. Somewhere below, Mrs. Wang moved about in the kitchen, the familiar rhythm of sounds signaling the meal preparation that had marked every day of his life on this ranch.

Three days of this. Three days sitting outside the door of Kate's temporary bed chamber, of reading until his voice went rough, of telling stories about ornery horses and Montana winters and the time James accidentally set fire to the wood shed—burning up their entire supply of firewood.

Three days of learning that Kate had a laugh like bells when she forgot about her worries, and a way of asking questions that made him dig deeper than he would have preferred.

Three days of wanting to push that door open and close the distance between them.

But the doctor had been clear. Scarlet fever spread through touch, through breath, through the invisible threads that connected people in close quarters. Kate might already be carrying it in her blood, waiting for symptoms to bloom. Until they knew for certain, she had to stay apart.

It seemed their conversations always existed with a barrier between them. Before it had been the darkness of night. Now a wooden door. What would it be like to look into her eyes and say what he really thought?

"Tell me another story." Her voice came quieter. "Something from when you were young."

He shifted against the wall, searching his memory. The happy ones were harder to find these days—buried beneath layers of frustration and that constant itch to be somewhere else.

But for Kate, he would dig.

"There was this one summer." He cleared a rasp from his throat. "I must have been seven or eight. James convinced me that if we built a raft, we could float down the creek all the way to town." He smiled at the memory. "Never mind that particular creek is about three feet deep in most places and town is twenty miles east."

"What happened?"

"We spent two weeks gathering logs and rope. Worked on it every spare moment, hiding our project in a spot by the water where we thought no one would find us." How important it had all seemed. "The night before we planned to launch, Father showed up at the creek."

"Your father was here? In Montana?"

"One of his rare visits." The words carried an edge he hadn't intended. He softened his tone. "We thought we were in trouble. We weren't allowed to go to town by ourselves yet."

"But?"

He shook his head, even though she couldn't see it. "He didn't scold us. Just stood there looking at our pitiful pile of logs and asked if we'd considered the rapids just before the sawmill. We hadn't, of course. Hadn't even known they existed."

The memory sharpened—his father crouching down to their level, pointing out the flaws in their construction with the same critical eye he brought to everything. Except this time, he hadn't stopped there.

"He spent the rest of his visit helping us rebuild it properly. Showed us how to lash the logs so they wouldn't come apart. Even helped us test it in the shallows." He swallowed against the tightness in his throat. "We never did float to town. But James and I spent the rest of that summer on that raft, fishing and swimming and pretending we were explorers."

Silence from the other side of the door.

Then, quietly, "That's a good memory."

"It is." He didn't add that those were the memories that hurt most now—the rare moments when his father had been present. When he felt like a real father instead of a distant monarch in England who oversaw their lives from the far side of the world.

"Thomas?"

"Yes?"

A pause. "What's your earliest memory? The very first thing you can recall?"

He closed his eyes to wander back through the fog of early childhood.

"Light," he said finally. "Sunlight through a window, I think. And the smell of lavender. My mother's scent, I think. I remember feeling warm. Safe."

Before he'd learned that warm and safe didn't last.

"That's beautiful." Her voice came barely more than a whisper. So much softer than the Kate she showed the rest of the world.

His Kate.

Silence settled like it had often, but something felt different this time. Tighter. Heavier.

He straightened, pressing his palm flat against the door as if he could reach through the wood to touch her.

"Kate? Are you all right?"

No answer. But then came a soft, hitching sound. The barely audible catch of breath that meant she was crying and trying to hide it.

His chest constricted. Three days of distracting her, of filling the silence with stories and questions and the sound of his voice. Three days of doing everything he could, but knowing it probably helped so little.

And Clara still lay in that sickroom, fighting for her life, while Kate sat alone with nothing but worry and a cracked door.

He shut the book and stared at the crack of light beneath her door.

Lord, I don't know how to do this.

Not the waiting. Not the helplessness. Not watching Kate drown in fear with nothing to offer but words.

If You're there—and I know You are—help me be what she needs. Help Clara live. Show me what to do for Kate.

He rose to his feet. The doctor's warnings rang in his mind—the risks of infection, the possibility that Kate was already carrying the fever without knowing it. If he went in there, if he touched her, he might end up sick himself.

But three days had passed. No fever. No rash. No sign that Clara's sickness had spread to her sister.

And Kate was crying alone in the dark while he sat uselessly in the hall.

He pushed the door open.

The room beyond was dim, curtains drawn against the afternoon light. Kate sat against the wall beside the door, her knees drawn up and her face turned away. She didn't look at him when he entered—just went still, like a deer caught in an open meadow.

"You shouldn't be in here." Her voice came out thick. "The doctor said—"

"I know what the doctor said." He crouched in front of her. "I don't care."

She lifted her head then, and the sight of her face nearly undid him. Red-rimmed eyes. Tear tracks cutting down her cheeks.

She looked exhausted, fragile in a way he'd never seen—this woman who would change her entire life to protect her sister, who faced down every challenge with that stubborn lift of her chin.

"Thomas—"

"Three days without a single symptom." He settled beside her, close enough to feel the warmth radiating from her body. "You're not sick, Kate. You told me so a few minutes ago. And I'm done pretending a wooden door can protect either of us from anything."

A sound escaped her—half laugh, half sob. "What if you're wrong? What if I'm—"

"Then I'll be sick with you." He slipped one hand around her shoulders and used his other thumb to brush a tear from her cheek. "But I'm not leaving you alone in here. Not anymore."

The careful control she'd been maintaining shattered like ice beneath the blow of an ax head. A sob tore from her throat, raw and ragged, and then she was reaching for him, her hands fisting in the fabric of his shirt as if he were the only solid thing in a world gone liquid.

He pulled her into his arms as something inside him broke too.

She came willingly, pressing hard against his chest. He gathered her close, one hand cradling the back of her head, the other wrapped around her waist.

She shook against him—great, wracking tremors that seemed to come from her deepest parts.

"I can't lose her." The words were muffled against his shoulder. "Thomas, I can't—she's all I have—"

He tightened his hold. If only he could absorb her fear into himself. "Robert's with her. He hasn't left her side. Mrs. Wang is making sure she gets everything she needs."

"But what if it's not enough? What if she's already too sick? What if I brought her all this way just to—"

"Don't." His voice came out fierce. "Don't finish that thought."

"I have to face it." Her voice cracked, and another shudder vibrated her body. "I have to be ready—"

"No, you don't." He pulled her tighter, willing her to believe his words. "Not today. Not yet. Clara is still fighting, and as long as she's fighting, so are we. Do you hear me?"

Something in her quieted, though her back still rose and fell with hard breaths.

Then she lifted her face to him. The movement brought her so close, the flecks of gold in her hazel eyes shimmered up at him.

"Thank you." Her voice came barely above a whisper. "For

these past days. For sitting outside that door. For reading to me. For..." Her words caught. "For not leaving me alone."

His throat tightened. How did he tell her that those hours had been as much for him as for her? That her voice through the crack in the door had been the only thing keeping him tethered when everything else felt like it was slipping away?

He cupped her face in his hands, traced his thumbs over the delicate line of her cheekbones. "Kate—"

Her gaze dropped to his mouth, and whatever he'd meant to say dissolved from his mind. Heat flooded him, chasing away the cold that had settled in his bones during those long nights of digging through snow and ice.

She wanted this. Wanted him.

The realization surged through his chest.

He leaned in slowly, giving her time to pull away.

She didn't. Instead, she rose up on her knees and closed the distance between them.

Fire flashed through his entire body. An avalanche—nearly overpowering.

Her mouth was desperate, salt-tinged from her tears. Her hands gripped his shirt, drawing him closer. This wasn't the careful brush of lips they'd shared at their wedding—this was need and fear and something far deeper he didn't have words for.

He kissed her back, tangling one hand in the loose fall of her hair while the other splayed across her back. She made a sound against his mouth—half sob, half something else—and pressed closer.

Her fingers loosened their grip on his shirt, sliding up to frame his face. The touch was gentle despite the urgency in her kiss, and the contrast made his chest ache.

He pulled back just enough to breathe, to search her eyes in the dim light. "Kate—"

"Don't stop." Her voice was ragged. Raw. "Please. I need—I just need—"

He understood. She needed to feel something other than fear. Needed to be held by someone who wouldn't let go. Needed proof that she wasn't alone in this.

He could give her that.

He kissed her again, softer this time but no less intense. Poured everything he couldn't say into the press of his mouth against hers—that she was extraordinary and brave and that watching her hurt was tearing him apart.

Her hands moved to his hair, fingers threading through the strands as she angled her head to deepen the kiss. He growled.

This was dangerous. Not because of scarlet fever or doctor's orders, but because of what it meant. Because kissing Kate like this—holding her like she was the only solid thing in his world—made California feel so much less important.

Made leaving feel impossible.

She broke the kiss first, her forehead dropping against his shoulder as she struggled to catch her breath. Her fingers still tangled in his hair, holding him close like she was afraid he might slip away.

"I'm sorry." The words came muffled against his shirt. "I shouldn't have—"

"Don't apologize." He stroked one hand down her back, doing his best to smooth out the tremors that still ran through her. "Not for this."

She pulled back just enough to look at him, and the vulnerability in her expression twisted in his chest. This was Kate without her armor—no sharp edges or defensive walls. Just a woman terrified of losing the person she loved most.

"I don't know what to do." Her voice broke on the last word. "I've always known what to do. But this—Thomas, I can't fix this. I can't make her better. I can't even be with her."

"I know." He brushed a strand of tear-dampened hair from

her face, tucking it behind her ear. "But you're not alone in it anymore. You have me. You have my family. We're all here, Kate. We're all fighting for her too."

Her eyes searched his face, like she wasn't sure his words were true. Whatever she found must have satisfied her, because she nodded slowly.

"I'm so tired." Her shoulders sank with the words, as though acknowledging them released some of the load she carried. "I haven't slept since— I keep thinking if I close my eyes, something will happen. Someone will come tell me she's—" Her voice caught. "That I missed my chance to say goodbye."

"You won't." He stood, drawing her up with him. She swayed, exhaustion evident in every line of her body.

"Come on." He kept one arm around her waist as he guided her toward the bed. "You need rest."

"I can't—"

"You can." His tone left no room for argument. "Lie down."

She didn't fight him as he drew back the quilts and eased her onto the mattress. Her body seemed to fold in on itself as she sank onto the bed, as though all the tension holding her upright had finally given way.

He pulled the covers up over her shoulders, tucking them around her with all the care his clumsy hands could manage.

She watched him through half-closed eyes, some emotion flickering there he couldn't quite name.

"I'll be right here." He settled into the chair beside the bed, close enough to touch if she reached for him. "I'll wake you the moment anything changes. The second Robert sends word. I promise."

"Thomas..."

"Sleep, Kate." He took her hand, threading his fingers through hers. "I've got you."

Her eyes drifted closed. For a long moment, she lay still, her breathing shallow and uneven. Then gradually—so gradually he almost missed it—her body began to relax. The tension bled from her shoulders. Her grip on his hand loosened, though she didn't let go.

He let himself watch the rise and fall of her chest, feel the steady pulse in her hand against his.

The light shifted as the afternoon wore on. Eventually someone would come—Mrs. Wang with dinner, or Robert with news from Clara's room. Eventually they would have to face whatever came next.

But for now, there was only this. The warmth of his wife's hand in his. The trust she now honored him with.

And for the first time in as long as he could remember, he wasn't running from anything.

He was exactly where he wanted to be. No matter where he went—including California—as long as he had this woman, he'd be home.

CHAPTER 23

Kate leaned against the doorframe of Clara's room, watching her sister push herself higher against the pillows. The movement was still slow, still careful, but it was movement. Five days ago, Clara had barely been able to lift her head.

"You're hovering again." Clara's voice had regained some of its familiar sweetness, though it came out thinner than usual. "I can feel you worrying from here."

"I'm not hovering. I'm observing."

"You're hovering." Clara smoothed the quilt over her lap, her fingers still pale beneath the red splotches that were starting to peel. "And you look exhausted."

She *was* exhausted—eight days of sleeping in fitful bursts, of straining to hear every sound from Clara's room, of holding her breath each time Robert emerged with an update. Even with Thomas holding her through these last five nights since they'd ended her quarantine, even with his steady presence anchoring her, the fear had carved itself into her bones.

But Clara's fever had finally broken two nights ago. Today she could sit up and had even regained enough strength to tease.

Kate had thanked Thomas a hundred times in her mind for staying.

But now, with Clara's eyes clearer and her voice stronger, a different, unfamiliar gratitude tightened inside her—directed upward, not sideways.

Had God been the one to heal her sister? How could she ever really know?

She forced herself to straighten, to release her grip on the doorframe, and refocused on her sister. "I'll stop hovering when you stop looking like a strong breeze could knock you over."

"Fair enough." Clara's smile was weak but genuine. Loose strands of her honey-blonde hair had escaped her braid and hung limp around her face. But her eyes held their familiar warmth.

"Thomas says you need to get out of the house." Clara folded her hands atop the quilt, her gaze too knowing. "He mentioned it to me this morning when he brought up my breakfast."

Of course he had. Thomas had been suggesting it since yesterday—gentle hints that fresh air would help her feel better, that Clara was improving, that sitting vigil wouldn't make her sister heal any faster.

"I'm fine here."

"Kate." Clara's voice carried that blend of affection and exasperation she'd perfected over the years. "You've barely left this hallway in over a week. Mrs. Wang told me you haven't even been down for meals."

"Someone needed to be close in case—"

"In case I needed you. I know."

"Kate." Thomas's voice came from the direction of the stairs, and she turned as he strode down the hallway. Mrs. Wang had trimmed his copper-brown hair sometime this week, though it still fell across his forehead in that unruly way that fit his personality so exactly. "I need to ride into Walnut Springs for Clara's medicine and a few supplies."

"Of course." She nodded. "I'll stay with Clara while you—"

"Actually." He stopped beside her in the open doorway. His gaze scanned Clara before finding hers with that steady warmth that had become her anchor these past days. "I thought you might come with me. My family's here to watch Clara, and Mrs. Wang has promised to check in every hour. You could use some fresh air."

Fresh air. The words tugged at something deep inside her—a longing she'd been pressing down beneath layers of worry and duty. She hadn't breathed anything but the close air of sick-rooms and hallways for days.

But leaving Clara, even for a few hours...

"Go." Clara's voice cut through her hesitation. "Honestly, Kate, there's nothing for you to do here except stare at me and fret. I'm mostly just bored now."

Thomas's hand found the small of her back, warm even through the layers of her dress. "We won't be gone long. The afternoon at most. And if anything changes, James can ride out to meet us."

She looked between them—her sister's earnest expression, Thomas's patient waiting. Both of them asking her to trust. To let go, just for a moment.

The tightness in her chest eased a fraction. "All right."

Relief flicked across Thomas's face. "Good. We'll leave in twenty minutes."

The moment she stepped onto the porch, the cold nipped at her face, and she drew a sharp breath at the clean bite of it. This winter wind carried the scent of pine and snow—so different from the stale air of a sickroom.

Thomas helped her into the wagon with his hands at her waist. The simple courtesy shouldn't affect her—she'd climbed into wagons countless times without assistance—but something had shifted between them these last few days.

Something she didn't have words for yet.

She settled onto the bench beside him, and when he released the brake and guided the horses forward, she let herself lean into his side. He lifted one arm, and she tucked herself against him as he wrapped that hand around her.

So easy, letting herself be with this man.

She'd spent so long holding herself apart, keeping walls in place. But Thomas had sat outside her door for three days, reading her books and telling stories into the darkness. Thomas had broken through when she needed him most. Thomas had held her while she fell apart and promised she'd never be alone again.

Maybe he was right.

The wagon rattled down the trail, and she let her gaze drift across the landscape. A fresh coat of snow now blanketed the hills in soft white, broken only by the dark spires of pines. The sky stretched overhead in the shade of winter blue that seemed to only live here in the Montana Territory—rich and sharp and impossibly vast.

"Better?" Thomas's voice rumbled near her ear.

"I didn't realize how much I needed this." She tilted her face up to the weak winter sun, filling her chest with cold air. "I feel like I've been holding my breath for over a week."

"You have been." His arm tightened around her. "We all have."

She let herself sink deeper into his warmth as the wagon wheels crunched through snow-packed ruts. The rhythm of it—the steady plodding of the horses, the creak of wood and leather—worked its way into her bones, loosening the knots a little at a time.

Somehow Thomas had known what she needed.

Each night this past week—after they'd ended her quarantine—they'd returned to his room to sleep, and he'd held her in the darkness, his body warm against her back. They'd talked for hours sometimes, trading stories and secrets she'd never shared with anyone.

He'd told her about the latest letter from his father. How the duke had mentioned that his cousin, Reginald Balfour—the one who'd kidnapped Thomas's oldest brother when they were all young boys, the man who'd been the reason the boys came to America to begin with—had begun pestering the queen again about their family's title. Thankfully, the monarch shut him down quickly this time. Thomas had laughed when he'd said it, a low, humorless sound in the dark, and Kate had felt the tension in his body. Even an ocean away, that man's shadow still reached for them.

And the kisses. Heat bloomed low in her stomach at the memory. The desperate press of his mouth against hers that first time, salt-tinged with her tears. The gentler ones that followed—in the hallway, in the quiet hours before sleep, stolen moments when the house was still.

He hadn't pushed for more. Hadn't asked for anything beyond what she was ready to give. That restraint, more than anything, had healed something inside her. She'd spent so long bracing for men to take, to demand, to prove her stepmother right about the nature of the world.

Thomas simply gave. Over and over, without asking anything in return. He made her feel safe.

"Thank you." The words came out before she could stop them. "For everything this week. For staying. For…all of it."

He turned his head to press a kiss against her hair. "There's nowhere I would have rather been."

The sincerity in his voice made her chest ache. She'd been so certain, that first day she met him in Butte, that she couldn't trust him. That his easy charm was just another mask, another manipulation. Now she couldn't imagine facing the past week without him at her side.

The road wound down through the pines, and Kate sank

into the moment. The creak of wagon wheels. The steady warmth of Thomas beside her. The clean bite of winter air against her cheeks. For the first time in days—weeks, maybe—something close to peace soaked through her.

"We should reach Walnut Springs within a quarter hour." Thomas adjusted the reins. "We'll stop at the doctor's first to get the medicine for Clara. Then I need to pick up some supplies from the mercantile." He paused, and the tone shifted in his voice. "And the livery. I'm hoping to get the last of what we'll need for California."

She froze as the word twisted inside her.

California.

She'd thought—hoped—maybe he'd set that aside. He hadn't mentioned leaving once since Clara fell ill. In the quiet hours of the night, wrapped in his arms, talking about everything and nothing, California had never come up. She'd let herself believe that maybe, just maybe, he'd changed his mind.

But he hadn't.

He was still planning to leave. To uproot them from this place that had begun to feel like home and drag them across the wilderness to an unknown future.

She pulled back a little—not far, just enough to create space where there had been none. The cold air rushed into the gap between them.

"Kate?" Thomas glanced down at her, confusion flicking in his hazel eyes. "What's wrong?"

Everything. Yet she couldn't say that. Could she?

She'd started to love this place. The sprawling ranch house with its massive stone fireplace. Mrs. Wang's quiet wisdom and fierce protection. The brothers who teased each other mercilessly but would clearly die for one another. Even Enoch, with his gruff exterior and gentle heart. Mandie and Rose, with their warm smiles and easy acceptance. And that precious baby.

They'd welcomed her. Made her feel like she belonged somewhere for the first time since her mother died.

And Thomas wanted to take her away from all of it.

"Nothing." Mayhap her voice came out a little too sharp, so she softened it. Though she couldn't quite bring herself to lean back into him. "I'm just...surprised. You haven't mentioned California in a while."

"The timing wasn't right. With Clara and everything." He guided the horses around a bend in the road, keeping his focus on the road. "But she's recovering now. Once she's well enough to travel, we can start making plans."

Plans. As if uprooting their lives was as simple as packing a trunk.

She tightened her jaw. *Could* she say something? Tell him that she wasn't sure she could leave? That the thought of abandoning this fragile sense of home made her chest ache with a grief she could barely put into words?

But they were approaching Walnut Springs now. Wooden buildings emerged through the trees ahead. This wasn't the time or place for the conversation they needed to have.

She swallowed the words pressing against her throat and fixed her gaze on the town ahead. "Let's just focus on getting Clara's medicine for now." Her voice came out steadier than she felt. "We can talk about the rest later."

Thomas didn't answer for a moment, and his gaze warmed the side of her face, though she kept her focus ahead.

At last, he said, "All right. Later."

The word hung between them—a promise and a threat all at once.

She drew a breath of cold mountain air, but it didn't hold the same crisp freshness. Just a burning ache.

CHAPTER 24

The main street of Walnut Springs stretched quiet in the early afternoon sunlight, a stark contrast to the chaos that still churned in Thomas's chest.

He shouldn't have mentioned California.

The moment the word had left his mouth, Kate stiffened beside him. The warmth had drained from her body like water through a cracked vessel. And now she wouldn't look at him, just kept her eyes fixed forward as though she wasn't even interested in the town.

But he couldn't keep pretending his plans had changed when they hadn't.

Had they?

He shoved the thought aside as he guided the wagon to a stop in front of Holbrook's Mercantile. The familiar storefront with its weathered sign and frost-rimed windows should have felt ordinary. Safe.

Nothing felt safe anymore. Too much turmoil churned inside him.

He set the brake and jumped down, his boots crunching on the churned snow. When he turned to help Kate, she was already gathering her skirts, her expression locked away like she did when she was upset but refused to show it.

"Allow me." He reached up and locked his hands around her waist through the layers of wool.

She hesitated for just a heartbeat before placing her hands on his shoulders. When he lifted her down, she weighed almost nothing.

Her feet touched the ground, but he didn't immediately release her. Couldn't quite bring himself to let go.

"The doctor's office is that way." He tilted his head toward the end of the street. "Dr. Morrison should have Clara's medicine ready. He knew we'd be coming sometime this week. I'll load the supplies from Holbrook's and meet you back here."

Kate's eyes searched his face, and something flicked there—disappointment, maybe, or resignation.

She stepped back, pulling out of his hold. "I won't be long."

She walked away, spine straight, shoulders squared against whatever the world might throw at her. Even upset with him, she moved like a woman who wouldn't be defeated.

You're going to lose her.

The thought struck like a fist to the gut. If he pushed to go west, would Kate refuse to accompany him?

California had felt like the answer. A fresh start. A place where nobody knew about the title he hadn't earned, the man who'd died because of his mistake.

But standing here on this frigid street, watching Kate's figure grow smaller down the boardwalk, certainty felt like a stranger.

He shook himself and turned to the mercantile. Supplies first. He could figure out his future later. If he changed his mind about California, they could use everything he purchased on the ranch. But at least he'd have things ready.

The bell over the door jangled as he stepped inside. Holbrook's smelled the same as always—a mixture of leather, coffee, pickles, and the mustiness of dry goods stored too long. Mrs. Holbrook stood behind the counter, deep in conversation with a woman he'd not seen before.

"—sheriff won't be back until Thursday at the earliest," the woman was saying. "My husband saw him off himself. Some business with the territorial marshal's office in Butte, apparently."

Mrs. Holbrook clucked her tongue. "Well, let's hope nothing exciting happens before then."

Thomas tipped his hat to them and headed for the aisle on the back wall that held building supplies. He needed more nails in case he couldn't find access to them where he settled. A chisel too, and an extra ax head. And more lamp oil and wicks.

The familiar act of scanning shelves and making mental lists settled his racing thoughts. Practical tasks with clear solutions.

As he examined a selection of rope, the door jangled again. That shouldn't be Kate so soon, but he kept an ear tuned to the sounds, just in case.

The footsteps sounded heavy. More than one person. And men, most likely.

"Mrs. Holbrook?" Definitely a man—his voice rough, with an accent Thomas couldn't quite place. "We need to send a telegram."

Something about that voice…

"Of course." Mrs. Holbrook's lighter tones carried easily through the store. "Just come down to this counter and write out your message."

Thomas moved deeper into the aisle, positioning himself behind a shelf of canned goods. Through the gaps between tins of peaches and jars of preserves, he could see the counter. Mrs. Holbrook had emerged from the back room, and two men stood before her.

His blood went cold.

Those men.

The one on the left was Jake—the same Jake whose fist left the bruise that had only just faded from Thomas's cheekbone. The man who'd been holding that girl in the Butte saloon, whose friends had tried to beat Thomas into the sawdust floor.

The other man...what was his name? He'd been in the fight too. The one whose nose Thomas had broken with his elbow.

What were they doing here? In Walnut Springs?

"We ain't good with letters." Jake's voice grated like gravel. "You'll have to write it for us."

"That's no trouble at all." Mrs. Holbrook pulled out a slip of paper and a pencil. "Where would you like to send it?"

"England. A place called Cumberland."

Thomas's hand tightened on the rope he still held.

"To Viscount Balfour," the second man added.

The world narrowed to a single point.

Cumberland. And Viscount Balfour...

That was his own title since his knighting. But these men couldn't be sending a telegram to him. He hadn't lived in England since he was two years old.

Which meant they were contacting someone else who used that title.

Reginald.

His father's cousin. The man who had tried to have Will kidnapped when they were children. The reason their mother had brought them to Montana in the first place—to escape his schemes.

"And what message would you like to send?" Mrs. Holbrook's voice kept its pleasant tone.

Did she think the direction odd at all? She had to. The Holbrooks had lived in Walnut Springs from before his family arrived. She handled the occasional telegram they sent to their father for urgent business that couldn't wait for a letter. She would recognize Cumberland.

Jake leaned against the counter. "Tell him we found our assignment right where he said it'd be. And tell him…"

The man paused, and Thomas pressed himself closer to the shelf, barely daring to breathe.

"Tell him we'll finish the job within the day."

Finish the job.

The words echoed in his head like gunshots.

These weren't random troublemakers. These weren't men who'd happened to be in Butte when Thomas walked into that saloon. They were assassins—hired by his father's cousin to eliminate the Balfour heirs once and for all.

And they planned to do it today.

His mind raced. How had Reginald found them? They'd been so careful all these years, living quietly, avoiding attention. Had someone from the hunting party talked? Had the knighting ceremony drawn notice none of them anticipated?

It didn't matter how. What mattered was that these men knew where the ranch was. Knew his brothers were there. And they were planning to attack.

Within the day.

He had to get home. Had to warn Enoch and James and Robert.

But first, he had to get out of this store without being seen.

He eased backward, keeping his movements slow and silent. The shelf of canned goods provided cover as he worked his way toward the front of the store.

Each step felt like an eternity. His pulse pounded in his ears, and every creak of the floorboards tightened his insides more.

Mrs. Holbrook was talking now, giving the fee and commenting on how long it took to send messages all the way to England.

He reached the door and kept his back to them as he eased the handle sideways. It took everything in him not to jump when the bell overhead sounded. Instead, he strode out and closed it behind him as if he didn't care a whit.

Kate. He had to find Kate.

He scanned the street, his heart hammering against his ribs. There—halfway down the boardwalk, just emerging from Dr. Morrison's office.

Relief flooded through him.

He strode toward her, forcing himself not to run. Running would draw attention. Running would make those men in the mercantile look out the window and see him. See *her*.

Kate's expression shifted when she spotted him—confusion replacing whatever emotion had been there before. He must look half-wild.

"Thomas? What's wrong?"

"We need to leave. Now." He took her elbow, pulling her back toward the wagon.

"Wait." Kate tugged away from him. "The doctor wasn't there. He left a note saying he'd gone to deliver a baby. He'll be back later today. We have to wait for Clara's medicine."

His jaw clenched. Every second they stood here was another second those men could finish their business and walk out of the mercantile. Another second they risked being seen.

"We can't wait." He kept his voice low. "Kate, please. Trust me. We have to go."

Her eyes narrowed. "What happened in there?"

"I'll explain on the way. But we need to—"

The mercantile door opened.

He grabbed Kate's arm and turned them both away from the store. His mind raced through options—could they make it to the wagon before the men noticed them? Should they duck into the alley between buildings?

"—appreciate your help, ma'am." Jake's voice carried down the boardwalk.

Thomas kept his face turned away, using his body to shield

Kate as he guided her toward the wagon with deliberate casualness.

Don't run. Don't look back. Act like nothing's wrong.

"Thomas, you're hurting me." Kate's whisper held an edge of alarm.

He loosened his grip but didn't let go. "I'm sorry. Please just keep walking."

Behind them, boots thudded on the boardwalk. Moving in the opposite direction, thank God. Toward the saloon, if he had to guess. These men would likely want a drink before they rode out to murder his family.

At last, he and Kate reached the wagon, and he dared a glance over his shoulder.

The two men were disappearing through the saloon door two buildings down.

He exhaled and turned to face Kate as he released her.

Her eyes flashed, and she crossed her arms like a barricade. "Will you please tell me what's happening?"

He swallowed. "Those men from Butte. The ones I fought in the saloon. They're here."

"What?" Kate twisted to look in the direction he had. "Are you certain?"

"They were in the mercantile. Sending a telegram."

Her gaze shot back to his face. "A telegram? To who?"

His throat tightened. "To my father's cousin. In England."

Her eyes widened. "Are they?"

He nodded, pressing his lips in a grim line. "Yep. The message they sent said they're planning to attack the ranch. Today."

Her face went pale. "Today? But your brothers—"

"Are completely unaware." He turned to the wagon again. "I have to warn them."

"Wait. Clara's medicine." Kate's voice rose.

"I know." He motioned for her to climb up. "I know, Kate.

But if we wait here, if they make it to the ranch before we do, Clara won't need medicine. None of us will need anything."

The brutal truth of it hung between them.

Kate's jaw worked, and a war played out in those pretty hazel eyes. Her sister's needs against the lives of everyone at the ranch. The practical necessity of medicine against the immediate threat of violence.

Finally she said, "Can't I wait here? Just a few hours. The doctor should return soon, and then I can rent a horse from the livery. I'll ride back as soon as I can."

Every instinct screamed at him to refuse. To throw her bodily into this wagon if necessary and get her away from this town before those men emerged from the saloon.

But the set of her jaw said she wouldn't be moved easily. And wasting time arguing when his entire family was in danger—

"Fine." The word tasted bitter. "But wait at the cafe. Out of sight. Don't go near that saloon. Don't let those men see you."

"I won't."

"And the moment—the very moment—the doctor returns, you get that medicine and ride for the ranch. Don't wait."

"I understand."

He grabbed her shoulders, perhaps too hard, but he couldn't help himself. "Kate, I mean it. These men are dangerous. If they see you—if they realize you're connected to us—"

"I'll be careful." She placed her hands over his, her touch steadying despite the fear flicking in her eyes. "Go. Your brothers need you."

Everything in him rebelled against leaving her here. Alone. With hired killers drinking two doors down.

But his brothers were at the ranch, completely unaware of the threat riding toward them. Enoch and James, working in the barn or out feeding stock. Robert with Clara, probably reading to her from one of his books. Mrs. Wang in the kitchen. Rose and Mandie with the baby.

All of them defenseless because they didn't know to be on guard.

He pulled Kate close, crushing her against his chest. He kept her there only a heartbeat, but he tried to pour everything he couldn't say into it...

Stay safe. Come back to me. I can't lose you too.

Then he released her and climbed up to the wagon seat.

"Thomas." Her voice stopped him as he reached for the reins.

He looked down at her.

"Be careful." The words came soft, but the weight behind them, the look in her eyes, pressed against his chest.

He nodded once. Then he released the brake and snapped the reins.

CHAPTER 25

The wagon thudded over another frozen rut, and Thomas shook the reins harder.

Faster. He had to go faster.

The horses strained against their harnesses, hooves churning the icy snow as they maneuvered curve after curve. The cold bit through his coat, but it didn't matter. The weight of everything he'd just learned pressed on his chest like a millstone.

Within the day.

How long had it been since he'd left Walnut Springs? Ten minutes? Fifteen? The landscape blurred past. Each minute put the ranch in greater danger.

His mind raced through the possibilities. How many men did Reginald hire? Just those two from the saloon, or were there more? Would they attack openly or try stealth? Even now, were there men stationed around the house, planning to converge from multiple directions?

And what weapons did they have? Rifles, most likely. His brothers kept firearms in the house, but they weren't expecting an attack. Weren't prepared for an organized assault by men who'd been hired specifically to kill them.

All he could see were his brothers' faces. Enoch's steady gaze. James's easy smile. Robert bent over a ledger, completely unaware that men were riding toward them with murder in their hearts.

Because of him.

The thought cut deeper than the wind.

He'd done this. His recklessness, his inability to leave well enough alone, his desperate need to play the hero in that Butte saloon—it had led those men straight to his family's doorstep. If he'd just walked away that night. If he'd ignored the girl and minded his own business like any sensible person would have done. If he'd listened to the voice in his head that whispered *this isn't your fight...*

But no. He'd had to interfere. Had to throw himself into danger without thinking, without planning, without considering for one moment what the consequences might be.

Just like always.

You've done it again. The voice in his head wasn't a whisper anymore. It was a roar. *Your mistake. Your recklessness. And now everyone will die because of you.*

His hands tightened on the reins until his knuckles went white.

His poor reactions had already caused the death of one man. Charles, the brave valet who'd stepped in to protect others when Thomas failed.

Would this most recent example of his recklessness take the lives of the people he loved most? His brothers and their families and the woman who'd been like a mother to them all?

And his own wife...

Kate was safe in town though.

Except not for long.

As soon as the doctor returned, she'd get the medicine and rush to the ranch.

Maybe even at the same time as Jake and his comrades rode

that exact trail. They'd gone into the saloon...to meet with other men? To get a final drink for courage? He had no way of knowing exactly when they'd come, only that it would likely be this day.

Quite possibly at the same time his wife traveled the same icy road.

If she saw the men, she would stay out of sight. She was smart. Savvy. She could protect herself.

Except she shouldn't have to.

He had vowed to protect her. To cherish her. To make sure she never faced trials or dangers alone. To put her—and her safety—above all else.

He pulled back on the reins, slowing the team.

Did he dare take the time to go back for her? She'd be safer in town than coming to the ranch with the fight close at hand. Why hadn't he thought to tell her to stay put until the danger was over? Until he came back for her?

He'd not been thinking. He'd only been reacting.

No more.

He reined the team all the way to a walk. Just ahead was a wider section where he could turn the wagon around.

Driving a wagon at high speeds through all this ice and snow was a foolish idea anyway. He should have taken time to get a single mount from the livery and leave the rig there. Later, when the danger was behind them, he could get all the animals sorted.

At last, he turned the team and set them in as fast a clip as he dared, back toward Walnut Springs.

Don't let me meet those men on the road, Lord.

He'd get to Kate, make sure she was settled in safety for the coming battle, then grab a horse from the livery and ride like fury to the ranch to help his brothers prepare for the fight of their lives.

CHAPTER 26

With both hands gripping the teacup, Kate's fingers were finally thawing from the intense cold outside.

She sat at a small table near the window of the boarding house cafe, positioned where she could see down the boardwalk to the doctor's office next door. She'd all but gulped the first few sips, but now the rich warmth of the liquid was working its magic to warm her. She should slow down now. She'd likely have hours to wait for the doctor, and Mrs. Patterson had been kind enough to let her wait here, out of the cold.

Thomas had been gone for nearly a half hour now. Racing toward the ranch to warn his brothers about the men who wanted them dead. And she sat here, useless, waiting for a doctor who might not return for hours.

Her hands tightened around the cup. Clara needed that medicine. The fever had broken, yes, but Dr. Morrison had been adamant—without the proper treatment to prevent complications, scarlet fever could return with a vengeance. Could settle into Clara's lungs or heart and finish what it started.

But Thomas's family faced death too. Immediate, violent death at the hands of hired killers.

She forced herself to take another sip of tea, though it had lost its comfort. Through the window, the street remained quiet. A few townspeople—mostly men—moved about their business, bundled against the cold.

If only she could see the saloon doors from here. How long would those men stay inside? An hour? Two? And when they emerged, would they ride straight for the ranch, or linger and make other preparations?

Movement caught her eye. The doctor's buggy rolled down the street, aiming toward the hitching rail in front of his office.

Relief flooded through her. She set down her cup and rose, already pulling on her gloves.

"Can I get you something else, Mrs. Balfour?" Mrs. Patterson looked up from the desk in the corner, where she looked to be writing a letter. "Is everything all right?"

"Yes—I mean, I need to go." Kate fumbled for coins, then left more than necessary on the table. "Thank you for the tea. The doctor's returned, and I need to catch him."

She didn't wait for a response.

The cold wrapped around her as she stepped onto the boardwalk, sharp and biting after the warmth of the cafe. She wrapped her cloak tighter and turned toward the buggy.

Dr. Morrison was just tying the horse as she approached. He looked exhausted—dark circles shadowed his eyes, and his movements carried the weight of someone who'd been awake far too long.

He glanced up at her, squinting against the winter sun. Recognition flicked across his weathered features. "Mrs. Balfour. I thought I might see you today."

"Clara's medicine." The words tumbled out as she reached him. "You said it would be ready—"

"Yes, yes. Come inside." He unlocked the door and ushered her into the cramped front room. The smell of herbs and antiseptic filled her nose as she followed him to the counter along the back wall.

"How is your sister faring?" He set down his bag and began rifling through a cabinet of small bottles and paper-wrapped packets.

"Much improved." Kate clasped her hands together to keep from fidgeting. "The fever broke yesterday morning. She's staying in bed, regaining her strength. The rash is still there, but I think it's no longer spreading."

"Excellent." The doctor pulled out a brown glass bottle and examined the label. "The tonic did its work, then. This next round should help rebuild her. A tablespoon three times daily, with meals, or at least a little broth."

He wrapped the bottle in paper, then handed it to her. "Now then." He picked up his bag again, already moving toward the door. "I'm afraid I must rush off. I only came back for a few supplies to help the new babe. The birthing was hard on the wee one."

"Of course." Kate gripped the package. "Thank you, Doctor. Truly."

He held the door for her, and they stepped out onto the boardwalk together. If possible, the cold stung sharper now, and the wind whipped harder, creeping under the edges of her coat.

"I'm glad you caught me, Mrs. Balfour. Give my regards to your husband and the others." Dr. Morrison turned to lock his door. "And tell that sister of yours to rest. I know women always want to do too much too soon, but—"

He straightened and stopped mid-sentence, his gaze fixing on something over her shoulder.

"Gentlemen. Can I help you?"

Kate turned.

Two men stood a few paces away on the boardwalk. Both were dressed plainly—work clothes that might belong to any ranch hand or drifter. The one on the left stood broad-shouldered, with a nose that looked like it had been broken recently. The other was leaner, a little taller.

"We're fine, doc," the thinner man said. "Just passin' through."

"Very well then." Dr. Morrison tipped his hat to them, then turned back to Kate. "I really must be going, Mrs. Balfour. Send for me if you have more trouble."

He moved past her toward his buggy, leaving her standing alone on the boardwalk with two men whose gazes hadn't shifted from her.

She should leave. Should turn and walk back to the cafe, to Mrs. Patterson and safety.

But her feet wouldn't move.

The doctor's buggy rattled down the street, and the sound of it faded too quickly into the wind.

The shorter man spoke first. "Pardon me, ma'am. You're Mrs. Balfour?"

Her pulse jumped, but she kept her expression pleasant. "Yes."

"Are you related to the Balfour family who run the ranch outside of town?"

The question was ordinary enough. Natural, even. Walnut Springs was a small community—everyone knew everyone else's business. If these were locals, they'd naturally be curious about a stranger bearing the Balfour name.

"I am." She forced her voice to remain steady. "I've recently married Thomas Balfour."

The words had barely left her mouth when a flicker lit the man's eyes. Recognition. Satisfaction.

Ice flooded her veins.

These weren't townspeople making polite conversation.

These were the men from the saloon. The ones Thomas had fought. The ones who'd sent the telegram to England. She'd just confirmed exactly what they wanted to know.

"Thomas's wife." The broad-shouldered one smiled, but it didn't reach his eyes. "That's real interesting."

She took a step backward. The cafe was behind her, but could she reach it before they caught her? What she could see of the street was empty—the few people out earlier had vanished into buildings or down side streets.

"Well, it was nice meeting you." She turned partway, trying to make the movement casual without putting her back to them completely.

Maybe a dozen steps to the boarding house. If she ran—

But they'd catch her. She could see it in the way they stood, weight balanced, ready to move. These weren't men who let prey escape.

Still, if she could get close enough. If Mrs. Patterson happened to look out the window…

"Now, now." The broad-shouldered man stepped around her to cut off her retreat, his bulk blocking half the boardwalk. "No need to rush off. We just want a friendly conversation."

"About what?" She shifted closer to the street. Maybe she could go straight across. No buildings lined the opposite side in this section. Just the sawmill perched down by the river. But it might be something.

"About your husband." The lean man shifted with her, his step longer, closing off part of her passage into the street. "And his brothers."

They nearly had her closed in.

Panic surged through her, pounding in her ears. How could she get out of this? They didn't look like words would change their plans. And she had no weapon. Could she cause a scene? Scream and bring someone running?

Only if there was someone close enough to hear her.

She dared a look down the street. First one way. Then the other.

The blow slammed hard in the back of her head, shooting black through her vision.

CHAPTER 27

Thomas gripped the reins a little harder as the wagon slid on an icy patch. Maybe he should slow the team on this last stretch before Walnut Springs. But everything inside him urged him to go faster.

To reach Kate, who was in the same town with hired killers.

What had he been thinking?

He hadn't been thinking. That was the problem. He'd been reacting—the same reckless, impulsive behavior his brothers had been warning him about for months. The very behavior that had led him into that Butte saloon in the first place, starting the chain of events that now threatened everyone he loved.

The road curved ahead, and he guided the team around a patch of ice that gleamed treacherously in the afternoon sun. His hands ached from gripping the reins, and the cold had long since seeped through his gloves.

The sound of hoofbeats reached him—coming from behind, moving fast.

His heart slammed against his ribs. Had Jake and his companion already finished their business in the saloon? But they wouldn't be coming from behind him. He'd meet them head-on.

He twisted in the seat, shifting the reins into one hand in case he needed to grab for the rifle.

A single rider emerged around the bend, pushing his horse hard through the snow.

Enoch.

Relief and confusion tangled inside him as his eldest brother closed the distance between them. Enoch's face was set in hard lines, his dark beard frosted with ice crystals from the cold.

Thomas pulled the team to a halt, the horses heaving and stamping in the sudden stillness.

Enoch reined in beside the wagon, struggling to catch his own breath as his horse blew white clouds. "Clara's taken a turn for the worse. Where's Kate?"

"A turn for the worse?" His gut twisted. "But she was improving—the fever broke—"

"It came back." Enoch's voice was grim. "Robert sent me after you in case you decided to spend the night in town. We thought Kate would want to know."

Clara. Sweet, gentle Clara, who'd been so weak already. Kate would be devastated if anything happened to her.

But there was more pressing danger. Danger Enoch didn't know about.

"Enoch, listen to me." He leaned forward. "Those men I fought in Butte. They're here. In Walnut Springs."

Enoch frowned. "The ones from the saloon? Why does...?"

Thomas shook his head. "They're working for Reginald. I saw them in the mercantile, sending a telegram." Thomas's throat tightened around the words. "To England. To Cumberland."

Enoch reared back. "How in the...?"

"I know." The connection seemed hard to fathom. "But I heard them. They said they found their 'assignment' right where he told them it would be. And they plan to finish the job within the day."

Enoch went still. "Today."

"They went into the saloon after sending the telegram. I left Kate in town to wait for the doctor and was heading back to warn you, but—" Thomas gestured helplessly at the wagon. "I realized partway back that I couldn't leave her there. Not with those men so close."

Enoch's gaze cut toward Walnut Springs, then back to Thomas. The calculation behind those blue eyes was almost visible—weighing options, assessing threats.

"Where is Kate now?"

"Waiting to get Clara's medicine." Guilt twisted in his gut. "Then she's planning to ride for the ranch. I can't risk her running into those men on the trail. I have to make sure she's safe."

Enoch nodded once. "Go. Take care of Kate. I'll ride back and get the others ready."

"Enoch—"

"We've prepared for this." His brother's voice carried the steel of a man who'd spent his whole life expecting danger. "Ever since we came to Montana, we knew Reginald might find us eventually. The house can be defended. We have weapons, provisions, plans mapped out. How many do you think there are?"

"I only saw two in the mercantile. But probably more." His mind raced through the possibilities. "They might be meeting the others in the saloon."

Enoch gathered his reins. "Get Kate. Get her somewhere safe. Once you know she's secure, if there's time, come back to the ranch. But her safety comes first."

The words should have chafed. Should have felt like another dismissal, another reminder that his brothers didn't trust him with the important work.

Instead, they settled something inside him.

Kate was his responsibility. His wife. The woman he was beginning to love with everything in him. And protecting her—making sure she didn't ride straight into danger—that wasn't running away from the fight.

That was exactly where he needed to be.

"All right." He gathered the reins tighter. "But Enoch—be careful. These men have been hired to kill, and they won't hesitate."

"Neither will we." Enoch's expression hardened. "Get Kate. Keep her safe. And Thomas?" He paused, his gaze locking with Thomas's. "Be careful."

Then he was gone, his horse's hooves throwing up sprays of snow as he galloped toward the ranch.

Thomas snapped his own reins and urged the tired team forward. The wagon lurched into motion, and he pushed them as fast as he dared on the treacherous road.

Hold on, Kate. I'm coming.

Walnut Springs emerged from the mountain pass like a collection of snow-dusted boxes scattered along the frozen river. He scanned the main street as he aimed the team toward the livery. No sign of his wife's familiar figure.

The boardwalks were mostly empty, the cold driving everyone indoors. The livery stood open, and he pulled the wagon to a halt.

"Howdy." The livery owner—a short fellow named Rufus who'd been shoeing horses in Walnut Springs for at least five years now—looked up from a harness he was mending. "Everythin' all right, Mr. Balfour?"

"I need a horse saddled." Thomas set the brake and jumped down. "I'll leave the wagon here and come back for it later, if that's all right."

Rufus set down his work and pushed to his feet, moving

toward the row of stalls with the unhurried calm of a man who'd spent decades around horses. "Something wrong?"

Everything. But he couldn't explain now.

"Family business. My wife came into town earlier—have you seen her? A pretty blonde woman wearing a blue dress."

Rufus shook his head as he led a sturdy bay gelding from its stall. "Can't say I have. Been in the back most o' the afternoon, though."

Thomas forced himself to breathe. Kate was probably still at the cafe next to the clinic. Still safe. Still waiting for the doctor.

Please let her be waiting.

"Let me know if she comes by." He started toward the door. "I'll be back for the horse soon."

As he trotted to the doctor's office, the building sat dark, the windows reflecting nothing but the pale afternoon sky. He tried the door anyway. Locked.

His pulse kicked higher. Where was she?

The boarding house sat next door, Mrs. Patterson's neat sign swinging slightly in the wind. He covered the distance in a few long strides and pushed through the door.

Warmth hit him first, then the smell of coffee and bread. Mrs. Patterson looked up from behind the small desk, her lined face creasing into a welcoming smile.

"Mr. Balfour!"

"My wife." The words came out in a bark. "Kate. Was she here?"

"Oh yes." Mrs. Patterson nodded to the tables by the window. "She was waiting for the doctor. Had some tea. But she left—oh, must be twenty minutes ago now. Said the doctor had returned."

Twenty minutes.

His stomach dropped. "Did you see where she went?"

"Just out the door, I'm afraid. I assumed she went to the

doctor's office." Mrs. Patterson's expression shifted, concern creeping in. "Is everything all right?"

No.

If Kate had gone to see the doctor twenty minutes ago and the office was locked, where had she gone?

He forced his voice to stay calm. "Did you see anyone else on the street? Two men, maybe? Strangers?"

The lines at Mrs. Patterson's brows gathered. "There were a couple of fellows I didn't recognize. Rough-looking types. They were standing near the doctor's office when I glanced out earlier." Her eyes widened. "Why? Mr. Balfour, is your wife in some kind of trouble?"

He was already moving toward the door. "If she comes back, keep her inside. Lock the doors. Don't let anyone in you don't know."

"Mr. Balfour—"

But he stepped out the door, and the cold once again struck him like a fist. He scanned the street in both directions.

Empty boardwalks. Closed shops. The wind carrying nothing but the distant sound of the river.

He strode toward the doctor's office, examining the snow-packed ground. Boot prints—dozens of them, overlapping, impossible to distinguish one set from another.

Wait.

There, just past the doctor's door. A scuff mark in the snow. And beyond it, drag marks leading toward the alley between the clinic and the boarding house.

His insides clenched even tighter as he followed the tracks.

CHAPTER 28

The cold seeped so deep into Kate's bones she'd actually stopped shivering.

That couldn't be good.

The rough rope that bound her wrists to the saddle bit into her skin with every tiny movement—either hers or that of the restless sorrel beneath her. The gag in her mouth tasted of sweat and dust and something metallic—blood, maybe, from where she'd bitten her tongue when they threw her onto the animal.

The camp—if it could be called that—was little more than a clearing in a stand of pines, hidden from the main road by a rocky outcropping and a short trail. Her mount was one of the five horses that stood tied to a picket line strung between two trees, their breath rising in white clouds.

The men had built no fire. Probably too much risk of being seen.

Instead, they huddled in a loose cluster a few steps away, passing a flask between them and speaking in low voices.

Five of them. The two from the boardwalk—the broad one

with the broken nose was Jake, and the lean, tall one they called Henry—plus three others she hadn't seen before.

All of them armed with rifles and revolvers. All of them watching the trail that led back toward town.

Waiting for someone.

At least they couldn't see the road to the Balfour ranch from here. At least not that she could tell.

She flexed her arms within the ropes again, twisting her wrists as much as she could. The leather gave almost no room to shift, much less work her hands out of its hold. Raw places had begun to chaff on her skin, but she didn't show the ache. Any sign of struggle would only draw their attention.

There had to be another way.

Would Thomas come back for her? Of course not. He was heading to warn his brothers about the danger. By now, he might be at the ranch, preparing defenses with Enoch and James and Robert. They'd need every person who could hold a rifle if these five—or more—rode down on them.

He wouldn't know she'd been kidnapped. That she'd been dumb enough to let herself be alone with those two lechers. Her throat tightened around the gag.

No one would come.

She was on her own. Just like always.

Except not quite like always.

Because this time, if she failed to escape, it wouldn't just be her life at stake. These men had taken her for a reason. They'd grabbed her the moment they learned she was married to a Balfour.

A bargaining chip. That's what Jake had said when they'd thrown her onto the horse. *If those boys put up too much of a fight, we've got a bit o' leverage now.*

They'd use her to force Thomas—or Enoch, or any of them—to lower their weapons. To walk into slaughter.

She couldn't let that happen.

She scanned the men again as Jake took a long pull from the flask and wiped his mouth with the back of his sleeve. "How much longer we gotta wait? I'm freezing my—"

"Shut it." A fellow with a beard nearly full gray cut him off with a bark. "Hank and Skeeter'll be here soon enough. Have to make sure no one followed 'em from town."

Jake shook his head. "No one's gonna follow. Half that town's too scared to look sideways at a stranger, and the other half don't care what happens to some woman."

"She's a Balfour. They'll care." Henry shifted his weight, his gaze cutting toward Kate before sliding away. "That family's got friends in this territory."

"Friends who'll be too busy burying the dead. We'll kill her along with the others once we know we don't need her." Jake spat into the snow. "Then we'll be halfway ta the border 'fore anyone knows what happened. Our pockets'll be lined with so much gold we won't ever have ta work again."

"I still don't understand why some English lord cares so much about a bunch of Montana ranchers." The youngest one in the group spoke for the first time, his voice carrying a bit too much whine. "Seems like a lot of trouble for—"

"It ain't your job to understand." Gray Beard's tone sharpened. "It's your job to shoot who you're told to shoot and collect your pay. You got a problem with that?"

"No, I just—"

"The Balfours ain't just ranchers." Jake interrupted, his voice carrying the lazy confidence of a man who enjoyed knowing things others didn't. "They're heirs. To some fancy English title. A duke of somewhere."

"Duke of Clarence." Henry snorted. "Our contact's a cousin or somethin'. Wants all the heirs taken out afore he handles the duke hisself."

"That's why we gotta be thorough." Jake's voice hardened.

"All four brothers. And any wives or children. No survivors. No witnesses."

Any wives or children.

Mandie and baby Catherine. Rose. Probably they'd assume Clara too.

And Kate herself, bound and gagged and utterly helpless to warn any of them.

No. She yanked against the ropes, hard enough that the horse beneath her sidestepped nervously. *No, no, no—*

"Easy there." The fifth man—the one who'd stayed mostly quiet—moved toward her horse and grabbed the bridle to steady the animal. He took her in with eyelids that didn't lift all the way, and one corner of his mouth tipped in a sort of leer that sent ice down her spine. "No point wearin' yourself out, sweetheart. You ain't going nowhere."

She forced herself to breathe through the gag, slow and measured, even as panic clawed at her chest. She had to figure out how to get away from this.

Thomas and his brothers would be ready for the attack, but she couldn't leave herself in the hands of these rakes. These murderers.

She couldn't untie herself though. Maybe the horse… If she could spook it at the right moment, send it bolting...

She'd probably fall and break her neck. With her hands bound to the saddle horn, she had no way to control the animal, no way to guide it toward safety. Branches would scrape her off, then she'd be injured and still at the mercy of these hired assassins.

God, help me. Show me what to do.

The prayer rose from somewhere deep. She'd stop praying when her mother died. Especially when her stepmother used religion like a tool…a way to manipulate the good opinion of others.

But Thomas and his family prayed. They spoke of God like

He was a friend, a father. Someone Who actually *cared* what happened to them.

Maybe... maybe she'd been wrong. Maybe her stepmother's version of God wasn't the only one.

If You're there—if You're really there—I need help. Not for me. For Clara. For Thomas's family. For Thomas.

The crackle of a large creature through the snow cut through her pleadings.

All five men turned toward the trail, hands dropping to their weapons. Her heartbeat surged.

Two riders emerged from the trees, their horses picking through the snow. The tension in the camp eased as quickly as it had risen.

"About time." Jake pushed off from the tree he'd been leaning against. "We were starting to think you'd gotten lost."

"Had to make sure we weren't followed." The first rider swung down from his horse with the easy motion of a man who'd spent his life in the saddle. "Town's quiet. If anyone noticed the woman go missing, they ain't makin' noise yet."

Yet. Kate clung to that word. *They haven't made noise yet.*

If Thomas knew, he would care. The problem was, he wouldn't know until too late. Until she was forced to become a bargaining tool.

Help me, God. Please.

"Good." Gray Beard moved toward his horse. "Then we ride. Get to our positions by dusk, then hit just after dark."

At dusk. That was...possibly three hours from now. Maybe two, judging by the position of the sun through the clouds.

Two hours to find a way out of this.

CHAPTER 29

The drag marks led through the alley and out the back, where they disappeared into a churned mess of hoof-prints and wagon marks in the snow.

Thomas's chest constricted until he could barely breathe. Were any of these from the men who'd taken her? Or just the usual town traffic?

Impossible to tell.

He scanned the tracks, then shifted his focus to the edges of the street. His best chance might be to follow this road and watch for prints that left the main route. He turned northward. This back alley would join up with the main road at the edge of town, then continue on the winding trail to Butte—almost a day's ride away.

But they wouldn't go nearly that far. Probably, they would circle around town to the west and find the road that led to the Balfour ranch.

As he strode forward, he scanned both sides of the street, especially the far right, as the buildings fell away near the edge of town.

There. A set of tracks—men's boot prints—branching off

toward the northeast. Recent, judging by the sharp edges that hadn't yet been softened by wind or fresh snow. Two pairs of tracks actually, now that he looked closer.

He followed the trail into the trees, striding as quickly as he dared while keeping his steps quiet. The snow here lay deeper, undisturbed by wagon wheels or regular traffic. The prints stood out clearly—two men heading northeast, their path winding between pines and around rocky outcroppings.

Away from town. Away from help.

He couldn't lose Kate. Not now. Not ever.

The trail curved around a rocky outcropping, and he slowed. Voices drifted through the cold air—low, masculine, too far away to make out words but close enough to set every nerve on edge.

He crept forward, using boulders and scrubby pines for cover. Thankfully, the snow muffled his footsteps.

The trees thinned ahead to reveal a small clearing. His heart nearly stopped.

A group of horses was tethered in a row, and on one sat a rider.

Kate.

From this distance, he couldn't see more than the rigid set of her back and that rich hair he loved to thread his fingers through when he kissed her. Was she injured? He couldn't see anything clearly.

She was alive though. *Thank You, God.*

He had to force his focus away from her to check for her captors. A cluster of men stood in a loose circle near the horses, passing something between them—a flask, probably.

Five.

Jake stood among them, his broad shoulders unmistakable even from this distance. And there—the other man from the mercantile. Three others he didn't recognize completed the group.

Five armed men against one. And Kate bound in the middle of it all.

Could he pick them off one by one? He had a rifle, but they would scatter before he got them all. Probably grab Kate and take off with her.

He'd have no chance to keep up with them on foot.

Could he cause a distraction and draw them away from Kate long enough for her to escape?

She was tied to that saddle, and the horse hitched to a tree. She couldn't just ride away. Even if he did manage to spook the horse enough for the animal to break free from its tether, if her hands were tied, a panicked horse would only put her in more danger.

Movement at the near edge of the clearing caught his attention. Two more men stomped through the trees to join the others.

His insides clenched. How had he not seen them approaching? They must have come from the left, the direction of the road to Butte. At least they hadn't walked near enough to see him.

Seven now.

All of them armed. Rifles. Revolvers. Probably knives too.

Seven against one.

His fingers tightened on his rifle. He was a good shot—better than good, really. Years of hunting in these mountains had honed his aim until he could drop a deer at a hundred strides.

But seven men? With Kate in the middle of them?

One shot, and they'd use her as a shield. Or worse.

A gray-bearded man moved toward his horse and swung into the saddle. "Mount up. We ride," he called to the others.

Within moments, all the men sat astride—Jake settled behind Kate. The sight of that man's arms around her sent heat flaring through Thomas. The lecherous murdering cad.

Thomas forced the rage down. Anger wouldn't help Kate. He needed to think clearly and not rashly.

They kicked their horses into motion, heading north through the trees.

He turned and sprinted back the way he'd come, branches catching at his coat as he crashed through the undergrowth. No time for stealth now. Speed was everything.

He couldn't stay with them on foot. Not through this terrain, not at the pace they'd be riding. By the time he made it back to the livery, they'd have a solid head start. He might lose them.

He'd have to trust they were riding to the ranch. Once he had a horse, he could take the main road, but stay off to the side. Out of sight.

Rufus should have the horse ready by now.

His boots sprayed snow with each step as he burst from the tree line and sprinted down the back alley. Through a path between two buildings. The shortest route to the livery.

Finally that building sat ahead of him, across the main road, its wide doors still open.

He charged the final distance. "Rufus! That horse—it's ready?"

The older man looked up from checking the cinch, his eyes rounding. "He is. What in the—"

"I have to go." Thomas grabbed the reins looped over the gelding's neck. "My wife's been taken. Seven men, heading toward our ranch."

Rufus's weathered face went pale. "You're gonna need help. The sheriff's gone, but we can round up some men. Give me fifteen minutes—"

Thomas swung into the saddle, and the gelding shifted beneath him, sensing his urgency. "I don't have fifteen." He slipped his feet in the stirrups and wheeled the horse toward the door. "If you want to help, bring whoever will come. Ride to the ranch after me."

He didn't wait for Rufus's reply. He had to get to Kate.

This time, he wouldn't stop. This time, he wouldn't let fear or doubt or the ghost of past failures slow him down.

This time, he would be worthy of the woman who made him want to stay.

CHAPTER 30

Every stride of the horse sent fresh pain lancing through Kate's body.

Her wrists had gone numb hours ago, the ropes cutting off circulation where they bound her to the saddle horn. But the rest of her felt everything—the rawness where the leather rubbed against her legs as Jake pushed her against the front of the saddle, the bone-deep cold that had settled into her like a permanent resident.

And Jake.

He sat behind her in the saddle, his arms bracketing her body as he held the reins, his chest pressed against her back in a way that made her skin crawl. Every so often, his grip would shift, his hands brushing against her sides or middle in ways that couldn't possibly be accidental.

She wanted to scream. To twist away. To drive her elbow back into his ribs until he released her.

But the gag stole her voice, and her bound hands stole her ability to fight. All she could do was hold herself as rigid as possible, trying to create even a sliver of space between his body and hers.

Helpless.

The word burned through her mind like a brand.

She'd spent her whole life fighting this feeling. Protecting Clara when her stepmother's cruelty turned sharp. Finding ways to survive, to endure, to keep some small piece of herself intact, no matter what was taken from her.

And now here she sat, trussed up like a market pig, utterly powerless to stop whatever these men had planned. They would use her against Thomas and his family. Use her to find their weaknesses. She had no doubt.

Thomas.

Was he at the ranch by now? Had he warned his brothers? Were they even now preparing defenses, positioning themselves to fight off this small army of hired killers?

Or had something gone wrong? Had the men's accomplices intercepted him on the road? Was he lying somewhere in the snow, bleeding out while she—

Stop it. She squeezed her eyes shut against the images. *Stop it. This won't help.*

The horse's rhythm changed as the trail began to climb, and Jake shifted behind her, his weight pressing harder against her back. She bit down on the cloth to keep from gagging.

God...

The prayer rose unbidden, desperate.

God, if You're there—if You're listening—please. Please let Thomas be safe. Please let him reach his brothers in time.

The trail curved around a rocky outcrop, and the trees thinned enough that she could see the sky ahead—pale gray, the sun already sliding toward the western peaks. How long until dusk? An hour? Less?

Please let them be ready. Let them pick these men off one by one before they can hurt anyone. Before they can use me against Thomas.

Her throat tightened around the prayer.

And please...please don't let me die out here. Not like this. Not before I've had a chance to tell Thomas—

What? What would she tell him?

That she'd been wrong to hold back? That he'd been the only person besides Clara to really listen. To see her. That somehow, in the short time they'd known each other, he'd become her family. Not just in name, but in the deepest parts of her heart.

She'd come to love him. And if he wanted to go to California, she'd be there at his side. Being for him what he'd come to be for her.

The horse stumbled on a patch of ice, and Jake's arm tightened around her waist. She flinched but could do nothing to stop him.

"Almost there," Jake said near her ear, his breath hot and sour. "We'll see how much those Balfour boys love their newest sister."

Sister. The word was meant to mock, but it struck a chord deep inside her.

She *was* their sister now. Part of their family. And they would fight for her the same way Thomas had fought for that girl in the Butte saloon—recklessly, desperately, without counting the cost.

That's what terrified her most.

The crack of a rifle shattered the winter silence.

Her heart seized.

For one frozen instant, nothing changed. Jake tightened around her, his body going rigid.

Then the world exploded into chaos.

Gunfire erupted from every direction—the sharp cracks echoing off the rocky outcroppings, making it impossible to tell where the shots originated. Men shouted. Horses screamed and reared.

The sorrel beneath her lurched sideways, and Kate's stomach dropped as the animal's hindquarters slid on ice.

Jake's arms released her—reaching for his rifle or trying to control the panicked horse, she couldn't tell which.

She did the only thing she could. Sank as low against the horse's neck as the ropes would allow, making herself as small a target as possible.

Another volley of shots. Closer now. The man to her right—Henry—cried out and toppled from his saddle, hitting the snow-packed trail with a sickening thud.

"Scatter!" Gray Beard's voice bellowed above the chaos. "Get to the trees!"

The horses bolted in different directions, some carrying riders, others fleeing with empty saddles as men dove for cover. Jake fought to control the sorrel, sawing at the reins, but the terrified animal had the bit between its teeth.

They careened down the trail at a dead run, branches whipping past Kate's face. She squeezed her eyes shut and pressed herself flat, praying the ropes would hold. Praying she wouldn't be scraped off by a low-hanging limb.

Jake cursed and finally managed to slow their horse, then turn it.

"Nobody shoot!" he bellowed. "We've got the woman! We got Balfour's wife!"

The gunfire paused, leaving an eerie quiet in its wake.

Kate's breath came in ragged gasps around the gag.

Then cold metal pressed against her temple.

She froze. Didn't dare even breathe.

"That's right!" His voice rang louder now. "Anyone takes another shot, she dies first!"

Silence. Even the horses had gone still, their sides heaving, eyes rolling white.

She had to think. Had to do something. She couldn't let her new family give up anything to save her.

She had no weapons. No way to free her hands. No way to escape.

But she had one thing Jake didn't expect.

She had a family she wasn't afraid to die for.

Kate threw her weight backward with every ounce of strength she possessed—slamming her head into Jake's face with a crack that shot all the way down her spine.

He howled, his grip loosening. The horse reared. The gunfire around them started again, fiercer than before.

Kate felt herself sliding—falling—the world tilting sideways as Jake lost his hold on her completely.

Her hands were still bound to the saddle though. Keeping her from leaving the animal completely. Her feet hit the ground at the same time the horse's did. The animal lurched, shying sideways, away from Jake crawling in the snow. Away from her at its side.

She scrambled to keep up with the sorrel. Could she grab the reins? Anything to stop the horse. Or maybe she could climb back on the saddle.

Being dragged by a panicked, bolting horse would be an awful way to die.

The horse wheeled, and her body swung out like a pendulum, her boots scrabbling for purchase on the icy ground. Pain exploded through her shoulders as the ropes yanked against her wrists.

A dark shape lunged from the trees, but she lost sight of it as the horse spun the other direction.

"Ho!"

That voice.

Even through the pain surging up her arms, that voice calmed inside her.

Then the horse slowed. Halted. The shots around them had ceased too.

"Easy there." Thomas's voice lowered, turning to a soothing croon. "Easy now. I've got you."

She couldn't see him—not with her face pressed against the

horse's shoulder, her arms trussed up on either side, blocking her vision.

But then a boot crunched in the snow close to her.

"Kate, are you hurt?" He kept that same calming tone. His voice not letting out an ounce of fear.

Something pressed against the rope around her wrists. Pulling it tighter for an instant.

Then the pressure released, freeing her hands from the saddle completely. In the same instant, an arm wrapped around her, scooping her up. Keeping her from falling to the snow.

Her entire body sagged, her legs buckling beneath her.

His arm tightened around her, his other joining as he pulled her close. Her back tightened against his chest. Thomas. His strength wrapped fully around her.

Then he slid to his knees, sitting her on his lap. "Let me get you free."

His hands fumbled in her hair. That awful gag.

The fabric pulled tighter. Then loosened completely.

Pain seared through her mouth, burning the corners of her lips. The remnants of that foul taste lingered, but at least she could get a clean breath now without smelling sweat and dirt.

Then Thomas reached around in front of her, his arms wrapping her as he gripped the rope still binding her wrists with one hand. The other wielded a blade that sliced through the cord in a single sawing motion.

As he peeled the rope off, a fresh burning stung the raw, open wounds the ties had created.

Her hands trembled. Her entire body trembled.

"I'm sorry." His voice broke on the words. "I'm so sorry, Kate."

Then his arms were around her completely, turning her sideways against him. He crushed her against his chest with a desperation that matched the wild pounding of her own heart.

She turned in his embrace, burying her face against his neck, and the tears she'd been holding back finally broke free.

"I've got you." He murmured the words against her hair. "I've got you. You're safe now."

Safe. The word didn't quite make sense yet. Her body still vibrated with terror, every nerve screaming that danger lurked just beyond the trees.

The sounds of men drifted around them. No more gunfire. Just grunts and low voices. Had the Balfours won completely, or did some of the killers escape? Maybe even now, they were taking aim from the trees.

She pulled back just enough to scan the clearing. "Are they —? There were seven of them."

Thomas's arms loosened but didn't release her completely. He turned them both so she could see the scene unfolding around them.

Enoch knelt beside a man in the snow, tying his hands to his feet, from what she could tell.

A few steps away, James worked over another form. Several bodies lay strewn about the rest of the clearing, but she didn't let herself linger long enough to see if they were dead or tied.

"Enoch!" Thomas called out instead of answering her. "We got all seven?"

His older brother glanced up from his work, that grim expression twisting through her. "All seven. We made sure to get a good headcount before we started the attack."

"Thank God."

"Amen." Only a God who cared could have accomplished this feat.

Enoch shifted his focus to her. "Are you hurt?"

She shook her head, though she didn't lift it from Thomas's shoulder. "No."

Enoch nodded, then met Thomas's gaze. "Two Stones and Heidi stopped for a visit, so he stayed behind to protect the place while we came to meet the threat before it could reach us. God prepared the way, I'd say."

"I'd say so too." Thomas's head shifted against her.

As Enoch returned his focus to his work, Thomas tightened his grip around her. He brushed his thumb across her back as they watched the final remnants of the ordeal come to a close.

"Are you sure you're all right?" His voice rumbled through her, his breath warming her ear and cheek.

"I am now." She snuggled in closer. Her body had finally stopped trembling. Maybe it really believed itself safe. Here in the arms of her husband—the man who'd promised to love and protect her, and had kept that promise against all odds. She pulled in a long, slow breath, then released it. "You made it back to the ranch in time then?"

His body tightened. "No, actually. I met Enoch on the trail and told him about the danger. He rode back to prepare, and I turned around to find you."

She pulled back to look at him. His copper-brown hair was disheveled, and his face streaked with dirt and sweat despite the cold. But his eyes held hers with an intensity that tightened her chest.

"Why? Your brothers needed you." Even now, worry began to twist inside her. It had all worked out though. She didn't have to be afraid. Yet why hadn't he returned with Enoch to protect his family?

One of his hands rubbed up and down her back. "You needed me." Pain flashed through his eyes. "When I couldn't find you. Then I saw those marks where they'd dragged you..." The raw emotion on his face—fear and relief and something deeper—made her chest ache.

"You came for me." She barely pushed the words through the knot in her throat.

"Always." His hand cupped her face, his thumb gentle over her cheek. "Kate, I will always come for you. Do you understand that? I will give everything I have to protect you. Always."

The certainty in his voice, the fierce protectiveness in his eyes undid the last of her defenses. All the walls she'd built, all the careful distance she'd worked her entire life to maintain, crumbled like ash.

"Thomas, I—" Her throat closed around the words she needed to say. Words she'd never said to anyone except Clara. Words that terrified her more than seven armed men ever could. "I love you."

The pain in his gaze flickered out, smothered by a heat that flared far brighter. "Kate…" So much emotion twisted across his face, she couldn't read it all.

Then he pulled her close, lowering his forehead to hers. "I love you too." His voice came rough, raw. "Kate, I love you so much. I thought—when I saw those marks—I thought I'd lost you before I ever had the chance to tell you."

A smile slipped out, and not even the pain from where the gag had rubbed the corners of her mouth raw could stop her. "You're not going to lose me. Not ever."

His mouth was on hers before she could draw another breath. Warming her, caressing her, pouring into her his love and relief and a thousand other emotions. So much she could barely breathe beneath the weight of it all.

His hand tangled in her hair, the other pressed against the small of her back, pulling her impossibly closer.

She kissed him back with everything she had, her arms wrapping around his neck. The cold, the danger, the terror of the last hours—all of it dissolved into the warmth of his mouth against hers, the solid strength of his body anchoring her to this moment.

At last, Thomas eased, the kiss turning into a languid lingering she never ever wanted to end.

This man. How had he come to mean so much so soon? And yet he did.

When they finally broke apart, both breathing hard, he pressed his forehead to hers. "I love you too."

Her smile wouldn't leave, and she didn't try to stop it.

"I guess we're about ready to take this group to town." James's voice pressed through the moment.

She pulled back from Thomas as heat climbed up her neck. Thomas didn't loosen his hold on her, just turned to his brother. "How many still alive?"

"Two. They're tied up, and we've caught enough horses to cart them all back to Walnut Springs." His expression softened as his focus honed on Kate. "You two get back to the ranch. Clara's fever came back, and I'm sure she'd do well to know you're safe."

A fresh surge of worry tightened through her. "The fever? No."

Thomas shifted beneath her, then rose, pulling her up with him. Once they were both on their feet, he wrapped his arm around her waist, tucking her close again. "We'll head there right now." But then he halted mid-stride. "The medicine. Did you ever find the doctor?"

Her insides tightened. "I did. He gave it to me right before—" Her voice broke. "I must have dropped it when they grabbed me."

"We'll find it." James was already turning to stride back to the cluster of horses his brothers had gathered. "One of us will bring it straight to the ranch, even if the rest of us have to stay in town a day or two."

Relief flooded through her, so strong her knees nearly buckled again. Thomas must have felt it because his grip shifted, taking more of her weight.

She didn't have to fix this alone. Didn't have to ride back to town herself, worrying about Clara the entire way. She could go to her sister and trust that others were also working for Clara's good.

She let Thomas lead her to a horse that stood nearby, reins dangling loose to the ground. He helped her up, then swung up behind her. His arms came around her, gathering the reins as his chest pressed warm against her back.

Nothing like Jake's suffocating weight. Nothing like the crawling fear of being held against her will.

This was safety. This was the man who loved her.

"Let's go home." Thomas's voice rumbled through her, and he pressed a kiss to her temple.

She let herself sink into him, her head resting back against his shoulder as the horse moved beneath them with an easy rhythm.

They were going home, yes. But home would always be with this man. Her husband. No matter where they chose to go.

CHAPTER 31

Sunlight pressed warm against Thomas's eyelids before he was fully awake.

He lay still for a moment, letting the quiet settle over him. The creak of the house settling, the faint murmur of Mrs. Wang's voice from the kitchen, the distant low of cattle somewhere beyond the windows.

He reached across the bed.

His hand found only rumpled sheets, already cool. Kate had been here when they'd finally fallen into bed last night—or rather, early this morning. He'd pulled her against him, and she'd come willingly, tucking herself into the curve of his body like she'd been designed to fit there. They'd both been so spent they hadn't managed more than a few murmured words before exhaustion dragged them under.

Now the space beside him held only the faint scent of her—lavender and that other aroma that was simply Kate.

He sat up, and a dozen aches announced themselves at once. His ribs. His shoulders. Even the raw places on his hands where the reins had bitten during that desperate ride. All would mend.

Kate wouldn't have gone far. Clara's room, most likely. Kate would want to be with her sister. That instinct ran deeper in her than breathing.

He pulled on his trousers, a clean shirt, and boots, then headed down the hallway.

The door to Clara's room stood open, but he stopped just outside. He and the rest of the family had spent a lot of time in this doorway over the past week and a half.

Kate sat on the edge of Clara's mattress, holding Clara's hand. And Heidi stood beside the bed, saying something about a tea and its healing properties. Maybe whatever was in those cups on the bedside table.

But Clara…she sat nearly upright on the bed. Looking almost as strong as she had yesterday before the fever returned. Her cheeks carried a flush that looked nothing like fever.

It looked like health. Like life returning to a body that had been fighting hard to keep it.

She was talking—actually talking, not the delirious murmuring or the weak whispers that came with her fever. Her voice still carried a rasp, and she paused now and then to catch her breath, but her eyes held their familiar warmth.

"—and she made me drink every last drop." Clara wrinkled her nose, though a smile tugged at her mouth. "It tasted like someone boiled tree bark in a mud puddle."

Heidi's laugh came low and easy. "That's because it *was* tree bark. The Salish have used it to bring fevers down for longer than any of us have been alive." She lifted one of the cloth bundles from the table. "This one will strengthen your body's own fight. I'll brew another batch before I leave."

"You've had scarlet fever yourself?" Kate's voice held an edge.

Heidi nodded. "When I was ten. Nearly killed me too. But I've nursed a good number of people through it since—Salish and white alike. The fever coming back the way it did yesterday, that's not uncommon. Sometimes the body rallies, then gathers itself for another push. But Clara here—" She reached over and pressed the back of her hand to Clara's forehead, then her cheek. "She's over the worst. I'd stake my favorite dress on it."

The knot in Thomas's chest eased. What a blessing to have Two Stones and Heidi here—especially since Heidi possessed this knowledge that seemed to have already helped Clara so much.

Kate must have sensed him at the doorway, because her head turned. The moment her eyes found his, her whole expression shifted. Her mouth softened, and the warmth in those hazel eyes made his pulse kick just like it always did.

"Good morning." She held his gaze for a beat longer than necessary, and it seemed to show the echo of everything they'd said to each other in that snowy clearing. *I love you.* Still new enough to send heat climbing up his neck.

"Morning." He glanced at Clara. "You look like you're feeling better."

"I look dreadful, and we all know it." Clara gave a tired smile. "But I'll take dreadful over dying."

"I'll take that trade too." He meant it more than she probably knew.

Kate straightened and tilted her head, listening. "I think I hear your brothers. Sounds like horses coming up the road."

Thomas moved to the window and peered out. Two riders approached through the morning sunlight—Enoch and James. Robert had already returned late the night before with Clara's medicine. These two now looked bone-tired, but uninjured, from what he could tell at this distance.

"I should go down." He turned back to the room. "Get an update about what happened in town."

Kate stood, smoothing her skirts. "I'll come with you." She glanced at Clara. "Unless you need me to stay?"

"Go." Clara waved her away with a hand that still trembled slightly. "I'm not planning to do anything more exciting than sleep for the next several hours anyway."

"I'll stay with her." Heidi reached for one of the cups by the bed. "You two go hear what your brothers have to say."

Kate pressed a kiss to Clara's forehead and murmured something he couldn't quite catch. Then she crossed to him, and he slipped his arm around her waist as they headed for the stairs.

They descended side by side, and every time they touched, it warmed through him—the brush of her shoulder against his arm, the quiet rhythm of her steps. Last night, riding home with her in his arms, he'd promised himself he would never again take for granted the simple miracle of having this woman beside him.

The front door opened before they reached the bottom step, and Enoch filled the doorframe. His brother looked like he hadn't slept—dark circles under those blue eyes, his jaw shadowed with stubble, his clothes carrying the rumpled look of a man who'd spent the night in a jail keeping watch over prisoners.

James followed close behind, equally worn but moving with a determination that meant he was running on will alone. Robert appeared from the direction of the kitchen, a cup of coffee in his hand and his shirtsleeves rolled to the elbows.

Rose emerged from the kitchen behind Robert, already reaching for James. He pulled her close with one arm, pressing his face into her hair for just a moment before straightening.

"How's Clara?" Enoch directed the question to Kate as he shrugged out of his coat.

"Better. Much better." Kate's voice carried a steadiness Thomas hadn't heard in days. "Heidi's remedies brought the fever down through the night. And Clara's sitting up and talking this morning."

James let out a breath. "Thank God for that."

"Thank God for Two Stones and Heidi showing up when they did." Thomas hung back near the base of the stairs, watching his brothers settle. Mandie had appeared from the parlor, and Enoch's arm circled her waist as naturally as breathing.

This. All of them, here and whole. The knot in his chest tightened, but it wasn't the old bitterness. It was something else entirely—something that felt too large and too fragile to name.

"Come sit." Mrs. Wang sounded from the kitchen doorway, as she always seemed to do at the exact right moment. "Eat first, then talk."

No one argued. Within minutes, the long dining table held platters of Mrs. Wang's biscuits and thick-sliced ham, a bowl of preserves, and a pot of coffee strong enough to raise the dead. The brothers and their wives arranged themselves around the table—Enoch and Mandie on the end, James and Rose on one of the longer sides with Robert beside her. On the other long side, Thomas held Kate's chair before taking the seat beside her. A small thing. But she looked up at him as she sat, and the quiet gratitude in her expression told him it wasn't small to her at all. Clara's chair sat empty, of course, and Mrs. Wang bustled in and out of the kitchen. Two Stones must be outside with the animals.

For several minutes, no one spoke beyond passing dishes and the scrape of forks against plates. Everyone too hungry and too tired for words. The biscuits were impossibly good, flaky and warm, and Thomas was on his third before he registered that the others had slowed.

Enoch set down his coffee cup and leaned back in his chair. "We put the two survivors in the jail. Doc Morrison bound up their wounds—one took a bullet through the shoulder, the other in his leg. Neither one's going anywhere. Sheriff says with our testimony and the telegram Mrs. Holbrook witnessed, there's more than enough evidence to hang them both for conspiracy to murder."

"As for Reginald..." Enoch's jaw tightened. "Hayes was straight with us. He has no jurisdiction over an English lord operating from across the Atlantic. That's our problem to solve."

The silence weighed heavy. This wasn't over.

"We need to wire Father." Robert said it like a conclusion he'd reached hours ago. "Today. He needs to know Reginald has escalated to hiring armed men in American territory. Maybe Father can finally get the English authorities to do something about him."

James turned his mug in his hand as he studied it. "We'll want to include enough detail to convey the severity without tipping our hand about exactly what we know. If Reginald has informants watching the telegraph lines—"

Thomas reached for another biscuit, though his appetite had faded. The conversation pulled at something in him—that old restlessness, the need to act instead of sitting around a table talking.

But Kate's hand found his under the table, her fingers threading through his. The touch anchored him, kept him from standing up and pacing like he wanted to.

Instead, he turned his agitation into words. "He could hire another crew inside a fortnight. Men like those aren't hard to find if you've got enough gold."

Enoch's gaze sharpened on him, and Thomas braced for the dismissal he'd grown so accustomed to. The pat on the head, the change of subject.

Instead, his brother nodded. "You're right. We need a plan for protecting this place that goes beyond hoping the next batch of thugs gets caught before they reach us."

James leaned forward, elbows on the table. "Thomas." His tone shifted—gentler, more deliberate. "Are you and Kate still planning to head for California?"

His throat tightened. California. The word that had driven him for weeks. The escape he'd been so certain he needed.

He glanced at Kate. Her hazel eyes met his, steady and clear.

No pulling back like she'd done on that ride to town—was that really only yesterday? No guardedness, no walls.

Just...permission. Trust.

She was leaving it to him. Whatever he decided, she would stand beside him.

The realization stole his breath.

He turned back to his brothers, and Kate's hand squeezed his beneath the table. Warmth spread through his chest, loosening all that had been wound tight for longer than he could remember.

"No." The word came easy. "Unless Kate wants to go somewhere, we'd like to stay here. On the ranch. With the rest of you."

Kate's fingers tightened on his, and when he looked at her, tears shimmered in her eyes. Good tears though. The kind that came with relief.

He added, "You'll need every hand you can get if Reginald sends more men."

Enoch studied him a long moment, those blue eyes seeing deep. Then he leaned forward, bracing his forearms on the table. "I'm glad you want to stay here. We'll need you. And more than that, we want you."

He cleared his throat. "And I've been thinking about how to make things easier for everyone. With three of us married now —" He glanced at Rose, then at Mandie, then at Kate. "It might be time to spread out a bit."

Thomas blinked. He hadn't expected this turn.

"I know we've..." Enoch paused, and for the first time in Thomas's memory, his brother looked almost uncomfortable. "We may have dismissed your ideas at times. Made it too easy to still think of you as the unruly youngster of the family."

Thomas couldn't speak. Couldn't have spoken if the house had been on fire.

"But you're not that anymore." Enoch's blue eyes held his,

steady and direct. "You're a man with a family of your own now. And you've proven that in ways that matter a great deal more than any of us gave you credit for."

Thomas's throat constricted. He stared at his brother, searching for any trace of pity or obligation. He found none.

"There are some good spots not far from the main house," Enoch continued. "South, along the creek, or up on that rise overlooking the east pasture. Close enough to help protect each other, but far enough to have your own space. Your own place." His gaze moved between Thomas and Kate. "If you and Kate wanted to build something, we'd all pitch in. Each couple can build their own life while still being part of the whole."

The words hung in the air like the first notes of a song Thomas had never dared imagine hearing.

Your own place.

Part of the whole.

Everything he'd wanted—not the running, not the escape, but the thing beneath it. The thing he'd been too afraid to name because naming it meant admitting how badly he wanted it.

A place that was his. A life he could build with his own hands. And a family that saw him—truly saw him—not as the youngest brother or the charming afterthought, but as someone whose presence mattered.

His vision blurred, and he blinked hard against it. Swallowed twice before he trusted his voice.

Kate's hand held onto his with a fierceness that said everything words couldn't.

He looked down at their joined hands, her slender fingers laced through his rougher ones. The burn marks on her wrists from the ropes were still raw and red, a reminder of what she'd endured. What they'd both endured.

And yet here they sat. Together. Home.

"I'd like that." His voice came out rough, stripped bare of the charm and the deflection and the easy humor he'd hidden behind for so long. "We'd like that very much."

Enoch nodded once—that firm, decisive gesture that meant the matter was settled.

James raised his coffee mug. "To building."

The others lifted their cups. Even Kate, who managed the motion left-handed because she didn't let go of his hand.

He didn't let go of her either.

As the conversation continued around them, Kate leaned into his side, just slightly. As if closeness was something she'd finally given herself permission to want.

He turned and pressed a kiss to her temple. She smelled of lavender and willow bark and the warmth of a woman who'd walked through fire and come out the other side still standing.

Home wasn't California. It had never been California.

Home was this table. These people. This woman whose hand fit so perfectly in his.

And for the first time in as long as he could remember, he had absolutely no desire to be anywhere else.

* * *

I pray you loved Thomas and Kate's story!

Would you like to receive a **free bonus epilogue of a peek at the next page in Thomas and Kate's story (including a glimpse into their happily-ever-after)!**

Get the bonus epilogue and sign-up for insider email updates at https://mistymbeller.com/mov-bonus-epilogue/

Then make sure you grab book 4 in the series for Robert and Clara's full story. As you can image, it's quite a doozy!

* Mail-order bride gone wrong
* He falls first/unrequited love
* Marriage of convenience

Turn the page for a sneak peek of *Mail-Order Lady,* book 4 in the Lords of the Rockies series!

SNEAK PEEK: MAIL-ORDER LADY

Chapter One

Fort Benton, Montana Territory – May 1870

She hadn't spoken in two hours.

Robert Balfour had been tracking the silence the way he tracked everything about Clara McKinney—with the part of his mind that had given up pretending it had better things to do.

The last words out of Clara's mouth hadn't been for him at all, but for Mrs. Wang—a question about the river. Before that, she'd noted the light glancing off the bluffs. Just small remarks. The sort people made when real feelings loomed to big to be spoken.

Fort Benton materialized out of the dust and the smell of the Missouri—a town built at the farthest point of navigable water, where the river ran too shallow for the big steamboats to go farther.

Everything that needed to go farther had to walk. A place of arrivals and departures. Of people strung between what had been and what might be.

That described the three of them well enough too.

On Front Street, a man lounged against the trading post wall, managing to watch without ever seeming to. Men passed back and forth along the road, sometimes in clusters, sometimes a singular determined stride. Casual commerce. Not anything he needed to worry about for Clara's safety. Probably.

But somewhere in this town, her mother might be waiting, even now.

"The hotel." Mrs. Wang pointed at the brick building on the left.

He reined in before it, then set the brake. Climbed down. Came around to hand Mrs. Wang out, and then turned to Clara.

She was already looking at him. The glance lasted less than a second—that assessing look she gave people she was trying not to react to—and then she took his offered hand and stepped down from the wagon.

"Thank you." She let go immediately. Then she turned toward the inn with her shoulders set the way they did when she was determined to force brightness into her world, no matter how dreary the outlook presented.

If only he could say something to help her. He'd been trying to do so for the ten days of their journey, but hadn't accomplished it yet.

"Ready?" he asked instead.

"Yes." She gave a firm nod. "Let's get it over with."

Perhaps her mother's steamboat hadn't arrived yet. They'd find out soon.

He picked up the bags and followed the women inside.

The lobby smelled of tobacco and old wood and a faint metallic odor—river water, probably, tracked in on boots and never quite dried. Stairs rose near the front door, beside a hallway leading back to a dining area. The main room held a desk and few chairs where people could gather.

Two men sat near the window, playing cards with the leisure of people who had nowhere else to be. Neither looked up.

The clerk at the desk did. A young man, perhaps twenty, with ink stains on his cuffs. His gaze skipped past Robert to settle on Clara with an interest that made Robert tighten his jaw.

"Good afternoon." Robert stepped forward. "I sent a wire ahead. Balfour."

"Ah, yes." The clerk turned to consult his ledger. "Got your message. Three rooms. That still suit?"

"It will."

The clerk's gaze flicked to Clara, then away. "Sign here, Mr. Balfour."

He signed. Took the keys. Paid for a week, though he had no idea if they'd need to stay that long. Or longer.

"Any steamboats arrive in the past few days?" He kept his tone casual.

The clerk rubbed his jaw. "One came in yesterday morning. The *Benton Belle*. Another's due tomorrow if the water holds."

Yesterday. Robert kept his expression neutral, though his pulse kicked up. If Mrs. McKinney had boarded that ship as she'd planned, she would be in town now. “Do you have a Mrs. McKinney staying here, by chance?”

"Not to my knowledge, sir." The clerk flipped back a page in the ledger, then another. "No one by that name's checked in this week."

He nodded. It didn't mean she wasn't here—only that she hadn't registered under her own name.

Or mayhap she'd found lodging elsewhere. Fort Benton had boarding houses. Private rooms above the saloons. A dozen places a person with means could stay if she wanted to avoid notice.

"Thank you." He collected the keys and turned back to Clara and Mrs. Wang.

Clara's expression remained bright and pleasant. The same face she'd worn at breakfast when Mrs. Wang had asked if she'd slept well. The same countenance she'd given him yesterday when he'd asked if she needed to stop and rest.

They climbed the stairs. The wood creaked under their feet, and somewhere above them a door opened and closed. The hallway at the top stretched long and dim, with sunlight slanting through a window at the far end.

Room seven. He unlocked it and pushed the door open for Mrs. Wang. She stepped inside, glanced around, then nodded. "Very good."

He crossed the hall to room eight and unlocked it. Pushed the door wide and stepped inside before he let Clara pass.

One window, overlooking the street. A decent latch on the inside. He checked it, then the door itself—solid, with a lock that didn't look recently repaired.

The room was plain but clean. A pitcher and basin on the stand. A bed and a narrow chair. A hook on the back of the door.

Adequate, though not nearly nice enough for a woman like Clara.

He still stood in the middle of the space when Clara appeared in the doorway.

"It looks lovely."

It didn't. It looked like exactly what it was—a frontier hotel room that had seen too many souls pass through without caring about any of them.

But Clara stood in the doorway with that expression on her face, the one that said she would find a gracious word to say about a tent in a rainstorm if she thought it would make someone else feel better.

"The lock is solid." He nodded to the door. "Keep it fastened when you're inside."

"Of course."

He set her bag on the chair. Checked the window latch again. Anything to keep his hands occupied and his mind on practical matters instead of the way she stood there, so beautiful and so perfectly composed. As if her mother weren't somewhere in this town with plans he couldn't yet anticipate.

"Robert."

He turned.

"You don't have to worry quite so much." She spoke softer now, soothing the edge from her words. "I'm not going to fall apart."

How could he answer that?

She wouldn't fall apart—that was the problem. She'd hold herself together through whatever her mother intended, and she'd do it with that careful grace and lovely smile. No one would know what it cost her except the people who'd learned to read the small signs. The way her hands stilled. The precise spacing of her words.

"I know you won't."

She tilted her head. Studied him the way she sometimes did, as if she were trying to solve him like an equation. "Then why do you look like you're preparing for a siege?"

"Because I am." He kept his voice level. "Your mother is likely in this town. She came here with a purpose. Until I know what that purpose is, I'm going to treat every possibility as a threat."

"That sounds exhausting."

"It's thorough."

The corners of her mouth lifted. Not quite a smile, but close enough that his chest tightened. "I'll lock the door. I promise."

He nodded. Then he moved toward the door, because standing in her room was beginning to feel like an intrusion he had no right to. "Don't open it for anyone until I'm back."

The smile touched her voice. "And how will I know it's you?"

"Three knocks, then two."

Was that a chuckle? "All right."

He went to check his own room before he could say anything else.

Mrs. Wang was in the hall when he came back out of his chamber. She'd removed her bonnet and smoothed her hair.

He didn't hesitate. "I'm taking the wagon to the livery. Stay here. Both of you." He gave her a glance to be certain she understood. "I'll be back within the hour."

She gave a nod, though her tone was dry. "We will not wander off into danger while you're gone."

He took the stairs two at a time and went back out to the wagon.

The street hadn't changed. Same lounger at the trading post. Same afternoon light slanting through the dust. He climbed up, released the brake, and guided the team down the road.

The livery sat two lanes back from the river, close enough that the smell of the Missouri followed him the whole way.

Irish met him at the entrance. A familiar face, though Robert didn't come to Fort Benton often for the man to recognize him. "Afternoon to you, sir. Looking to stable your team?"

"For the week, possibly longer." Robert climbed down and gathered the reins. "They'll need grain. It's been a long journey."

"Will do." The man took the reins and ran a practiced eye over the horses. "These Balfour stock?"

Robert stilled. "You know my family?"

"Know of 'em. Your brother Thomas was through here last fall with a few horses. Fine animals." The man patted the nearest horse's neck. "These have the same look about them."

Of course Thomas had made an impression. He always did.

Robert pulled his attention back to the matter at hand.

"Anything else I can do for you, Mr. Balfour?"

"No. Thank you." After paying the liveryman, he added a little extra, then turned back toward the street.

The walk to the hotel should have cleared his head. But too much pressed in.

The *Benton Belle* had arrived yesterday. Mrs. McKinney could be anywhere in this town. She could have already spotted them on the street. Could be watching the hotel right now.

He lengthened his stride.

He'd read her letter a dozen times over the past month. The hand was elegant, the sentences carefully measured—the sort of writing that hid effort behind grace. *My daughters,* she'd called them, which Kate had snorted at.

Kate was not her daughter. Kate was Richard McKinney's child from his first marriage, the girl Margaret had spent twenty years treating as a complication rather than a child. That Richard had split the inheritance between his wife and Kate—including leaving Kate's birth mother's belongings specifically to her, things Margaret had presumably kept for two decades—suggested a man settling accounts in his final days that his wife would not have sanctioned while he was alive.

How had Margaret received that news? Probably not graciously.

The hotel lobby was empty except for the clerk, who barely glanced up from his ledger. As Robert took the stairs, his mind counted them like usual. Sixteen. The hallway at the top stretched quiet and still.

He knocked on Mrs. Wang's door first. Three, then two.

She opened it right away, a smile in her dark eyes. "All is well here."

"Good." He glanced past her into the room, though of course there was nothing unusual to see. "I'll check on Clara, then go make some inquiries around town."

"She has not left her room."

He nodded and crossed to Clara's door. Three knocks, then two.

A pause. Then the sound of the lock turning, and Clara

opened the door. She'd taken off her traveling cloak and tidied her hair, though a few strands still escaped near her temple. She looked tired. Actually tired, not just the careful version of tired she usually let people see.

"The horses are settled." He cleared the dust from his throat. "I'm going to walk the town. See what I can learn."

She nodded, but didn't step back from the doorway. "You think she's here."

"*The Benton Belle* arrived yesterday. If she kept to her plan—"

"She always keeps to her plans." Clara's tone was matter-of-fact, but her fingers gripped the doorframe. "What will you do if you find her?"

A question he'd been turning over since they'd left the ranch.

"Talk to her. Find out what she wants." He paused. "What she thinks she can claim."

"And if what she wants is me?"

The words hung between them. Clara's face stayed pleasant—that careful, practiced pleasantness—but her knuckles turned white against the wood.

"Then we'll deal with it." He kept his voice level. Professional. As if this were simply another legal matter to be managed. "You're not a minor. She has no legal authority over you."

"Legal authority and actual power aren't always the same thing."

They weren't.

He held her gaze, but kept himself from sinking into those blue eyes. "I won't let her force you into a marriage you don't want. No matter who the man is."

Especially if he's three times your age and looking for a decorative young wife to manage.

That was the marriage arrangement she'd schemed already. The one that drove Clara to answer a mail-order bride advertisement. The one that sent Clara and Kate all the way from South Carolina to the Montana Territory.

Ordering a bride for Thomas had been Enoch and James's plan mostly, though Robert had seen some wisdom in it. Thomas needed a wife to settle down with. Thankfully, the best someone for him had turned out to be Kate, not Clara.

Yet would Mrs. McKinney still try to enforce that agreement? Or had she devised a new plan in the months since Clara fled?

"I mean it." His voice held a hard edge, but he didn't soften it. "Whatever she's planning, we'll counter it."

Clara studied him a long moment. Something shifted in her expression—not quite relief, but maybe the beginning of it. "Thank you."

He should leave. Go search the town. But his feet stayed planted in the hallway like they'd grown roots.

"Robert." She tilted her head. "You can go. I'll be fine."

Right. Of course she would.

He forced himself to step back. "Lock the door."

"Three knocks, then two." The corners of her mouth lifted again. "I remember."

He turned toward the stairs before he could do something foolish like promise her things he had no right to promise. Before he could say he'd been watching her for weeks now and couldn't seem to stop. That the silence in the wagon had felt like pressure against his ribs because he wanted to know what she was thinking and had no right to ask.

The street outside hit him with dust and noise and the smell of horses.

Better. This was better. Something to focus on besides the way Clara's fingers had gripped the doorframe.

Fort Benton possessed two boarding houses, lodging above all three saloons, and private rooms scattered through buildings that served other purposes during daylight hours.

Mrs. McKinney would choose somewhere with a veneer of

respectability. The boarding house on Second Street, probably. The one that catered to travelers with pretensions.

He'd start there.

The afternoon sun pressed against his shoulders as he walked. A freight wagon rumbled past, loaded with furs that smelled like blood and smoke. Two men stood outside the gunsmith's, talking in low voices that cut off when he passed.

The boarding house sat back from the street, fronted by a narrow porch with carved posts that someone had painted white last season. Lace curtains hung in the windows. A sign beside the door read "Mrs. Dunmore's Rooms—Respectable Lodgers Only."

Respectable. That would appeal to Margaret McKinney.

He climbed the steps and knocked.

The woman who answered was perhaps fifty, with iron-gray hair pulled back in a severe bun. She looked him over with the assessment of someone who'd learned to judge character quickly.

"Afternoon." He kept his voice polite. "I'm looking for a Mrs. McKinney. I believe she may have taken a room here."

Mrs. Dunmore's expression remained neutral. "And who might be asking?"

"Robert Balfour. I'm an attorney." Not fully. He'd done the study course, but hadn't had the opportunity to apprentice or take the exam.

She studied him another moment, then stepped back. "Come in, Mr. Balfour."

The front room appeared spotlessly clean, with dark wood furniture and more lace. A vase of dried flowers sat on a side table. The kind of attention to detail that spoke of a woman who ran her establishment with firm rules.

"I do have a Mrs. McKinney staying here." Mrs. Dunmore closed the door behind him. "Arrived yesterday on the *Belle*. Took my best room."

Of course she did.

Robert's pulse kicked up, but he kept his face impassive. "Is she in at present?"

Mrs. Dunmore grasped her hands together at her waist. "She went out about an hour ago. Said she had business to attend to in town."

Business.

The word settled like lead in his gut. What business could Margaret McKinney have in Fort Benton except the kind that involved her daughter?

"Did she say where she was going?"

"Not to me." Mrs. Dunmore's tone suggested she found this lapse in manners noteworthy. "She's not overly forthcoming, your Mrs. McKinney."

Not *his* Mrs. McKinney. But he didn't correct her.

"When she returns, would you tell her Robert Balfour called? I'm staying at the hotel on Front Street."

Mrs. Dunmore's eyebrows lifted. "You want me to tell her you're looking for her?"

Maybe he should say *no*. Keep the element of surprise. But better to get the meeting over with. And he could be watching for her. "Yes. Please tell her."

Mrs. Dunmore nodded. "I'll pass along the message, Mr. Balfour."

He thanked the woman again and let himself out.

The street had filled with afternoon traffic—wagons hauling freight toward the levee, riders heading in from the prairie, a cluster of men outside the saloon. He scanned faces, looking for a woman of middle age with blonde hair and the bearing of someone who'd spent her life enforcing social hierarchies.

Nothing.

But she was out here somewhere. In town. On business.

He turned back to the hotel. She might be at the land office, checking records. Or the telegraph office, sending messages. Or

—and this lodged like a stone in his chest—she might be at the hotel already, asking the clerk which room Clara was in.

He quickened his pace.

Get MAIL-ORDER LADY, book 4 in the Lords of the Rockies series, at your favorite retailer!

Did you enjoy Thomas and Kate's story? I hope so!
Would you take a quick minute to leave a review where you purchased the book?
It doesn't have to be long. Just a sentence or two telling what you liked about the story!

To receive a free book and get updates when new Misty M. Beller books release, go to https://mistymbeller.com/freebook

ALSO BY MISTY M. BELLER

Lords of the Rockies

Mail-Order Duchess

Mail-Order Baroness

Mail-Order Viscountess

Mail-Order Lady

Brothers of Sapphire Ranch

Healing the Mountain Man's Heart

Marrying the Mountain Man's Best Friend

Protecting the Mountain Man's Treasure

Earning the Mountain Man's Trust

Winning the Mountain Man's Love

Pretending to be the Mountain Man's Wife

Guarding the Mountain Man's Secret

Saving the Mountain Man's Legacy

Sisters of the Rockies

Rocky Mountain Rendezvous

Rocky Mountain Promise

Rocky Mountain Journey

The Mountain Series

The Lady and the Mountain Man

The Lady and the Mountain Doctor

The Lady and the Mountain Fire

The Lady and the Mountain Promise

The Lady and the Mountain Call

This Treacherous Journey

This Wilderness Journey

This Freedom Journey (novella)

This Courageous Journey

This Homeward Journey

This Daring Journey

This Healing Journey

Call of the Rockies

Freedom in the Mountain Wind

Hope in the Mountain River

Light in the Mountain Sky

Courage in the Mountain Wilderness

Faith in the Mountain Valley

Honor in the Mountain Refuge

Peace in the Mountain Haven

Grace on the Mountain Trail

Calm in the Mountain Storm

Joy on the Mountain Peak

Brides of Laurent

A Warrior's Heart

A Healer's Promise

A Daughter's Courage

Hearts of Montana

Hope's Highest Mountain

Love's Mountain Quest

Faith's Mountain Home

Honor's Mountain Promise

Texas Rancher Trilogy

The Rancher Takes a Cook

The Ranger Takes a Bride

The Rancher Takes a Cowgirl

Wyoming Mountain Tales

A Pony Express Romance

A Rocky Mountain Romance

A Sweetwater River Romance

A Mountain Christmas Romance

ABOUT THE AUTHOR

Misty M. Beller is an ECPA and *USA Today* bestselling author with over 1 million books sold. She writes romantic mountain stories, set on the 1800s frontier and woven with the truth of God's love.

Raised on a farm and surrounded by family, Misty developed her love for horses, history, and adventure. These days, her husband and children provide fresh adventure every day, keeping her both grounded and crazy.

Misty's passion is to create inspiring Christian fiction infused with the grandeur of the mountains, writing historical romance that displays God's abundant love through the twists and turns in the lives of her characters.

Sharing her stories with readers is a dream come true for Misty. She writes from her country home in South Carolina and escapes to the mountains any chance she gets.

Connect with Misty at www.MistyMBeller.com

www.ingramcontent.com/pod-product-compliance
Lightning Source LLC
Chambersburg PA
CBHW020917060726
47591CB00004B/1291
9781965918463